The Words of Every Song

Liz Moore is the author of the acclaimed novels *Heft*, recently optioned as a feature film, *The Unseen World*, which has been optioned for television, and the *New York Times* bestseller, *Long Bright River* which has also been optioned for film. A winner of the 2014 Rome Prize in Literature, she lives in Philadelphia.

ALSO BY LIZ MOORE

The Words of Every Song
Heft
The Unseen World
Long Bright River

The Words of Every Song

Liz Moore

WINDMILL

1 3 5 7 9 10 8 6 4 2

Windmill Books
20 Vauxhall Bridge Road
London SW1V 2SA

Windmill Books is part of the Penguin Random House group of companies
whose addresses can be found at global.penguinrandomhouse.com

Penguin
Random House
UK

First published in the United States by Broadway Books,
an imprint of Penguin Random House, Inc., New York in 2007

First published in Great Britain in paperback by Windmill Books in 2021

www.penguin.co.uk

A CIP catalogue record for this book is available from the British Library.

ISBN 9781786091147

Printed and bound in Great Britain by Clays Ltd, Elcograf S.p.A.

The authorised representative in the EEA is Penguin Random House Ireland,
Morrison Chambers, 32 Nassau Street, Dublin D02 YH68

For my family

I was handsome, I was strong
I knew the words of every song
Did my singing please you?
No, the words you sang were wrong.

—LEONARD COHEN, *"Teachers"*

Contents

Acknowledgments

I wish to thank the following individuals:

my agent, Nina Collins, and Matthew Elblonk, both of Collins Literary, for their hard work, vision, and guidance;

my kind and talented editor, Gerry Howard, and Julie Sills and Andrea O'Brien of Broadway Books;

my producer, Rob Galbraith, and all of the musicians I've had the pleasure of playing with or knowing, especially the other three members of the Liz Moore Band;

Matt Umanov and Matt Umanov Guitars, and all of my friends there;

the writers and professors with whom I studied at Barnard College—especially Roddy Doyle, Mary Gordon, and Timea Szell, who all read this manuscript and gave me their thoughtful criticism—and the dedicated teachers of the public school system of Framingham, Massachusetts;

my colleagues at the Morgan Library and Museum, especially Patricia Emerson and Karen Banks, who showed me the other side of publishing;

the many friends and loved ones who provided support or inspiration for this book, including Adriana Gomez and the Gomez family, Mac Casey, Bergen Cooper, Sarah Israel, Vani Kannan, Olivia Liff, Danny Reisbick, Leah Seligmann, Julie Valka, Christine Vrem-Ydstie, and Courtney Zenner;

and my family members—all readers, writers, and thinkers themselves—especially Steve, Chris, and Becky Moore; Cheryl Parkhurst; Donald and Susan Moore; Beth Parkhurst and Bill Card; Leslie and Patrick Dennis; and Geoff, Claire, Nicole, and Charlie Parkhurst.

I am endlessly grateful for your love, support, and guidance.

I.

THEO, MOVING FORWARD

I.

Theo Brigham, while walking up Tenth Avenue on his way to meet a band, decides impulsively to visit an art gallery. It is the sort of decision he rarely makes and usually regrets. The gallery itself does not matter, he thinks; it is the idea of it, the surprise, the defiance of his own expectations of himself. He sends furtive glances north and south and then darts left into the first gallery he sees, maintaining his pace as he does so, fairly careening into an open doorway with a rusted-over frame—no, a frame that has been painted to look like rust. He pauses for a moment on the threshold of the place, peering inside, savoring a bit the odd sensation of shyness. He so rarely puts himself in situations like this one. Rarely makes entrances he has not planned on making.

From the doorway, he can see various installation pieces, two of which resemble giant greeting cards. One says, "Love! Love!" One says, "Trust? Ho ho!"

Then Theo catches the eye of an official-looking woman, who smiles coldly and says, "Welcome to ArtSpace."

Theo walks out. He breathes deeply, congratulating himself on his brief adventure, feeling that he has once again fulfilled some unspoken promise. But now he must turn his mind to other things: he is going to his fourth industry showcase this week, and he has a terrible hangover. In his messenger bag is a planner. Today's date has written on it, in Theo's neat handwriting: *Edgedwellers. 3 pm Sound-Off. 19 yr olds—good for next drive? Call Cynthia re: manager.*

Theo is not thinking of the Edgedwellers when he walks into the lobby of Sound-Off Studios at three P.M., or of their incompetent manager, or of the secretary, Cynthia (though today is her thirty-second birthday, and he will buy her a bottle of champagne later). No, today Theo is thinking of being a very young man—sixteen—and hearing Springsteen's album *The Ghost of Tom Joad* for the first time. He was sitting in a car with a girl.

♮ ♮ ♮

Here is Theo in Sound-Off's lobby, which is lined with signed and framed posters of the Stones, Fleetwood Mac,

Phish. Others too. All famous faces. Theo knows what he will find at the end of the hallway and through the heavy padded door: four terrified kids trying to look cool. He hopes these ones don't have acne. One of the three acts he's seen this week did. Acne throws him off.

Through the door Theo goes, enjoying as always the immediate hush that falls over the room when he enters it. He quickly takes in the Edgedwellers, who don't have acne, but do have annoyingly short hair. Tony the sound man is lurking in a corner, fiddling with the sound board.

"Hey, guys," says Theo. He walks up to the stage and shakes their limp nineteen-year-old hands in turn and prays none of them has masturbated recently. Each straightens a little when Theo greets him, and Theo is amused by their too obviously planned outfits: retro rock T-shirts and Converses all.

Theo can tell they are surprised by his appearance, and he likes this feeling; he is slim and tall and quite young-looking, even for his twenty-six years. The Edgedwellers might think that he is their age, and this gives him an advantage. He's the one with the contracts sticking out of his messenger bag. He's the one with the messenger bag, come to think of it: an ideal thrift store find. Exactly the right amount of wear. Theo sits on a couch twenty feet from the stage and waits for the band to play.

The lead singer is not a good-looking kid. He decides to be brave and he walks over to Theo, who is now reading a text message from his girlfriend—"bond st 2nite 10pm"— on the smallest cell phone the kid has ever seen. The kid notices this halfway through his walk and he isn't sure whether it is a good idea to interrupt Theo, but he has already started walking and he can't turn around now. It wouldn't look smooth.

Theo knows the kid, whose name is Kyle, is standing in front of him, but he takes a few beats before he looks up.

Kyle says, "I just wanted to thank you because we're, you know, we're really grateful that Titan brought us out here to New York, and we want to say that we're hard workers." Immediately Kyle knows this wasn't a good idea and he should have just played the fucking song. God, thinks Kyle, why am I so uncool?

The other Edgedwellers are still pretending to tune, but they are looking at Kyle, who has taken the hit for them, they know. Each of them is silently thankful that he is not Kyle right now. They wait for Theo's response.

"Yeah," Theo says.

Kyle makes a hasty retreat.

Theo knows already that he won't sign the Edgedwellers, that he will send them back to California with broken hearts but a good story to tell their friends, who will ask them about it incessantly for the next year and then forget about it. The Edgedwellers will forget about it too, later in life, much later, when they are Officedwellers, when they are so far from the Edge that the Edge could buy them a Rolling Rock in a bar and they wouldn't know. One will start a family but have a string of affairs. One will come out of the closet. One will kill himself.

But how could Theo know all this? He puts on an expression that flutters between bored and bemused, lights a cigarette, leans his head against the wall, and waits for them to play their shitty emo pop meets indie rock.

Theo is unhappy.

II.

There is an old rummager on Bond Street and he is sifting through garbage cans. He is whistling "Star Dust," a song that strikes Theo as lovely and comforting as he jogs by, messenger bag jostling against his left side uncomfortably— for he is late again to meet his girlfriend, Luz. Lovely, comforting, yes, thinks Theo, checking himself; but unhip. Whistling has always struck him as terribly unhip. Farmers whistle. Old men whistle. Theo cannot imagine himself whistling, ever, even by himself, even though he likes the sound of it and it reminds him of his father.

The rummager eyes Theo's back and remembers suddenly and painfully that "Star Dust" was always the last song they played at his high school dances. Once he had a girl named Esther who wore her hair in braids.

Now Theo stops, huffing, in front of the restaurant. Through the window he can see that Luz is there already, sitting with her friend Amelia. Luz is the kind of thin that makes people follow her around rooms with their eyes. She is tall and tan—"and young and lovely," thinks Theo, imagining that if he were a different kind of person, more casual, less afraid, he might tell her she looked like the girl from Ipanema and then do something silly like give her a noogie or tickle her. He smiles, imagining it—Luz would like that. She dresses purposefully. She is in her last year at FIT, and her wardrobe is a small work of art. She has six rings, all plain bands made of different colored stones, that she wears no matter what. She takes them off each night and puts them in a little mother-of-pearl box by the side of the bed, dons them each morning and holds up her smooth dark hands to inspect them. She says she got them from her mother, but Theo suspects they are from a former lover, the way she caresses and cares for them, the way she fingers them absentmindedly when she speaks of the past. She has kept her hair long all her life, and she brushes it so it gleams.

Luz will eat out only at sushi restaurants, so she and Theo have tried nearly all of them in the city: Neo, with its wooden floors and bamboo poles; the various Harus, with their overpriced meals and overly sticky rice; the original Nobu, with its endless waits and posh crowds. Bond Street is their favorite.

Luz should be happy, thinks Theo. She's twenty-two, she's lovely, and she's sipping water that she has turned into a sick kind of diet lemonade with a lemon wedge and Sweet'n Lo. But he can see that she's upset and he knows it's probably something he's done. He shifts his focus to his own reflection and considers himself. He is decent-looking. He might pass for a good person. He thinks briefly about leaving. If he turned around now, if he went home to their apartment and packed up his things—for Theo has few items of his own besides clothes—if he got on a plane and flew somewhere (Costa Rica? He's heard it's temperate and relatively nonpolitical), what would she do?

But now her face is so lit by candles, so breakable and young that for a moment Theo imagines he has mistaken her for someone else entirely, a child, a schoolgirl. And now Amelia has seen him and waved to him, and he is caught.

III.

When Theo was sixteen, he had a girlfriend. Amy. He had a girlfriend named Amy and he had a band named Ruin. And he had baseball cards, and a baseball autographed by Roger Clemens, and a clock radio set to wake him up at six-thirty A.M. for school each day, and two parents, and a dog named Sam, and best of all he had an old, old Chevy that he pretended to know things about—mechanical things, practical things—but really just admired for its beauty and for what he supposed to be its romantic history. He loved thinking about the people who owned it before he did, and he made up tales about them for Amy while driving her around. Amy was blond and raggedy. Boys liked her because she was easy to talk to.

He thought he was profound and he thought everyone else was overeager. His love and hate of high school alternated with astonishing frequency and vigor. What is it, what is it, what is it that makes him remember this year— of all years!—with such fondness, though? Perhaps that his band Ruin won Boston's annual Battle of the Bands, sponsored by WBCN. Perhaps it was Amy. Perhaps it was because he discovered *The Ghost of Tom Joad*. He often thinks, now, of ways to stuff these memories into a sort of supermemory: a memory of driving in his old, old Chevy, his beautiful car, with Amy in the front seat and his bandmates in the back, listening to *The Ghost of Tom Joad* on the way to the Battle of the Bands. Of course, this never happened, never all at once like that—of course, if Theo could remember better, he would realize that sixteen was painfully bad for him in most ways. But how he dwells on it now, walking about New York; how the longing to be sixteen again hits him sometimes between the eyes and coaxes ridiculous guttural sounds from him, especially when he is drunk; how it comes crashingly down about him when he sees himself in storefront windows, when his reflection catches him off guard!

IV.

That night. After dinner. At home. Luz and Theo make sad and tragic love and then lie on opposite sides of the bed. Theo thinks, This is ridiculous; this is a movie. All of Luz's long fawnish limbs are gathered and twisted together and her spine is facing Theo. He traces it with a finger but makes sure not to touch her skin, thinking that at some point he should really tell Luz he thinks she is too thin.

Luz turns over urgently and Theo is pleased, thinking, Here we go; here's where we talk. But Luz is just dreaming of something larger than she is, just fighting some sleep creation. Her dreams lately have been of elaborate murders, but she has not told anyone this.

Her skinny arm flops onto Theo's chest, and he is crying suddenly. Theo has not cried in a few years, and he has forgotten the saltiness of it. Crying makes him think of hot, angry embarrassment: how liquids appear so suddenly, how the throat aches, how the tears themselves fall, terribly loud and hot, onto the pillow one after another, leaking over the bridge of the nose. Their trails cool quickly and soon he is snuffling, trying to suck in mucus noiselessly but failing. Luz wakes up.

"Darling." She sits up, and her small-breasted torso looks heroic and Greek in the light from outside. She touches his forehead, and this small act of sympathy is just enough to turn the crying to panicky sobs. Theo is reduced.

"Darling, what's the matter?" When Luz says "darling" it sounds like "darrrleen." She's from a family of wealthy Venezuelans.

Theo can think of nothing to say, and considers telling her just this but decides against it.

"You're too thin," says Theo. "You look sick."

Luz retracts her arm from his forehead as if hot tea has been spilled on it and, with great dignity, settles back into pretend sleep, facing the wall again.

Again, the wall of her spine faces Theo.

V.

This is the story of why Theo is now working for Titan, Inc.

It begins with the first time Theo went to an industry party in New York, at the home of a Russian man he had met in his first production class at Tisch. Theo had intended to be a screenwriter, but all of his scripts kept being about music. The Russian had just started a small but fashionable record label that the majors were interested in distributing. The man was looking for new talent, and he invited Theo to a small gathering at his SoHo loft.

The gathering turned out to be about fifty people in the biggest apartment Theo had ever seen. He was nineteen and most impressed by two things: a white shag rug that occupied a third of the floor space of the area, and a large group of models who stood in a corner and took turns snorting up in the bathroom and eyeing the Russian as if he were a plate of french fries. Theo felt out of place in his Dockers and a polo shirt. It was 1997. The fashion was to look as if you had just gotten into a fight and had emerged stylishly abused.

At one point, the Russian turned off the music and made an announcement: "Guys, this is Theo! He's going to do some production for us, if he wants to," and at this point he winked at a rather drunk Theo, who raised his glass in the air in a jolly toasting gesture and immediately regretted it.

The models glanced at him. The Russian was waving an empty wineglass and messing with the CD player. He continued: "Check this shit out. Theo's first single. Fucking brilliance, my friends."

Alcohol delayed his reaction, but in a few moments Theo's heartbeat began to quicken. He opened his mouth to object. The noise of the party was overwhelming. Theo cringed in anticipation: his first single featured lousy song-writing by a music major who would drop out of NYU the following semester, lousy singing and playing by a local band, and, most significantly, lousy production on Theo's part. He would be exposed as a fraud, he thought. Kicked out of the party. He watched the Russian place the CD in the machine and he stood rooted in place until the first few wavering, echoing notes resounded through the loft.

Theo blinked. The models were bopping their heads around. The execs flashed thumbs-up signs at Theo. Theo left for the bathroom and slapped himself around a bit. He looked at himself in the mirror. Three gin and tonics and a Sam Adams were pooled in his stomach, but he couldn't make them come back up.

He emerged to find the Russian listening rapturously to the single while smoking a cigar with amazing ferocity.

The Russian said, "I want to work with you. You've got something, man. You're it."

Theo said, "Thank you." Then he left.

Theo realized three things that night. First, that he would never be a producer. Second, that everyone in the business was faking it. Third, that he could fake it too.

It became simple for Theo to fit in. He got over marveling that no one ever tossed him out of these parties; he went to one a week in college, met Luz, made some good connections, and ended up working A&R for Titan upon graduation.

That's why he is where he is.

VI.

"Why do you love me?" says Theo to Luz.

"Because you are only mine," says Luz. She is looking out the window of their apartment. Theo has gotten ready for work and is putting on a tie—his once-a-year tie for Titan's once-a-year pep talk, during which the head honchos meet with the A&R crew and give each a resounding pat on the head or the rump, depending.

"You are mine alone," she says again, surprising Theo with this poetic turn of phrase. Luz is very good at speaking, even in languages that aren't her own. Her answer makes Theo feel guilty: he is thinking of his various indiscretions over the past year. There was the cocktail waitress, and a few band members (never ones Theo was working with; he has his rules), and an old flame who was in town for Christmas. All of them were meaningless, he tells himself, and in fact he always thought of Luz while with these other women. Still, the weight of his actions creeps up on him now, and he crosses the room to be closer to Luz, sitting on the bed next to her and kissing her on the forehead. One day I will be faithful, he says to himself. When I'm married I will be faithful.

"You will be late again," Luz says. "You're always late!"

VII.

Theo meets with Jax Powers-Kline, the president of A&R at Titan Records. She spends the first five minutes of their meeting together bitching about how one of her two personal assistants, Cynthia, has been turned into the secretary/receptionist for the entire A&R division. "Cost cutting?" she says. "Try efficiency cutting! Cynthia can barely keep track of my schedule, let alone yours and Tom's and Dick's and Harry's!" She predicts that this policy will change once Corporate realizes their mistake.

Theo, who walks by Cynthia every morning and has noticed a drastic change in her mood—for the better— since having been relieved from constant contact with Jax, just nods sympathetically.

"Anyway," says Jax. "Enough of that. I want to talk to you about your performance."

Theo sits still.

"It's been a while since you've signed anyone, Theo. What was your last sign? The Stark Ravers? A year ago?"

"You know my philosophy, Jax," says Theo. "I'm a perfectionist."

"To be frank, Theo, it's not like the Stark Ravers have done all that well."

"I've got my eye on a few with real potential."

"Who?"

"There's this band called the Burn," says Theo. "Real potential. Lead singer with attitude. Chick singer. Siobhan O'Hara. That's what's hot right now. Rock 'n' roll."

Theo has the tendency to speak in very short sentences when he's trying to affect nonchalance and coolness.

"Yeah?"

"Yeah. They're almost ready. I've been working with

them for a while. Girl's young still, so she's got a lot of growing to do."

"When can we see them?"

"Soon. Meeting with them next week."

"Okay," says Jax. She waves a hand. "Just keep doing what you're doing."

Theo leaves her office and passes Titan's biggest star, Tommy Mays, on his way out. He wonders if he'll ever sign someone like Tommy Mays. He hates to say it, but he has his doubts. Sometimes the faking it catches up with him and he wonders if he's been overconfident.

In her office, Jax makes eye contact with the life-size cardboard Elvis cutout she keeps in the corner. Cynthia buzzes her and tells her Tommy Mays is here to see her. "Tell him to come in," she says. She thinks Theo might be a lost cause. But like he himself said about that girl, he's young still. He's got some growing to do. He was wearing a tie. That was cute.

VIII.

Luz and Amelia always have lunch on Friday because Luz has no Friday classes at FIT, and today they have decided on the newest of New York's many sushi restaurants, a little place in Chelsea. Luz gets there first and sits outside. It is warm for October. Today she is wearing an outfit that makes her feel attractive and capable of anything: a short patterned Versace skirt that she bought for half off at Century 21; a thrift store T-shirt that says wow! on the front in orange letters, which she has mutilated and pinned back together; boots that she thinks might be described as "combat-influenced but ultrafeminine" in *Vogue*; and large hoop earrings.

Luz looks around for Amelia and makes eye contact with a man at a nearby table who is reading Proust and looks like a musician.

"What's your name?" asks the musician. He has already romanticized Luz into a modern-day Guinevere and he will go home tonight and write a bad song about her.

"Luz," she says.

Amelia arrives and the conversation stops before it can start, but Luz is delighted and she wiggles her toes inside her ultrafeminine combat boots and takes her long hair out of its ponytail to show it off to the musician, who keeps one eye on her and one on Proust for the rest of his lunch.

Luz is so happy that she eats two California rolls instead of her usual one.

IX.

Another showcase. Number five. Another band passed over. These were more difficult to turn down than the last—talented, but far too old—and Theo hopes no one else grabs them and makes them big. Theo wishes for their immediate failure.

Last night, Theo unearthed his copy of *The Ghost of Tom Joad* and left it on the kitchen table for himself so he'd remember to bring it to work. Now he's fumbling around in his messenger bag for an old Discman he dug out of his closet this morning.

He looks up once the headphones are in place, once Springsteen is urging him forward. Suddenly—there, across the street, at a sidewalk café—he catches a glimpse of the most stunning woman he's ever seen. She is sitting at a table, looking particularly lost. Is she a tourist? She has that overwhelmed look about her. She is rhythmically kicking one crossed leg at the ground like a child and clutching her water glass at its base. Theo closes his eyes and opens them and she's still there.

Watch. In thirty seconds, Theo will realize that it's Luz, but the realization will come too late; for now he has seen her as a stranger—a thought that Theo cannot unthink. He will not go to her.

Instead, Theo will stare as she turns to speak with a man next to her; as she waves to Amelia; as she eats her California rolls in a particularly joyful way. Theo will watch her, from a Chelsea bench, as she pays the bill and stands and yanks at her short skirt and walks on thin legs away from the restaurant and Theo.

Theo won't go home tonight. Tonight, Theo will sleep at a friend's apartment, feeling as if he has been halved; he will sleep in a half-empty bed, will sleep with Springsteen's album going off in his ears and two hands that grope sleepily for their missing counterparts. He never kept much in the apartment anyway. It will be easy for him to pick up his things while Luz is at work the next day.

Theo will leave a note. A note. That's all.

Next week, Theo will wake and go to work and hear another band that he will sign solely on the basis of the looks of the blond female lead singer, thinking of Jax and what she likes, and he will hate himself a little bit.

In two weeks, Theo will turn his ankle walking drunkenly down into the subway and will wear a cast for the next few months.

In a year, Luz will get pregnant by a man she meets at a party in Williamsburg and will have an abortion. She will notice the coldness of the waiting room seats and will buy an ice cream cone the next day—her first in years. Later in life, she will discover photography. She will have three girls after marrying a man named Fabian. She will die at 102, having outlived her husband and all but one of her children.

And Theo: he will spend most of his life in New York City, rising through the ranks at Titan and becoming a senior vice president, at which point he will retire to the North Shore of Massachusetts, to spend his days boating with his wife, Marie, a former editor, and hosting dinner parties. He will whistle. He will not have children but he will acquire an extensive collection of records, which he will listen to, and watch the sea from his window and look back upon these things: sitting in a car with a girl; moving forward on a Chelsea street in autumn; watching a lover without being seen; being close to any sort of edge but this desperate edge, this edge between earth and water.

♮ ♮ ♮

But that's all some other day.

Now Theo is here, oblivious, standing on Tenth Avenue with his green messenger bag, falling in love with a woman he never really knew anyway. He will not know the pain of that until it is a memory, distant and hallowed, until it is a dream.

2.

SIOBHAN IN LOVE

I.

The day the second-most-famous gun in the history of
rock 'n' roll sent its lethal shot through the red parts, the
gray parts, the lively parts of Kurt Cobain's mouth and
brain, Siobhan had gotten her first period. She had been
sitting in an English class with Sister Mary Perpetua. At
the class's end, she rose to find a spot on her chair and
knew immediately that its twin was probably blooming
across her plaid-covered ass. She sat back down abruptly.
She didn't know what to do. Jamie Kerr had seen, she

knew, and might tell his friends later, but he said nothing to her—he just looked shocked and left.

The class filed out and Siobhan was stranded, hands folded, mouth distorted into a panicky smile, face-to-face with a puzzled nun. She wondered if she could run from there to her house without anyone seeing her stained uniform. But it was too late: Sister Mary's expression had changed and she was going to talk.

"Is anything wrong, Siobhan?" asked Sister Mary Perpetua.

Siobhan had started crying. She was in eighth grade. "I'm leaking," she had said. She couldn't make herself say it to a nun: "period." It was like "panties" or "vagina."

Sister Mary Perpetua paused and looked scared. "Siobhan, do you mean that your friend is here?"

Siobhan didn't know what the hell the sister was talking about. She kept crying and covered her face with her hair.

♮ ♮ ♮

Later she would reflect—inaccurately—upon the idea that she and Kurt Cobain might have started bleeding simultaneously. Really he had done it the day before it was announced on the news, but Siobhan liked to be romantic about certain things. Her dad always watched channel seven after dinner.

The news anchor, female: "It's a tragic day for fans of the Seattle-based band Nirvana. Lead singer Kurt Cobain is dead at the age of only twenty-seven in an incident that police are calling an apparent suicide. Cobain was known to have been addicted on and off to narcotics."

She had said it like "Cobain."

"*Cobain*," said Siobhan, and she thought of the toilet paper in her underwear and how astonishingly white it had been when she had layered it there earlier. No question: it was ruined now. She still hadn't told her dad she needed pads.

"You like them? Nirvana?" asked her dad, pointing at the anchorwoman with his beer.

Siobhan nodded.

Her dad shook his head in disgust. Kurt Cobain's sad eyelined gaze considered their dark living room from the TV screen. "Feckin' eejit. Killin' yourself is throwin' away God's greatest gift." He took a thoughtful gulp and glanced at Siobhan. "Remember I said that."

"Dad," said Siobhan. "My friend is here."

Her dad had looked around the room. "What the feck are you on about?"

♮ ♮ ♮

That night, in her small room, in her small house in Yonkers, Siobhan had lit candles she had taken from the ground by the statue of the Blessed Virgin in front of St. Jeremiah's. She fumbled under her bed for a copy of *Rolling Stone* that she had borrowed from her friend Kathleen Hanrahan. She was crying again because she had found a box of tampons among her mum's old bathroom things, still stuffed into the hall closet as if she might need them again. Siobhan had tried to put one in, but it was the kind with the cotton sticking out of the top and it hurt like hell. She couldn't imagine ever being able to use one—she wondered if she had read the instructions right. She had thrown it out and changed the toilet paper in her underwear.

Now she was sitting on her bed with candles on the windowsill (presumably holy—they had been blessed by the Virgin, in any case) and a *Rolling Stone* open to Kurt and a little pocketknife she had gotten from her little brother, Hugh. And she was crying. Kathleen had called her and told her how he died: a gun in the mouth. Siobhan tried to imagine that. Getting the gun. Writing the note. Sitting down. Picking up the gun. Putting it in your mouth.

Pulling the trigger.

Siobhan, looking for an appropriate tribute to the life and death of Kurt Cobain, was working away at her inner ankle with the pocketknife. She was carving "K.C." just below where her sock would end. It hurt, but not the way the tampon had hurt her and not the way the shot would hurt. She closed her eyes and dug the knife in far enough to really hurt but not bleed too much. She multiplied by a thousand: Would that be death? Would that be a bullet in the mouth?

Kurt was watching her from the magazine. He was beautiful, really beautiful, angelic and blond. Painful to look at.

II.

Siobhan lives in Williamsburg now. She's on the bus, on her way to an important rehearsal in Manhattan. She and her band have been getting good press recently, and an A&R guy is going to be there, one who's been prowling around the band for the last few months without offering them anything. Waiting to see if he has competition, Siobhan figures. She thinks it's funny—she imagines sending the band flowers with notes like "Thanks for last night—you were *great*. Yours, Geffen Records." Or planting boxes of chocolate from Universal around the rehearsal space.

Her cell phone rings. It's Hugh.

"Hi, pal," she says into the phone. She says it quietly because she's embarrassed of cell phones—they remind her of businessmen and go-getters.

"Hello?" says Hugh. "Siobhan?"

"Yo," she says a little louder.

"Hello?"

"Hi, Hugh!" Siobhan says. "Hi!" The old man next to her rattles his newspaper.

"What up. So, aaaah. You know the thing I was telling you about tonight?"

"Nope." Siobhan is still annoyed at having to shout into her cell phone on a bus.

"Yeah, so anyway, there's gonna be this ill party at my friend Stats's apartment, and I was kinda like, to my friend Stats I was like, Yeah, I think I can get them to play. Remember what I was asking you?"

"I'm on my way to rehearsal and I'm not the only one in the band, Hugh."

"Yeah, but you're the lead singer."

"Mike R. has to work after rehearsal."

"So you're not gonna do it?" There is a whiny edge to his voice.

"I didn't say I could definitely, pal."

"Fine, you're totally fucking me over, but that's fine. I'll just tell Stats my sister's too cool for his party. No, that's fine. We just won't have music."

Her cell phone beeps at her and she sees her friend Lenore is calling her.

"Hugh, Huey," she says. "Lenore's on the other line. I'm sorry."

Hugh hangs up on her. He will pout for the next hour and then beat a friend in basketball, which will cheer him up.

Siobhan feels bad. There's some girl that Hugh's been trying to impress. But she's late for rehearsal and the bus is stopped in traffic and Hugh's always been a baby.

The old man with the newspaper takes a page and rips it into evenly sized shreds, one of which he wads into a ball and pops into his mouth.

He turns to Siobhan and winks. "Can't be too careful!" he says cheerily through a mouthful of recycled paper and black ink.

♭ ♮ ♭

Siobhan runs up two long flights of stairs to the loft they use for practice. Everyone is sitting around when she gets there. Katia and Pete and the A&R guy are smoking up in a corner. Mike G. is tuning up. Mike R. is glaring at the door and he doesn't alter his expression when Siobhan walks through the frame. Siobhan has been late to every rehearsal this week, and Mike R. is pissed off. He set up this meeting with the A&R guy personally.

Siobhan smiles apologetically at Mike R., gestures with her chin toward the A&R guy—who looks perfectly content and is taking an enormous hit from Pete's three-foot bong—and shrugs.

The A&R guy looks up in a stoned way and notices Siobhan. He gets up and walks over: "Hey there."

"Hi, Theo," says Siobhan. She turns away to get her Fender out and tune up with Mike G.

Theo is annoyed that Siobhan never pays much attention to him. He's more used to bands who crave his attention, who make fools of themselves for it. He backs off and leans against a wall coolly. He considers saying something like, "Oh, man! You know what, I've got a meeting now." But the Burn is musically tight, they've got catchy rock songs (*real* rock, thinks Theo), they have an obsessive and dedicated, if modest, fan base, and they've got something important: a female lead singer. Theo knows chick singers are going to be the next big thing. He wants in on it. He's going to get fired if he doesn't sign someone good soon.

He's really high.

The band starts playing and Siobhan gets into it, does

the little bent-kneed thing, bobs up and down with her legs pressed together. She swings her head back and forth when she's playing guitar and raises her eyebrows when she sings.

Sometimes she wonders if she's imitating someone else—the way she moves, the way she sings—but mostly she's too busy drowning in notes, keeping up with her own breath, to think.

It is only when playing music that she feels truly at ease in the world. Her whole life, she feels she has been working hard to know who she is; when she is playing before an audience, she is able to say to herself, "Well, this is who I am," and believe it.

III.

Siobhan's parents met in Dublin in the late 1970s. Her mother, Patricia, was a student at UCD. Her dad was a barman. Patricia was majoring in Irish literature. She liked *Ulysses* because of the sound of it and because she loved Joyce's fascination with her own history.

Patricia and her friends used to sit in pubs for hours and get drunk and talk about boys—men? it was such an awkward age—and Yeats and U2. They were all young and foolish and horribly torn between Catholicism and the impressive club of academia. At school, they laughed at wrinkled old incense-smelling religion, along with Joyce and Freud and the others. At home, they said their rosaries with guilty fervor and went to Mass with their mums and das like all Catholic girls did.

One night Patricia got to the Burren before her friends did, and she went up to the bar and ordered a pint.

Siobhan's dad—the barman—said, "Okay, but it'll cost you." He was trying to be funny, but that was what came out.

Patricia looked at him like he was weird and said, "Has the price changed, or what?"

Frank—that was Siobhan's dad—said, "No, I was just trying to think of something to say to you. You and your friends always coming in here and me never saying anything to you."

After that, he asked her to dinner.

♮ ♮ ♮

Siobhan liked to hear that story when she was younger. Patricia was best at telling it—she related Frank's verbal incompetence in a hilariously exaggerated way—and Frank always pretended to be mad but laughed at the end. "Okay, but it'll cost you!" Patricia would say, low-voiced, hysterical.

Siobhan was twelve when her mum died. It was unexpected, and that was the worst part, Siobhan always thought. Her mum had gotten ill and waited to get better. Two weeks later she was gone; they said it was an infection that could have been easily cured had Patricia seen a doctor right away.

Siobhan never understood why anyone would say that. Rubbing it in like that. Making her mother look foolish, like the victim of something, when she was the smartest person Siobhan knew. Smarter than her dad, certainly. Smarter than her teachers.

Her dad had let Siobhan and Hugh stay home from school for a week, and then he sent them off. Partly, Siobhan thought, it was so he could have the house to himself to look at photo albums and cry. When she went back to school it was as if nothing had changed; her friends kind of tiptoed around her a little bit, but that was it. She knew that the sisters had told her classmates about her mother while Siobhan was at home.

A lot of them came to the memorial service, dragged there by their own Irish parents. The mums swooped down on Siobhan and Hugh and Frank and gave teary hugs and words of encouragement and trifles. The dads frowned a little stiffly and shook Frank's hand and said, "If there's anything . . ."

Siobhan's classmates hung back shyly until they discovered one another and then chatted, even laughing sometimes. Siobhan could see the only way they could make themselves feel sad was by picturing their own mums dying. Then their eyes would get teary, a little, and they'd glance at Siobhan guiltily.

Siobhan went home after the service and up to her room. She put on Nirvana's *Nevermind*. Hugh came into her room—normally he knew better than that—and crawled up onto her bed nervously. Siobhan ignored him but let him sit with her and listen.

Downstairs, her dad was on the couch, curled into himself with pain, wondering what he was going to do with a nine-year-old, a twelve-year-old, and the rest of his life.

IV.

If there's one thing Siobhan hates, it's lying. She is sitting across from Jax Powers-Kline, president of A&R at Titan Records. She's doing it; she's offering them the deal that the other members of the Burn are practically pleading for, have their tongues on the table for. Mike G. and Mike R. are sitting next to each other and Mike R. keeps hitting Mike G. emphatically under the table whenever the exec says something impressive—which is clearly her only job.

"The Burn is hot right now," says Jax Powers-Kline. "No pun intended." She chuckles. She has never heard their music before, but she has read Theo's notes and they're worth signing. She's done this a hundred times before. "I love your work. I want to help you make it better. I want to make the Burn the best it can be. And I want to make sure the entire country—the entire *world*—gets a chance to experience the power of your music. So what do you say? Do we have a deal?"

Pete and Mike R. try to disguise their excitement, stuttering something about having the lawyer look at it, but Siobhan isn't listening. She is gazing at her reflection in the mirrored wall across from her. She has gained weight in the past year and she can see the exec calculating already how best to encourage her to lose it.

The band takes the paper contract—Mike R. accepting it and holding it as if it were an infant—and says they will look it over. The band files out and Siobhan rises from her chair last, at once picturing the stain on the chair of her eighth-grade English class, at once picturing Kurt Cobain in his final year, eyes pleading for mercy from an audience that was nameless, immense, and overwhelming. Then the shot. Then the blood.

Then the knife. Then the blood.

V.

Hugh has come to her apartment in Brooklyn with his things. It's the day before Christmas. The two of them are taking the train to Yonkers—Hugh with his enormous suitcase for a month at home; Siobhan with her little one for a few days, and her acoustic guitar. She doesn't feel like bringing an amp.

Christmas has become perfunctory in their house. It's a relic of the past. It's a reenactment of all of the Christmases before Siobhan turned twelve. Their dad still puts out stockings with candy in them that he has bought from the Irish imports store on McLean Avenue.

He joined the Rotary Club after their mum died. He kept busy that way; he had made a group of friends he bowled and played cards with. He still works at the same bar he's worked at since coming to America; bartending is the only part of Ireland he has not left behind. There he has a small set of loyal friends and regulars who know his name and use it fondly. But the house is still empty at night and, though he won't admit it even to himself, he misses having Hugh and Siobhan home with him. He and Hugh fought continually while Hugh was in high school, after Siobhan moved out. She held them together.

But now his two children are coming home for Christmas, and he has cleaned up the place a bit, put up a wreath on the front door and a tree in the living room (though he felt a bit womanish doing it), and he answers the doorbell with a swollen heart.

Hugh and Siobhan are standing there, bundled up for winter, suitcases in hand.

"Hello, you two," says Frank. "Come in then."

♮ ♮ ♮

After their Christmas Eve dinner—chicken meals from Boston Market and shortbread cookies that Siobhan made yesterday—and after opening presents—Hugh gave Siobhan a mug that said #1 SISTER and Siobhan called him a cheap bastard—they retreat to their separate corners. The house was always old and it's gotten older, drafty in its retirement.

Hugh walks into his room and collapses onto his bed. He is thinking of Angela, the girl he's been dating casually for three months. He likes her better than she likes him. He likes her better than any girl he's met before. He might be in love with her, actually.

Frank is sitting on the edge of his bed, eyes closed. He is remembering moving to America with Patricia, filling out forms, taking exams. He remembers making her tea and worrying together blissfully about how they'd manage to pay the rent, a baby on the way, another after that. They worried as a way of showing love.

Frank's eyes are still closed. He is pulling a thread from his very old sweater. He is praying for the happiness of his children.

♮ ♮ ♮

Siobhan opens the door to her childhood bedroom and the familiar cold hits her like a wall. In the near-dark she finds her way to the light on the bedside table, stubs her toe on the bed, says, "Fucking A." She collapses, holding her foot, in agony. She finds the lamp from her place on the floor and it sheds light on all the junk she's kept under her bed for years.

Kurt Cobain stares up at her from the cover of *Rolling Stone*.

Siobhan is frozen—meeting him like this, unexpectedly, seems too much to bear. She takes the magazine out from its dusty place and touches Kurt's eylined eyes. His mouth—his wounded mouth. His nose.

The only man I've ever loved, she thinks—and is abruptly hurt for herself, realizing the truth of it and the sadness.

She stands and hobbles to the window. Outside, it has begun to snow.

Her mum. Kurt Cobain. Downstairs, her dad in his bedroom, maybe drinking, maybe not. Hugh, lovesick and funny. James Joyce in the ground in Ireland. Her family in America. Her ancestors across the Atlantic, thousands of them, all lined up in perfect Irish succession, all of them watching her.

And here's Siobhan: in love with a dead man with desperate eyes, a man she's never met, a man she bled for twice.

3.

TOM, WHO CANNOT SAVE THE WORLD

I.

The babies are crying again. Tom is still asleep, but he won't be for long.

Right now he is in the midst of a lovely dream: In it, he is at his mother's cabin in Vermont. It is late autumn and the reservoir is so low that a mile of beach stretches between the house and the water. Tom's older brother, who has been dead for ten years, is alive and talking to him about philosophy while they walk along the beach.

"Ben," says dream-Tom, "I'm scared of my life." He turns to his brother, who has disappeared but is still there.

"Tom," says Tom's invisible brother. "What's that noise?"

♮ ♮ ♮

He's up, he's up. Camilla is lying still to his left, and he gets out of bed carefully so she doesn't wake. This is the first time she's slept in thirty-six hours. Having two daughters twelve months apart was not her idea. Tom fumbles for his robe in the dark. The small squeals down the hall are increasing in frequency and volume. The girls will turn hysterical in thirty seconds if the nipple of a bottle is not placed in both of their mouths.

Tom is fully awake now, barreling down the hall toward the kitchen, where he nukes two bottles of formula for less than the recommended time, and then into the babies' room. His wife has decorated it in shades of green. It was Camilla's mother's idea to have the girls sleep in the same room, despite the difference in their ages—despite the fact that Clara sleeps better than Alice but Alice wakes her up. Camilla's mother has been into some neo-hippie/New Age stuff this year, and read someplace that siblings that sleep in the same room have better relationships later in life. Camilla bought into it and Tom didn't feel like arguing, though tonight he thinks he might have a case.

He turns on the soft baby light and shuts the door behind him, feeling slightly unsure what to do next. There's two of them. One of him. It's not fair. He doesn't have a chance.

"Shhhhh, shhh," says Tom uselessly. He can never figure this part out. The girls' howls don't desist, and Tom puts the bottles down on the nightstand and then bends to scoop up Alice—the younger of the two, only four months old—from the left crib. He plugs one bottle into her mouth. From the other crib, sixteen-month-old Clara's cries turn to screams. He hands Clara the other bottle, half bending into the crib while balancing Alice on his hip, and then has a sudden vision of her choking—she's lying down, and you're supposed to prop them up, right? He yanks it away again. This does not further his cause. Clara is barely pausing for breath while she screams. He puts Alice back in her crib and she immediately starts up again.

"Let's be rational here," he says to Clara and Alice.

When at last he has arranged two babies in his lap and they are suckling greedily from their bottles, Tom leans his head against the back of the chair and thinks how strange it is that he loves these creatures—strangers, really.

"I haven't known you guys for very long at all," he says. "Isn't that weird?"

They don't think so.

♮ ♮ ♮

An hour later, and the three of them are still awake. The girls are alert and smiley in their cribs, gurgling and cheering. Ready to play at three o'clock in the morning. Tom's eyes are closing, but each time he makes for the door Alice whimpers threateningly. A police car goes by and casts its blue and red stain across the wall. Tom wants to cry. Most of all, he wants to sleep. He has to leave tomorrow and he's going to be wasted.

He reaches for the guitar that's propped in the corner. The old thing is hopelessly buzzy and will never be tuned, but it was Tom's first and he can't get rid of it. He drops the low E to D and does his Leonard Cohen impression:

"It's *fooouurrr* in the moorning, the *eennd* of December, I'm *wriiiiting* you *noooow* just to *seeee* if you're better . . ."

The girls are out cold.

Tom watches his daughters sleep, feeling ancient and comforted in the tradition. He imagines his own parents watching him, and theirs watching them. He wants to shelter Clara and Alice like a willow tree forever.

Their little heads are still and their soft backs rise and fall together. They cannot know these things: on Alice's eighth birthday, a man with a camera will follow their family and friends into the skating rink at Chelsea Piers and their father will rip the camera from his hands. Clara will cry and Alice will not speak to Tom for the rest of the day.

On her first day of sixth grade, Clara's English teacher, in a noble attempt to make her students love poetry, will play the first single off Tom's latest album and will ask the class to analyze its lyrics. Clara's classmates will of course know who she is and will laugh.

Alice will be asked to her prom by a boy she has loved since age thirteen. He will come to the apartment to meet her father and then will not dance with her for the rest of the night.

II.

Tom and Camilla have been fighting. Recently, everything triggers them—what to have for dinner, whether to hire a housekeeper, where to find a babysitter. And now Tom is packing to go away again. It's January, the time of year that the band gets ready to go on tour.

Camilla has always gone with them before, but now they have the girls and the idea of two babies on a tour bus is unappealing. Camilla's mother is coming to stay with them while Tom is away.

It seems strange to Camilla not to be leaving. She has always packed up her things like Tom and the rest of the band and hopped on one of the buses, driving for hours and hours and staying in strange hotels. Watching Tom bent over his guitar with inspiration late at night after a show. Stopping for lunch at little joints along the way and taking everyone's order so they wouldn't have to get off the buses and possibly face a mob. Standing around backstage and marveling at the sheer number of people in the audience. Terrified at the way they loved her husband.

The girls, especially. Such young girls and all of them

screaming, some of them crying from love for Tom. She remembers being desperately in love with Jon Bon Jovi, and she wonders if these girls hate her. She wonders if she is supposed to feel guilty for being married to Tom, or grateful, or undeserving. Sometimes she feels all three.

Most of all she feels overwhelmed. She and Tom met in the midnineties (when we were babies! she thinks, often) and dated for years before getting married. He and the band got famous sometime during this period, but she can't even really remember when. It still feels new, though, this life under scrutiny. It's a life of comparison, really—imagining what it would be like to be normal again, or to walk to the grocery store with her husband without a fan stopping him for an autograph, or to move to the suburbs and be happy and build snowmen in a small snow-covered yard.

♭ ♮ ♭

Now Tom is bent over his suitcase, stuffing his shoes in on top of a pile of shirts. His manager, Glen, is sitting on their bed and talking about merchandise. Camilla watches Tom from the doorway and smiles. He's always packed in the weirdest order.

"Let me," she says. Tom startles.

"It's okay," he says. He sits on the suitcase and zippers it from that position.

Camilla laughs and rolls her eyes at Glen. She looks at Tom, who is triumphantly lifting his closed suitcase off the bed. "Are you going to say goodbye to the girls?"

♮ ♮ ♮

Camilla's mother is on the floor with Clara and Alice in the living room, and she is making crazy cooing noises. She sees Glen and Tom with his suitcase and picks up Alice, making her little hand wave.

"Say bye-bye to Daddy! Bye-bye, Daddy!" says Camilla's mother, of whom Tom has always been afraid.

Tom picks up each daughter in turn and kisses them both hard.

"Bye-bye," he says, and feels stupid.

"Awwww," says Glen. Tom wants to deck him. He's been getting more and more annoying in recent years. Glen claps him on the back and says, "Let's get the show on the road, Tommy!"

♮ ♮ ♮

Camilla, Clara, and Alice watch. Tom is walking out the door. He's walking to the elevator. And the door is closing. Camilla waves to the metal door. She turns and faces her daughters, feeling as though she's forgotten something, or something has forgotten her.

III.

The show tonight is at a stadium in New Jersey. The band does a sound check at two and then heads to the hotel.

At six P.M., they climb back onto the bus to do the show. They pull into the alley that goes behind the place, passing a crowd that has already begun to assemble— though no one will be let in until seven. The windows of the bus are tinted, Tom knows, but he still feels strange staring through them at this horde of young people who have, by now, seen the buses and are hitting each other affectionately and screaming. He feels as if they must be able to see him, standing here stupidly, leaning on the Formica slab that serves as a table.

Tom has the conviction that if these people knew him, they might hate him. They probably would have made fun of him in high school, anyway. He watches as three girls run toward the bus and Tom is afraid, just for a moment, that they will be caught beneath its wheels, crushed like animals. But they stop just short of it and content themselves with howling at its sleek black sides.

The bus moves on and the guards shut the gates behind them, keeping the fans out. The three girls stop and collapse in laughter. One of them is dressed in a shirt she has made that says I LOVE YOU TOMMY! and she is freezing. It's January, and the sun is going to set soon. Her friends are dressed more sensibly.

Leila is the name of the girl in the homemade shirt. She is in love with Tom, really in love with him, she thinks. She cannot imagine being in love like this ever again. Her friends all claim to love him too, but she's not sure they understand him. She's not sure they've listened to his words like she has.

She and her friends are singing now: "If you're alive,

why aren't you living?" She loves that song. Leila looks around and has an uneasy feeling of hatred for all of his other fans, which she works to suppress.

She and her friends are all seventeen. They drove to this concert at four and have been drinking beer ever since. They're a little tipsy.

IV.

The opening act walks offstage. Siobhan and the other members of the Burn are sweaty and elated. This is the biggest crowd they've ever played for, by far. They are unsure of themselves and their legs feel light and bothered. This has happened quickly: Theo Brigham somehow managed to place them on tour with Tommy Mays when the original opening act dropped out. The signing, the contract, and now this: all in just over a month. Is this how it happens? thinks Siobhan. Is this how fame happens to everyone? The crowd is still cheering and Siobhan wonders if the Burn will ever have this kind of draw on their own. It's a bit scary. She's not sure she wants it. But the other members of her band are jumping up and down, screaming. They've had their taste of the big time and they want more. Siobhan is worried.

They pass Tom, who is slumped in the concrete hallway, meditating on the opposite wall. He looks as though he's had a couple of drinks. Siobhan's heart flutters a little—she remembers going to see his band when she was seventeen.

Tom looks up. "That was great," he says. "Have fun?"

Siobhan nods and says, "Good luck!" too chirpily. Immediately she feels like a little kid again. Mike G. snickers and runs down the hall like an airplane.

♮ ♮ ♮

When Tom is onstage, his mind wanders. He'll be in the middle of a song and suddenly thinking about dinner. Or about the girl in the front row with the shirt that says I LOVE YOU TOMMY! Or about his father.

Tonight, he is also thinking about his wife and his daughters, wondering if they're asleep yet—it must be about ten o'clock because the band has played ten songs already. He hopes Clara and Alice are sleeping well.

They're in the middle of an old song. This is one off their first album for Titan. It was their first single. The crowd loves it because they all know it and it's upbeat and fun and it has lines like "If you're alive, why aren't you living?"

Tom hates this goddamn song. Titan made him write it and Titan makes him play it.

They're in the middle of an instrumental break and Tom is pacing the stage with his guitar, acting hot and bothered because the song requires it. He bends his knees— he shakes his ass. He stomps up to his lead guitarist, Jeff, who grins and then goes back to looking intense. Tom has to fight back his urge to roll his eyes. Jeff is young and cute and girls like him and he tries very hard to keep it that way.

Tom walks over to the mic in time to deliver the last chorus. He's sung it so many times that he dreams it sometimes. Is Camilla having a hard time with the girls?

♮ ♮ ♮

Leila watches Tom and cries. Her small hands are clutching her necklace at her heart and she is standing perfectly still while, all around her, people are dancing and singing. She has never been so close to the stage even though she's seen the band eight times before. She is in the front row— the *front row*—and she can see each bead of sweat work its way down Tom's face. Her two friends scream and shout and cry out, "Marry me, Tommy!" in unison sometimes.

Leila wonders if they can see the wedding ring on his finger. She closes her eyes and wipes tears from them. She is overwhelmed by the music, absolutely drugged by it. She is sobbing. She looks up at Tom and suddenly he is looking at her too—looking right at her and singing. She freezes.

♮ ♮ ♮

Tom is blinded by the lights onstage. The crew turns them up full force during the loudest parts of his songs. He squints down into them and blinks. He can't believe he's thirty. When did that happen? He remembers turning twenty-one. That was a fun birthday.

The song ends, finally, and Kai, the drummer, bangs out the final beats. He tings the triangle ironically a few times, deadpan bastard that he is. Tom walks back to the elevated drum set, where his beer is sitting. He takes a quick swig and feels better. He likes getting a little drunk onstage. It's powerful.

Back at the mic, he says, "Thank you for comin' out! Thank you, New Jersey. Jers*eeeee*." He retreats and the crowd is screaming for more. He could say anything. It wouldn't matter.

♮ ♮ ♮

She is absolutely silent. She is wanting more. Leila has not told her friends this yet, but she has discovered what hotel the band will stay at tonight.

V.

After shows, the band usually goes back to their hotel and sits in the hotel bar and gets drunk. They've done this since they started. It's tradition. Tonight, Kai and Jeff have found a piano and they are pounding out a drunken version of "Heart and Soul." Kai has borrowed sunglasses from a waitress and is pretending to be Stevie Wonder. Tom laughs. Kai is so funny sometimes. Jordan, the bassist, is in the bathroom. Jordan has developed a bit of a bad habit since the band took off.

Jeff is making eyes at the waitress. Tom feels like telling him he doesn't have to try so fucking hard. She'll sleep with him either way.

Tom is at the bar, working away at his sixth beer. He feels good. He wants to call Camilla and tell her how much he loves her—a lot, he thinks, so much. He takes out his cell phone and dials.

On the third ring, Camilla answers frantically: "Hello?"

"I love you," says Tom. "I love you, Camilla."

"You love me?" says Camilla.

"Yeah."

"Tom, it's one in the morning. You woke up the babies."

"Are they crying?"

"Yes, they're crying now. I have to go," says Camilla. "Are you drunk, Tom?"

"I miss you."

Camilla has hung up.

Across the bar, Jeff and Kai and Jordan have lost interest in the waitress and have moved on to three girls who look too young to be in a bar. One of them looks familiar, Tom thinks. Maybe they were at the show tonight.

The room has become blurry all around him. He walks toward the band and the girls, winding left and right. He sits in their booth and puts his head down on the table.

"Dudemeister," says Kai.

"Good show!" says one of the girls. One of her friends giggles. The other is silent, staring at him, her mouth open.

"Thanks," says Tom. "Thanks very much." He sips his beer and waits for them to ask him for an autograph, or to leave.

They don't. The two girls nearest to him are staring at him hungrily. One of them says, "So are you staying here tonight?"

Tom looks at her. "How old are you?"

The girl is caught off guard. "Twenty-one," she says. She's lying. "How old are you?" Her friend laughs. The quiet one looks like she might cry. All three of them are wearing shirts that barely cover their belly buttons, and tight jeans.

"I'm thirty," says Tom.

"You're an old man," says Jeff.

Tom nods sadly. He is an old man. Kai and Jeff and Jordan are ordering drinks for the girls now.

Under the table, Jeff puts his hand on Leila's leg. She feels sick from too much beer and from being what she is: just another fan. Easy. They think she's a slut. She's dressed like one. She is looking at Tom, pleading with him in her head, thinking maybe if he can see her, really see her, he'll rescue her. But his head is down on the table again, and she's never seen anyone look sadder. Jeff's hand moves to her side and he touches her face.

No one can save her.

"You wanna go someplace quieter?" he asks in her ear.

Kai and Jordan are teasing Leila's friends and they are shrieking with laughter.

"Yeah," says Leila. She wipes a tear off her cheek. Her eyes are down. She has kissed two boys before.

♭ ♮ ♭

Tom picks his head up in time to see Jeff walking out of the bar, holding the hand of the quiet girl. But she's too young, thinks Tom. She's just a baby.

"Jeff," he says. "Jeff."

The music in the bar is too loud, and Jeff disappears with the girl out the door. Tom's drinks are swimming around in his head. He wants to see Camilla. He wants to see his daughters.

♭ ♮ ♭

Leila, in the elevator, is dreaming of the first concert she ever saw. She was in the second-to-last row. She was fifteen. Tom, in the lights onstage, had looked like an angel.

4.

CYNTHIA, GODDESS OF CHASTITY AND OF THE MOON

I.

While walking through Times Square on her way to Titan, Inc., Cynthia sees what she has been dreading for four months: a big fat billboard with Lenore on it. Lenore with her hands in her back pockets, looking limp-haired, looking strung out. Lenore with a '61 reissue Gibson SG hanging too low on her tall sharp frame. Below the picture is this caption: "Lenore Lamont—her Titan Records debut!

Available everywhere this fall." Her first thought: They're advertising early; it's only April. Her second thought: This means that they think Lenore's going to be huge. Her third thought: I am going to cry or vomit.

But she didn't. She held it in and kept walking.

Certainly, she'd had warning. In December she had answered the phone and Bernie had said, "Have you heard about Lenore?"

"Bernie, you asshole," Cynthia said, "I don't give a fuck about Lenore."

She had hung up the phone and pulled her hair and racked her brain for what could possibly have happened; feared momentarily that Lenore had died; grieved prematurely and against her will; looked on Lenore's Web site and breathed a deep sigh of relief that there was no death announcement; and, finally, saw that Lenore had been signed. To Titan. It said it in bold letters in the News section. Of all the record companies in New York, Lenore had been signed to Titan.

It irked Cynthia still that she hadn't known before Bernie. She was the one who worked for Titan, damn it, and she didn't even know.

Each day for the last four months, all day long, Cynthia has watched for Lenore, has expected to see her walk out of the elevator bank and onto the top floor of Titan, where Cynthia works as the secretary, or receptionist, depending on which way you look at it. She used to be one of two personal assistants given to Jax Powers-Kline, the president of A&R at Titan, but Corporate turned her into a secretary for the whole A&R department recently, citing cost issues. Jax still treats her like her personal secretary, though, and Cynthia can do nothing but accept it: one cannot negotiate with Jax.

Cynthia's desk faces the elevator doors almost exactly. If the doors opened on Lenore one day, it would be a face-off. It is simultaneously Cynthia's biggest fear and her great hope that one day the elevator doors will open and Lenore will walk out. So far this has not happened. No one at Titan knows she has ever even spoken to Lenore Lamont, of course; no one at Titan knows anything about her. Theo Brigham might know something of their relationship, because he is friends with Siobhan, the lead singer of the Burn, and Siobhan is friends with Lenore, but he has never mentioned it, out of respect—or perhaps because he was uninterested.

The closest Cynthia has come to Lenore since they broke up is hearing her murmured name in the halls of Titan, Inc. More and more frequently she hears it—"Lenore Lamont"—on the lips of some exec or other on his way in or out. Lenore is, according to most, the next big thing.

So Cynthia has known this was coming anyway. She's had fair warning. But face-to-face like this, blindsided by a billboard on Broadway. Cynthia wants to kick out like a child; her eyes go blurry; her head starts pulsing the way it does before a migraine.

And now—Cynthia checks her watch—she will be late for work.

But it doesn't matter. She's always late anyway.

II.

The morning after Cynthia's first night with Lenore, she had woken slowly and had experienced an overpowering sense of disorientation, which was unusual for her. Admittedly, she was used to sleeping in strange beds. She was alone in this one. The sheets were red. The room was small and filled with sunlight. PJ Harvey was on the stereo. It had taken her a full ten seconds to place herself. When she did, happiness overwhelmed her smoothly, and she regarded the room with new eyes. It was Lenore's room, and it was as perfect and lovely as Lenore herself.

There was a mirror across from her, mounted on the wall, and she sat up to look at herself. The back of her hair was mussed. She tried to smooth it. She wiped her mouth and the corners of her eyes. Cynthia wondered if Lenore had left; if she was embarrassed or regretful, if she would return.

And then Lenore walked in, fully clothed, smoking a cigarette. It was possible that she had been up for hours. She did not smile, but she didn't look upset either; she looked at Cynthia curiously, impassively.

"You're up," she said at last.

"Come here," said Cynthia, and patted the bed. Lenore crossed the room obediently and sat down, keeping her back straight and her hands on her knees. She faced the window and looked outside intently.

"How do you feel?" asked Cynthia, because she couldn't think of what to say. She wanted to touch Lenore's back but found she couldn't muster the courage. She felt embarrassed, suddenly, to be naked under the covers. In the dark she had been brave, unthinking. But now it was morning and Lenore was sitting there, fully clothed already. She felt a bit guilty, a bit dirty, a bit corrupt.

The angle between them gave Cynthia a view of Lenore's profile that Cynthia had considered many times before. It was a very nice profile. Lenore had very long hair then, and it was in a ponytail, and her eyes were wide and thickly lashed, and she looked five years younger than she was, and she looked even younger when she turned away from the window and slid childishly, conspiratorially down on the bed to face Cynthia, as if they were at a sleepover.

Then Lenore said, "Are you my girlfriend?" Cynthia had been asked the question before. Usually the answer was no. "Am I your girlfriend?" Lenore asked again, and gazed at Cynthia earnestly. She held her cigarette in her hand, resting it on her rib cage. It was only the cigarette that leant her the air of an adult. Everything else about her was innocent, sweetly unaware and childish, brimming with youthful vigor.

"Do you want to be?" asked Cynthia, surprising herself, all at once nearly trembling with greed.

"I think this is a good idea," said Lenore. And looked at her again: "You're my first girlfriend."

♮ ♮ ♮

It was a lie. Later Cynthia would find out that it was a lie. But the memory remains dear to her because of her happiness at that moment, her feeling that she was luckier than anyone in the world to be naked beside Lenore Lamont in Lenore's bed, with PJ Harvey on the stereo. She knew instinctively that it was a lovely day outside, warm and breezy, and she thought that she was going to teach Lenore about life.

III.

When she gets to work her telephone indicates that she has already missed ten calls. Unfortunate, as at least five of them will have been Jax. She settles down behind the desk and takes a breath, feels the personality melting off her. She is completely different here. She takes orders. She is meek. She complies.

She surveys her surroundings.

The top floor of the Titan building, just east of Grand Central Station, is always warm. The heat has no clear source; there is no radiator and there are no ducts in the ceiling of the great foyer, which is bordered on one side by windows, on two sides by impressive offices, on the fourth side by a bank of elevators.

Against the large wall of windows facing west, there is a ficus tree that Cynthia mists each morning and each evening before she leaves. When the sun sets, the tree casts its shadow across the marble floor and she is comforted by its familiar slow progression toward her desk.

Cynthia sits out in the center of the high-ceilinged room, so she always feels a bit marooned. The hall is full of echoes and the music of Titan's latest find. Cynthia checks behind herself occasionally to make sure no one has crept up. It would be easy to startle her out there in the middle of everything.

Her job is to smile when the doors open and greet the people she knows or knows of. To those she does not recognize, she says, "Welcome to Titan. How may I direct you?"

But those who are allowed access to the top floor of Titan are an important breed. Cynthia thinks she's maybe asked that question twice.

IV.

Jax Powers-Kline comes in for the day two hours after Cynthia. She never says hello. Today is Monday and she is wearing tight jeans tucked into cowboy boots and an orange velvet blazer. The elevator doors open. Without lowering her copy of the *Times,* Jax knows that the secretary is smiling at her. She pauses before exiting and waits to hear it:

"Hello, Jax. How are you today?"

Jax was out until four A.M. last night and she's not in the mood. She inhales, lowers the newspaper just enough to see the secretary. Raising it again, she reads as she walks to the right and dodges the central desk, hoping the secretary won't talk again. She fumbles beneath the paper, still reading, for the handle of her door. Then she has it open and just for a moment the life-size cardboard figure of Elvis that Jax has set up in her office peers out into the foyer. Jax shuts the door behind her.

A moment later she emerges, sunglasses on, cigarette in hand, and takes a long slow drag. It feels good. She holds the smoke in while she addresses Cynthia.

"Give it to me straight, Cynthia." She always says that. She thinks it sounds punchy and cinematic.

Cynthia reaches for the planner—it's the only thing on her desk besides a phone and computer—and opens it to the page marked "Jax Powers-Kline." She says, "You have a lunch date with James at one-thirty at Haru. A three-thirty meeting with Mr. Romero, a five o'clock manicure. And the Burn is having their drop party at the Bowery tonight."

Jax exhales. "Cynthia," she says.

"Yes, Jax?"

"Cynthia, who in the fuck is James?"

Yesterday, Jax had yelled from her office to Cynthia that she was meeting James for lunch at Haru at one-thirty. Cynthia had gotten up from her chair and walked to Jax's door.

"James who?" she had asked.

"James! James! You know James," Jax had said, using her cigarette for punctuation. She had been on the phone.

But Cynthia does not remind Jax of this now, only says, "I don't know, Jax."

V.

Cynthia and Lenore met when they were on the same bill one night at Arlene's Grocery. Five years ago, Cynthia

drummed for a singer named Drake who—Cynthia realizes now—really couldn't sing at all. But back then he had
the look. Hipsters had taken over New York and Drake
had better vintage T-shirts than anyone.

He also had one of the nastiest smack habits Cynthia
had ever witnessed. The night she met Lenore, he was still
floating ten minutes before the show. Cynthia took him
into the bathroom and hit his face and hit his arms and
splashed his face with water, trying to get him up and get
him out. But he was smiling; he was somewhere else. His
head lolled onto his chest and his eyes looked up at her
from far away.

The door opened and Lenore came in, before she was
Lenore, when she was just some woman—practically a
teenager back then—in the hideous bathroom of a rock
club.

"Check him out," said Lenore. Drake was still smiling,
eyes closed now.

Cynthia said nothing. She was contemplating leaving
Drake where he was and walking out. He had done this
same thing two or three times before. Always, the clubs'
employees took it out on her because she was the sober
one. But something about Lenore made her want to stay.
Something about Lenore made her heartbeat quicken.

"We're on in ten," said Cynthia. "Supposed to be, I
mean."

"What's his name?" Lenore asked.

"Drake."

"Drake," said Lenore. She put a hand—long-fingered,
red-nailed—on his forehead. Cynthia thought it must have

been cold. It looked cool, comfortable. She wanted it on her forehead too.

"Drake," said Lenore again, and from her back pocket she pulled out a small clear bag. She waved it back and forth in front of his lazy gaze. "You want some of this, Drake?" Inside the bag was fine white powder. Lenore took out a mirror, cut four fat lines out, rolled a dollar bill. She did two. Then she held it under Drake's nose.

"Do it," she said to Drake. But she was looking at Cynthia. Drake emerged momentarily from his coma and obeyed. In a minute he was up, and in ten they were on.

That's how Cynthia met Lenore, and that's how Drake died. Not that night, of course. Later. Last year. Cynthia went to his funeral and stood in the back and the worst part was that she only really went because Drake was responsible, in some strange way, for Lenore.

They played "Stairway to Heaven" at his funeral. No one cried except Drake's mother, who wore a black dress and a black veil and wailed like an electric guitar.

VI.

The phone rings.

"Titan," says Cynthia.

"Cynthia," says Theo. "It's Theo."

"Yo!" says Cynthia. Theo is the only person at Titan that she likes. Last fall he bought her a bottle of champagne—

it was for her thirty-second birthday—and she was so touched that she didn't even tell him she was allergic. She was still with Lenore at the time and she brought it home and handed it to her. Lenore had popped the cork out the window and drunk the whole bottle in one sitting. All of this flashes through Cynthia's mind in the second it takes Theo to go on.

"I need to ask you a favor," he says.

"No," says Cynthia.

"Please?"

"Okay."

"Make sure Jax is coming to the Burn's show at the Bowery tonight," says Theo.

"She knows," says Cynthia. "It's on her schedule."

Both Cynthia and Theo know this means nothing, and Cynthia can almost hear him roll his eyes on the other end of the phone.

"Cynthia," says Theo. "You're killing me here."

"What do you want me to do?"

"Tell her Madonna called and she'll be there," says Theo. "I don't know. Help."

"I'll try," says Cynthia.

Cynthia knows what Theo is doing. He needs the whole company to be on board to ensure the Burn's success. They've just come off a tour opening for Tommy Mays, Titan's biggest act. Their album is out this month. If Jax doesn't care about them—if she lets them fall into the abyss of bands Titan signs and forgets about—they're doomed. Big labels tend to get behind only one or two new

acts a year, and right now it looks like Lenore is monopo-
lizing the attention of the highest-ups.

Of course she is, thinks Cynthia, and vows to do everything she can to help the Burn.

VII.

Cynthia and Lenore started the band because Lenore's
drummer moved to California and she decided she wanted
an all-girl band anyway. She was like that. She would decide on things frantically, frenetically, and then she could
not be convinced of the existence of any other way but
her own. In this way she chose Cynthia as her drummer.
Later, as her girlfriend. Last, as her ex-girlfriend, her ex-
bandmate. Cynthia does not now recall being part of these
decisions. She thinks of them as if they were natural disas-
ters: unstoppable, unswerving. Predestined.

"I liked your show at Arlene's. We can rehearse next
Thursday," said Lenore, the first time she called, a week after she and Cynthia met. As if it were natural that they
would—back then, before they knew each other at all.

"How did you get this number?" asked Cynthia, more
out of curiosity than anything.

"White pages," said Lenore. "So Thursday?"

♮ ♯ ♮

They found a guitarist and a bassist, but they never mat-
tered. Their names were Sheila and Jo-Jo, respectively,

and they did as they were told because they were grateful and they weren't that good. Their rehearsals were strained. Lenore gave them no advice at all. "That rocked," she would say, if a song did. "That sucked," she would say, if a song did. It was up to Cynthia to fix things, to make things work. She stayed up late at night writing guitar parts that she would record to cassette and give to Sheila to learn, note by note. She built bass lines on the four bottom strings of her electric guitar and met with Jo-Jo separately to teach them to her before each rehearsal. Lenore wrote songs in G, mostly, and sometimes in E. They were predictable. Some were bad, even. But she made up for it onstage.

♮ ♭ ♮

Cynthia had never seen Lenore perform before their first show together. Based on their rehearsals, she had always gone on the assumption that Lenore must be good onstage, the way one might look at a woman and guess at her skill in bed. She was intense when she rehearsed, staring at herself in the mirrored wall opposite the band in the room they rented at Ultrasound, turning and gazing coolly at her bandmates when she felt like it. But their first gig showed Cynthia a part of Lenore she had only guessed at—the lustful part, the dangerous part. She thinks of it now as the first time she was hurt by Lenore, or the first time she realized she would be hurt eventually by Lenore.

Because everyone wanted her. It was a communal need, almost a surprising need: everyone in the room hungered for Lenore, and Lenore hungered for herself, and the music was hardly important at all.

Lenore pulsed with an unnatural intensity, like her veins were outside her skin, like she would be cool to the touch even in a spotlight, even sweating as she did. And Cynthia wanted to touch her very much. More than that, she wanted to *be* touched by Lenore with a nearly religious fervor. It was all she could think about. She watched her from behind and lusted and lusted and felt like she would never want anyone again the way she wanted Lenore at their first show: Lenore, who leaned into the microphone and said, "Hello, New York," as if it were the most natural phrase in the world; Lenore, almost astonishingly tall; Lenore, who shook out hair that might not have been washed in a week and started Cynthia's pulse racing.

When Lenore took Cynthia home with her that night, it was like drinking water after a drought—it was like the sudden gracious fulfilling of a need that had been part of Cynthia for her whole life, a need she had not known was there until that night. After they had come together violently and then fallen apart again, Cynthia did not sleep, but watched Lenore asleep. She was the stillest sleeper Cynthia had ever seen; her face was almost corpselike. She lay perfectly flat on her back, her arms by her sides, her legs stretched out endlessly toward the foot of the bed.

"Lenore," said Cynthia soundlessly. She mouthed the word as if she were invoking something, and became frightened there in the dim quiet of Lenore's room. "Lenore," she said aloud.

Lenore's eyes opened and she turned toward Cynthia, as alert as if she had been awake for hours.

"What is it?" she asked.

"Nothing," said Cynthia. "Just seeing if you were okay."

VIII.

Jax returns from lunch at Haru and tries to cross the lobby unmolested by the secretary, but fails.

"Jax," the secretary is saying. "I have a message for you."

"Not now," says Jax, and shuts the door.

Inside her office, the shades are half drawn, as she likes them. The large room has been done in shades of deep red and brown. These are the colors of the house she grew up in. Her parents have not ever seen her office—she has not ever invited them—but should they ever have the chance to, they'd be surprised at the similarities to their own home in Brooklyn Heights.

She hears a timid knock on the door and ignores it. It's bound to be Cynthia, the godforsaken secretary, whose professed and proven interest in music landed her a job that should have gone to someone much younger and—let's face it—much more attractive than she. Since Corporate switched her to department secretary, she has been the first person their guests see upon exiting the elevator; she's the de facto face of Titan. It is only Jax's unwillingness to invest training time in a new secretary that prevents her from firing Cynthia based on her awful short haircut alone. Recently Cynthia has been ducking out early too, and coming in late. No dedication, thinks Jax. This must change. Jax's personal assistant, Mimi, is a sweet young thing with aspirations to be just like Jax. Mimi follows Jax to concerts and events after work, asking for advice on everything from clothes to makeup to her career. As annoying as Jax finds her, there's still something nice about her overt admiration. Come to think of it, isn't it part of Cynthia's duties to come to a concert or two now and again—to show her support for Titan artists, as an employee of Titan? For such a music buff, she doesn't seem to really like music.

The knocking starts again.

"Go away," says Jax. "I'm on the phone."

A pause.

"I can see when you're on the phone," says Cynthia through the door. "I can see everyone's lines from my desk." Normally she would not be so bold, but this is for Theo.

"I'm on my cell phone," says Jax. "Seriously, I'll talk to you later."

"Okay, I'll just wait outside here," says Cynthia.

The nerve. Jax walks to the door and throws it open, looking at Cynthia incredulously.

"Yes?" she hisses.

"Just wanted to remind you about the concert tonight."

"*What* concert tonight?" asks Jax.

"The Burn's. At the Bowery. It's on your schedule."

"Oh," says Jax. In fact, she had had no intention of going to that concert. The Burn is some midlevel band that Theo has a hard-on for. They don't fit in at Titan, not really; she signed them to please Theo, gave them some speech about greatness—her standard. If they sell twenty thousand records she'll be surprised. Everyone's focusing on Lenore Lamont now anyway. "Something came up," she says. "Do me a favor and tell Theo?" She starts to shut the door.

"Um," says Cynthia. "I've heard they're really good."

"Of course they are," says Jax. "They're a Titan band, aren't they?"

Cynthia makes sympathetic eye contact with the Elvis cutout briefly before the door slams shut. She contemplates knocking again, then decides she needs more ammunition.

Before she can move, the door opens again abruptly. "You should go, though," says Jax, who has just had a moment of inspiration: a new way she can torture the secretary. "New company initiative. Everyone's gotta go see one show a month. Today's April thirtieth. Have you seen a show yet?"

♮ ♯ ♮

She isn't kidding. Cynthia, who had planned on meeting her friend Bernie for a drink after work, must now call him and cancel. She would invite him to the show, but she does not like to mix work with her social life; she is partially embarrassed of the people she works with, and partially embarrassed of her friends. Bernie acts huffy and then settles down.

"Quit your job—it sucks," he says, before hanging up.

Cynthia knows this. When she accepted the job as Jax's personal assistant, she had fantasies of moving up through the ranks, maybe eventually doing A&R, if music didn't work out. Then she was still with Lenore, still in a band, and she felt hopeful—thought possibly that the connections she made through Titan would be useful when the band was ready to be signed. Now she is thirty-two, and bandless, and in music, thirty-two is ancient. She knows this more than ever from working here, so really, she should be focusing on her professional career. But the fact is that Cynthia doesn't have a college degree. She went to secretarial school after high school because her parents had sensed that she would never make it through four years of higher education—they had barely coaxed her through high school—and they wanted her to have some way of sustaining herself. It's true that not everyone at Titan has a college degree, but the vast majority of them do, and, frankly, Cynthia's attitude is often poor. She knows this. Her effort is minimal. Other candidates are more likely to gain entry into a different part of the company. She knows she will probably spend most of her adult life behind a desk, and she has almost resigned herself to this fate. Always, her mind circles back to one final reason to stay—Cynthia is something of a hypochondriac, and Titan has wonderful benefits—and then she nods to herself and settles back into work.

IX.

Lenore and Cynthia moved in together nearly as abruptly as they started a band together.

"I'm being evicted," said Lenore, after she hadn't paid her rent in two months. "Can I bring my stuff over tomorrow afternoon?"

"Yes," said Cynthia reflexively, too surprised to think. She had learned already that Lenore was skilled at surprising people into things with her bluntness. And even though Cynthia was wary because she had not lived with anyone in five years, she was excited because it was Lenore, and Cynthia was desperately in love with her and wanted her nearby as much as possible.

So they moved in together, and Cynthia became a bad person. She really thought she was. "I am a bad person," she said to herself out loud from time to time. What she meant was this: she became sneaky. Lenore was penetrable to her all at once. All of her things within easy reach, and Lenore out so much.

Cynthia began with the photo album. It was the second day after Lenore moved in. A year before, maybe more—before they were sleeping together anyway—Lenore had flipped through it with her casually, brushing past pages of pictures of herself with different women and men. "This was Hannah. This was Graham," she said, pointing to one picture at a time, always using the past tense. At the time, Cynthia hadn't paid particularly close attention. She remembered one or two. One was of a woman (nearly a girl! nearly a girl!) sitting next to Lenore on the subway and angling for a kiss. Lenore was laughingly fending her off. Who took that photo? wondered Cynthia, in retrospect. Was it one of Lenore's friends that Cynthia knew? The question overwhelmed her.

Lenore's photo album occupied a good deal of her thoughts before she and Lenore moved in together. She was desperate to see it again; she dreaded seeing it again. She imagined Lenore with every one of her past loves, and felt somehow that the photo album was the key to them. She tried to remember how Lenore acted in the pictures, whether the look in her eyes was more loving, more compassionate, than it was for her. Or was she exhibiting some behavior that she withheld from Cynthia? Like putting her hand on Cynthia's knee, or her arm around Cynthia's shoulders. These were things that Lenore had never done and Cynthia had always wondered about: simple acts of love and possession and pride that Lenore seemed to reject implicitly. Suddenly, the photo album became the answer to all of these questions, and Cynthia found herself wishing that she could remember it better. She had seen it so early on—it was almost a conversation starter; it was early enough in their friendship that they were awkward together, or Cynthia was awkward with Lenore. Later, it was all she could do to stop herself from asking Lenore to see it again, which was unthinkable.

When they moved in together, it became so available. She looked at it whenever she knew Lenore would be out for a long time. It brought her incredible pain. She imagined Lenore making love to every person in every picture— the men and the women, the young and the old. She imagined them crying out her name. She imagined them laughing late at night in bed.

It was strange, she thought, that she had never met any of these people. Even stranger that Lenore never spoke of them. It was as if they did not exist for her anymore, as if they had ceased to exist for her once she put them between the transparent plastic layers of the pages of the photo album.

Cynthia wondered if she would be in Lenore's photo album someday. She was not there yet. Instinctively, she knew it would be a bad sign the day she found a picture of herself in Lenore's book. Still, it irked her that Lenore had never asked for one: Cynthia had plenty, taken by friends at shows, taken by Cynthia with false nonchalance. She showed pictures to Lenore whenever she got them, but Lenore always seemed uninterested.

Uninterested. That was a word that Cynthia hated, but more and more it seemed to her that it described Lenore.

X.

Just before five o'clock, Theo calls Cynthia again.

"What's the word on Jax?" he asks.

"Not good," says Cynthia. "Doesn't look like she'll be going. She's making me go, though, and write a report. Does that make you feel better?"

"Okay, I've got something else," says Theo. "You ready?"

"Hit me."

"What if I could promise Jax that Lenore Lamont would

be making a surprise appearance at the Burn's show tonight?"

Cynthia's heart stops. She wonders if Theo can hear her
breathing. She cannot speak.

"Next big thing, right? She'd go if Lenore's there."

"Yeah," says Cynthia. "Yes."

"Tell her for me, okay?"

XI.

Their last week together, Cynthia and Lenore had been
fighting. They were always fighting. They would fight and
then Lenore would leave or Cynthia would leave and go
for a walk, or if the fight had been bad, one of them would
stay with a friend. During these times apart, Cynthia would
realize (a realization that always seemed newer, fresher
than it ever had before) with crushing certainty how much
she needed Lenore. She would have elaborate breakup
fantasies: she imagined herself standing in the shower and
wailing, imagined clutching herself and doubling over in
emotion, imagined crying on the subway and earning sympathetic glances from strangers. For Cynthia, there was always a sort of pleasure in these fantasies, a satisfaction that
only comes from self-righteousness. And then, inevitably,
her thoughts would turn to the more painful consequences
of losing Lenore. She could not bear the thought of waking up without her for too many mornings in a row. She
could not bear the thought of doing without Lenore's body,
of being separated from her physically. But it was the

thought of losing the chance to play with her onstage that always sent Cynthia spinning; watching Lenore play without knowing that, later, she would share a bed with Lenore—that was impossible. It would not do. And so she always apologized.

♮ ♯ ♮

They had been fighting on the day Lenore left, but Cynthia always thought she would come back. When she didn't the first night, Cynthia had the breakup fantasies she liked: the kind that made her feel sorry for herself, the kind that gave her grim pleasure. The second night, she was worried. The third night, her self-righteousness turned to loathing and she felt afraid. She crawled to the shelf in the living room where Lenore kept her photo album and she opened it for maybe the thousandth time and she turned it, page by page. She felt terrible pity for everyone. The girl with Lenore on the subway: What was she doing now? Cynthia was certain that Lenore had hurt her somehow. The bitch. The bitch. Kiss her, she said to Lenore in the photo. She just wants a kiss.

"Did she pull your hair in bed?" Cynthia asked the girl. "Did she ever say your name out loud?"

Then she had an idea. She stood up and went into the bedroom and found a picture she had of herself and Lenore playing together. It was a good picture of Lenore, but most pictures were. More surprisingly, it was a great picture of Cynthia. She looked intense and appealing. Her right hand was raised, about to come down on a tom. She took it and brought it back into the living room, where the photo album was open on the floor. She stuck it in behind the picture of Lenore and the girl on the subway. There, she thought. She was in Lenore's photo album at last.

Cynthia was still sitting on the floor, still looking at the album when the door opened and Lenore came in.

"I'm leaving," said Lenore. It was cold outside. Her nose was running and she wiped a hand under it. "Why are you looking at my pictures?"

Cynthia didn't respond. She picked up the album and turned it toward Lenore and pointed at the girl. "What's her name?"

"I'm leaving," Lenore said again. Looked. "Her name was Julia." She walked out of the room, into the bedroom. She began packing. Cynthia could hear her opening drawers and closing them quietly. She sat on the floor and looked at poor Julia, begging for a kiss, young enough to break, young enough to be in school, and Cynthia realized that none of her breakup fantasies had been right. She would not cry in the shower tomorrow or on the subway. Instead she would burn slowly from the inside with grief— at work, she would think of waking up that first morning with Lenore; at home, she would play Lenore's songs and remember being on a stage with her; between, she would think of Lenore at odd times. For the rest of her life. She would dread Lenore's success with the same force that she dreaded her own failure.

She was still in the same position on the floor two hours later when Lenore emerged from the bedroom, her things slung about her haphazardly. Before her on the floor, the album was open to the same page.

Lenore walked toward her and bent down and Cynthia thought for a moment that she was going to kiss her good-bye. Instead she picked up the album and gazed at it for a moment, a small affectionate smile on her lips.

She looked at Cynthia and then down at Julia.

"She was my first girlfriend," she said to Cynthia.

She left.

XII.

Again with the knocking. Jax seriously considers getting up from her desk, where she is reading about herself on Gawker.com, opening the door, and greeting Cynthia with the words "You're fired." Instead she screams, "WHAT!" and waits for a response.

"Another message," says Cynthia, and her voice is quieter and more serious. She has been considering her options.

"Is it from Theo?" asks Jax. "I don't want it if it's from Theo."

"Can I come in, Jax?" asks Cynthia.

"Fine," says Jax. "Come in."

Cynthia opens the door and approaches Jax. "It is from Theo," she says, "but he has some news."

"What is it?"

"Lenore Lamont's gonna play tonight."

"With the Burn?" asks Jax, suspicious. She pauses. "Why?"

"I think she's friends with Siobhan," says Cynthia, knowing that she is, working hard to battle the lump in her throat. Goddamnit, goddamnit, she thinks. She cannot speak of Lenore without the threat of tears.

"Siobhan? Oh, the singer girl. Right." Jax is interested. She thinks Lenore Lamont might be Titan's biggest success story this year. She has what's cool right now: that chick-with-guitar thing (electric, not acoustic—that's key), that effortlessly-hot-chick thing. She's a little dirty, and that's great. Joan Jett for the new millennium. Joan Jett meets Avril Lavigne. "Yeah, tell Theo I'll be there."

"Really? Because . . . I guess this means that . . . I actually had plans tonight, so if you're going . . ."

Jax looks at her secretary and the urge is there again; she thinks of firing her.

"Yes, Cynthia?"

"Maybe I could sit this one out," Cynthia says, finally. The most annoying thing about Cynthia is her long pauses between statements. She hesitates when nervous.

"I don't think so," says Jax. "Unfortunately, Titan needs all its employees to come out to one show a month, as I've stated. Moral support; you know."

"Can I go to a show tomorrow?"

"Tomorrow is May first."

"Can I go to two shows in May?"

"Cynthia, really," says Jax. "It seems to me that you aren't committed to Titan. If you aren't, that's fine," she says. "But don't waste your time here. Seriously, Cynthia," says Jax. "If I don't see you supporting the Burn tonight, I think I

might tell you to consider looking elsewhere for employ-
ment."

Jax rises from her desk. It is five o'clock, and she has to
go home and change now that she will be seen in public
tonight.

XIII.

Cynthia mists the ficus before leaving. She collects herself
and her things, turns off her computer, and presses the
down button for the elevator. Outside it is lovely and warm:
the start of an early summer. Her heart and her mind are
filled with Lenore. How is it, she asks herself, that love
can end for one but not another? Lenore still fills her;
she is Cynthia's first thought upon waking, her last before
sleeping. But Lenore has done nothing to contact her
since leaving. Never even once. It's as if their relationship
of four years did not happen at all. Even Cynthia can feel
herself distilling their time together into moments that
she does not want to forget: a trip to the Jersey Shore to
stay with friends of Lenore's, during which Lenore was ex-
ceptionally kind and sweet to her; a visit to Cynthia's family's home in New Hampshire; a bathtub filled with hot
water; that first morning together; that first evening
together.

What was it in the time between that drove them apart?
Cynthia has so often heard the refrain from her little circle of friends—"It wasn't your fault; it was Lenore"—that
she almost believes it, but she wonders at times if she

really did drive Lenore away. She cannot bring herself to hate Lenore, not even a little bit. Her internal rhetoric is hateful, the thoughts she thinks in words, but her feelings for Lenore are still loving and tender. In most ways she still thinks of Lenore as she did way back when: as a child that she could care for. She is older than Lenore by seven years. She allows herself one folly: a fantasy that maybe when Lenore is older, wiser, she will see the light and come back to Cynthia. She will realize her mistake.

This is the start of summer in New York, and all around her couples are sitting outside at restaurants, laughing, eating. Just what I need to see, says Cynthia, and tries to laugh at her own expense, but she cannot even muster dark humor.

Cynthia usually loves the city in the summer. It's so much more open than it is in December or January. Everyone is outside. Everyone is in love.

She walks past a display of TV sets in some electronics store and sees they are all playing the same music video. Three women gyrate silently in time to some inaudible song.

The Burn is playing at eight o'clock. She could just walk downtown. She could just stand in the back of the Bowery, say hello to Jax once, perhaps slip out early.

XIV.

Siobhan and the Burn are backstage. Theo Brigham walks in.

"Where's Lenore?" he says.

"I don't know, man," says Mike R., the lead guitarist. "You're the one that asked her to play."

"Siobhan asked her to play," says Theo. "Siobhan called her."

"You told Siobhan to call her," says Mike. "Right, Siobhan?"

"I don't know," says Siobhan. "I don't remember." Mike is pissed that Lenore is singing at their album release party: it's *their* album release party. Lenore will get her own next fall. She's already got a goddamn billboard in Times Square, and that's something the Burn can only dream about. Siobhan doesn't really care. She's friends with Lenore, for one thing—they've been playing the same circuit forever—and she knows why Theo has arranged this. Siobhan has forced herself to stop caring about the little details of record making. It would kill her if she paid attention. She just does what she's told. Recently she has gotten recognized twice, and these are her first experiences with fame: once, a young woman who told her she had seen her open for Tommy Mays in New Jersey; once, a father walking with two children who grabbed her shoulders enthusiastically and planted a kiss on her cheek.

She likes it now, the way one likes to see one's name in the newspaper, or to be interviewed on the local news, but she will not always. In five years she will tire of fame suddenly and move to the south of France to wait tables in obscurity, though she will come back to New York in the end.

She looks at Mike now and gives him a subtle shake of her head: the universal sign for "It's not worth it."

"She'll be here. She's usually late," says Siobhan.

Theo is pacing back and forth, which is hard to do in the tiny room they're in. The sound guy comes back to ask Mike one last question about the mix he likes in his monitor, and then they're on.

XV.

Cynthia, having stopped for a few drinks to bolster her courage on the way down, is late. She stands outside for a moment, hesitating. She could still turn around. She does not know if she's on the list; she figures that her Titan identification might be enough to get her in. Then again, maybe not. Depends on who's working the door. She tries the man with the list.

"I'm not sure if I'm on here," she says. She has never mastered the bravado that others in the industry seem to pick up effortlessly.

"What's your name?" asks the man with the list.

"Cynthia Kelley."

The man scans the sheet. "Nope," he says, and looks away. Cynthia wants to tell him she's not trying to get out of paying, that she just didn't know. Instead she walks to the box office, which conspicuously lacks a line.

"How much?" she asks the girl.

"Thirty-five," says the girl at the window. Cynthia

blanches for a second; she knows she does not have that much in her wallet, and, because of her recent purchase of a sweet vintage drum set, she has only about fifty dollars in her bank account to sustain her until her next paycheck. She fumbles for her debit card anyway, aware that if she does not find her way into this concert, another paycheck might not be coming.

"But it's sold out," says the girl. "So."

Cynthia looks around. This might be a perfect way out. She imagines the conversation: "I'm sorry, Jax," she would say. "It was sold out." Then Jax would say, "Why didn't you get yourself on the list? That's perfectly within your power." Then Jax would say, "You're fired."

Fortunately, the man with the list puts down a walkie-talkie and calls her over. "Cynthia Kelley?" he says. "You with Titan?"

"Yeah," she says.

"Go on in," he says. "They're expecting you."

Cynthia heads for the door, feeling mildly vindicated. She crosses paths with Theo as he comes out of the venue, talking agitatedly on his cell phone. "She said she'd be here," he says. "She promised."

Immediately Cynthia feels the same sort of physical reaction she felt when she saw Lenore on the billboard. Illness. Grief. She is surprised at herself: she should be relieved that Lenore is not coming, and also she should have known. Lenore was many things, but reliable was not one of them. Still, she had been anticipating a glimpse of Lenore, and to be deprived of this is like losing Lenore all over again. Just one little glimpse: that's all she wanted. One small glimpse from the safety of a darkened room.

♭ ♮ ♭

Inside, she looks around for Jax but cannot find her. The Burn is already onstage, playing too loud, dressed in their drop-party best. She heads upstairs, flashing her Titan ID as she goes; for this concert, the upstairs is reserved for the label. She looks all around but still cannot find Jax. She recognizes some low-level execs but feels too shy to say hi. She is certain that they will wonder what the secretary is doing here, unaware of Jax's latest abusive policy. As she is contemplating whether or not to spend more money on a drink, Theo comes in, and she approaches him, relieved.

"Hey," he says. He looks distracted.

"Hey, Theo," says Cynthia, trying to be cool. "What's up?"

"Not much."

"Have you seen Jax?" asks Cynthia, casually. She would rather die than let Theo know she has been bullied into being here.

"Ha," says Theo.

"What?"

"Very funny."

"I don't get it," says Cynthia.

"She's not coming," says Theo. "You knew that, right? Jax isn't coming. We're basically fucked. The room is packed and no one important's here to see it."

Cynthia spends one half second wondering if she will ever be the type of person important enough to be called important, and another one remembering Theo's telephone call and realizing the implication of his revelation.

As if in answer to her question, the Burn stops at the end of a song and Siobhan says, "We've got a treat for you guys. A *reeeeeeal treeeeat.*" Siobhan is shy when she's not singing, and sometimes she disguises this shyness by dragging and slurring her stage banter into a semblance of nonchalance. She would prefer it if Mike or Katia or someone else would just talk, and they used to until Theo told them that that was weird, that Siobhan needed to be a real front woman so as not to confuse the audience. "Please welcome my friend Lenore Lamont," she says, and the room breaks into applause. Most of the kids there are here to see the Burn, but they've all heard of Lenore too. She's still underground enough to be considered cool, but she's getting big enough to earn new fans as well.

Next to Cynthia, Theo buries his head in his hands, imagining what Jax would think if she were here. He hopes someone is videotaping this, at least. Maybe he can show it to Jax later.

Cynthia approaches the front of the upstairs section as if in a trance. She puts one hand on the railing of the balcony and sees Lenore come onstage. She cannot tell if there is a lull in the noise that marks her entrance or if her hearing has cut out; suddenly all of her senses are consumed by Lenore. It's funny, the things we feel when we have not seen a loved one in some time: that no time has elapsed at all, that it has been a millennium, illness, shyness, bravery. The disbelief that once you shared a bed with this person. The desire to share a bed once more.

All of this before Lenore has sung a note or said a word. She has walked onstage, kissed Siobhan (Cynthia now hates Siobhan), waved to the crowd. She looks like herself, but she has cut her hair shorter. She is wearing some kind of dark eyeliner that makes her look like Chrissie Hynde. She is wearing a short skirt, and her legs are pale and lovely. She picks up the guitar that the tech has propped on a stand for her, plugs in, and slings it about herself so it falls at her hips.

"Hello, New York," she says. Her voice is like a twelve-year-old's. Nothing has changed.

Theo is saying something to Cynthia but she cannot hear; she leaves him and walks to the stairs, sprinting down them, taking them two at a time, walking toward the stage, toward Lenore. She stops far enough back so that she is certain Lenore cannot see her. Lenore and the Burn have chosen to play one of Lenore's songs that Cynthia helped her write, and Cynthia allows herself to believe that Lenore had guessed she might be there. It is easy, sometimes, to convince herself that Lenore has forgotten her completely, has moved on so thoroughly that if they ran into each other on the street Lenore's look would be one of utter confusion.

We spent four years together, thinks Cynthia. I am worth something to her. She must know me. She is playing a song that I helped her write. Right now, she must be thinking of me.

But Lenore, as she looks out at the crowd, shows nothing but a sort of affected passion for the music: her brow furrowed the right way, her right foot pounding the floor in time to the music—the right way. Cynthia wonders if she ever knew her at all; she tries to remember the name of Lenore's hometown in Minnesota, and she can't. She takes this as a sign.

You were mine, you were mine, she thinks. Once you were only mine. Now Lenore is everyone's, and Cynthia is no one's. Don't let me live my life behind a desk, she says to anyone who is listening.

She turns and leaves.

♮ ♯ ♮

Outside, the intersection is empty but for a few solitary pedestrians. The man with the list is smoking a cigarette and looking depressed.

Cynthia decides to walk home and starts up the Bowery. She looks up suddenly and is confronted with a full moon. How could anyone call that moon a man? she thinks. The features in her broad, wise face, the pity in her eyes. She is a weakening woman. She is old, cold, and weary.

What happened to you? thinks Cynthia. Compassion overwhelms her. She closes her eyes and feels that she is being orbited by a great and glorious weight. Beyond her is the city. Beyond that, the sea, steadily reflecting what it is not, slowly being pulled toward daylight.

5.

CHE'S BIG BREAK

I.

"It's in the drums. The bass hits you, the guitar hits you, but the drums come in and you're fuckin' hooked. *Bakka, b-bakka, b-bow bow bow bow slam.* Feels good. Damn, that's good."

"Fuck yeah."

"I mean, just, *b-bow bow bow!* And you don't even know what's happening. You're like, 'Whoa, whoa, what's goin' on?' 'Cuz this is like nothing you've heard before. *B-bow bow bow!*"

"I know, man. It's like, it's like."

"You know?"

"Totally."

"*Yeeeow.* Good shit. *Ka-pow pow tisssh.*"

♮ ♯ ♮

Che is examining himself in the mirror of the bathroom down the hall of his dorm. His hair is alarmingly large. His eyes are alarmingly small. He hasn't slept in a few days. Or showered. He lifts his arm tentatively and then lowers it to his side, fast. He's run out of deodorant.

It is his twentieth birthday, and he has an exam at nine A.M. The class is called Psychology of Drug Use and Abuse—a name that is always good for a laugh among Che and his friends. They like blowing lines of Adderall off the big green textbook. The irony.

Che is trying to get a comb through his hair but it just gets stuck and kind of hangs there. Che laughs. He considers wearing it out like that, like an Afro pick.

"You wanna piece uh this? Do you? *Do* you?"

Che's reflection: "No, I was just, I mean . . ."

"I will *kick* your ass, son. Not even playin'."

Che pounds a fist into his palm and checks out his bicep. Not as big as it could be. Nonexistent, kind of.

Back in his room, Che decides to take a break before his exam. He packs a bowl and lights it. His roommate, Ty, mumbles something from the top bunk across the room and reaches a sleepy hand toward the smoke.

"Dude," says Che. "Dude, you wanna get high in your sleep?"

Ty opens his eyes and rubs his face and Che cracks up.

♮ ♮ ♮

At 9:10 A.M., Che is asleep on his bed. Somewhere else on campus, a professor of psychology is passing out exams.

II.

"Again."

"If you wasn't runnin' games then it could have been the same—"

"Shit. Hold on." Che gets up from his place at the computer and trips across the dorm room toward the kid at the mic. The kid's name is Lewis but he goes by L-Money.

Che checks the connection between two cords on the floor and makes frustrated noises.

"What's up?" asks L-Money. He takes off his headphones. He's getting annoyed. Che has been promising him a demo for two months, ever since L-Money gave him an eighth on credit.

"I don't know, man—the thing's not showing."

"What thing?" L-Money checks the time on the little clock he wears around his neck just like Flavor Flav.

"You know, like on the computer. The, um, the volume thingy. The input."

Che goes back to the computer and looks to see if everything's in place. "Okay, again."

"If you wasn't runnin'—"

Down the hall, a door slams. This always happens. Che gets up and opens the door to his room. "SHUT THE HELL UP, ASSHOLES!" He closes the door again, sits back down. "Go ahead."

"If you wasn't runnin' games, then it could have been the same. But you caused me much hurt and you caused me much pain. You and me, ma, and a bottle of champagne—"

"Oh, man." Che starts laughing. "You're not, like . . ."

"What? What?" L-Money rips off the headphones and stands up. He's considerably taller than Che, and a whole lot wider.

"I mean, no offense. I mean."

"You don't like that? Just say it. You don't like that?"

Che thinks for a moment. He opens a drawer in his desk and pulls out a joint. He lights it and extends it to L-Money. A peace offering.

L-Money kicks over the mic and walks out.

III.

Che likes thick girls, girls who can fill out their jeans. In his psych class there is a girl named Kendra who walks like a truck. Her lips are glossy. Her nails are pink. She smells like tea, sometimes like vanilla.

Che tries to sit near her, but he gets to class late most

days. Today he has made a special effort to be there on time, and he overshoots—Kendra's not there yet. He stops in the doorway, walks to the bathroom. When he gets back she's sitting there with her glossy lips and her thick self. Che starts sweating.

He walks over to where she's sitting and she glances at him, kind of, but she's talking to her friend. Che is stumped as to whether to sit right next to her or one seat over—if there's a space between them, there's a chance someone might sit there, so he does it. He sits right next to her.

Kendra gives him a weird look and kind of scoots over in her chair. Who is this guy? There's like fifty other chairs in the large lecture hall. She turns back to Renee.

"Anyway, *she* was like, 'I don't like him like that,' and then he goes, 'Yes, you do, you know you do.' "

"NO he didn't."

Che clears his throat. This is his chance. Class is going to start in five minutes.

"Excuse me, ladies." He leans in. Real smooth.

Kendra and Renee look at him.

"I was wondering if one of you girls might have a pen?"

Kendra looks at Renee, who reaches into her backpack and produces a pink pen. She gives it to Kendra. Kendra gives it to Che.

Che takes it and says, "Thank you." He pauses. He hasn't really thought through what comes next. He opens his mouth.

Then Renee asks, "So are they still together, or what?" Kendra turns back to her. Class starts.

And Che's notes that day are pink.

IV.

"Here's what's sweet about it."

"About what?"

"I'm gonna tell you. Okay, right here. You hear that? The . . . the . . . *bam*, right there."

"You're talking about the cello loop thing?"

"The, yeah, the *bwow bwow baaaooo*, that part there."

"Could we do that?"

"We could totally do that. Yo, you know that kid Mitch? Looks like John Cusack? Glasses?"

"Yeah."

"He plays cello. Oh, shit, man. We could totally . . . we're gonna get him to do a keyboard with cello sounds. Like three octaves of cello notes. Then we're gonna add it to our beats, dude."

"Fuck yeah."

Pause. "Ty, you know that girl Kendra in my psych class?"

"Thick one?"

"Yeah."

"Yeah."

"I talked to her today."

V.

Jumping through puddles after a heavy rain has stopped, Che is reminded suddenly of being young enough not to know better. This is more of a conscious choice for him.

His sneakers are falling apart anyway. Public Enemy is pulsing through the little white wires of his iPod. "Fight the power . . . you've got to FIGHT the powers that be."

He is thinking hard. Trying to make a list in his head of ways that he and Ty can get the music they've been working on out there. He and Ty had a serious talk once about whether going corporate was worth it, and the answer they came upon was yes. "Because once you're famous," Che had said, "you can just do whatever the fuck you want. You've gotta sell records before you can change shit, you know?"

Che knows. For this reason, his list includes the following options:

1. Build a fan base for acts they work with from the ground up, starting with small clubs. (Too time consuming, thinks Che. We'd be forty by the time anyone got noticed.)

2. Send demos of said acts to major labels and hope to be noticed. (Too unrealistic. Also, a lot of labels won't even listen to unsolicited demos. No good.)

3. Make friends with that girl Sara in his philosophy class. Isn't she the daughter of someone at Sony? (Isn't she also really annoying? Che doesn't know whether he can handle sucking up to her.)

4. Get internship at major label. Work way up. Get demos to right people. (But who *are* the right people anyway? And Che isn't sure he could make himself get up for an unpaid internship on the weekends.)

5. Get internship at indie label. Def Jux? (Same problem.)

Che is stumped. "FIGHT the power," says Chuck D. Che tries to jump over a puddle and lands directly in the middle of it.

6. Send demos abroad. Isn't Italy an up-and-comer on the hip-hop scene? (Maybe for Italian hip-hop.)
7. Focus on own record label. (Possible . . .)

The sky opens again suddenly. Che ducks down the stairs into the subway. Water is running down them in a slow drain toward the tracks. He puts the minimum amount onto his MetroCard. He hears the train approaching and bolts toward the turnstiles, rushing down the second set of stairs. The doors start to close behind him and then he sees a woman through them. She looks miserable and wet. Not thinking, Che sticks his hand between the subway doors. They open enough to let him wedge himself farther between them, and the woman squeezes past him. Then the doors clamp indignantly closed.

"Thank you," says Jax Powers-Kline. She is abrupt about the words. On her lips they sound foreign to Che, though she has no accent.

"No problem," says Che.

VI.

When Che and Ty started doing demos for the kids in their college, they just wanted practice. They did it for free from their dorm room. Sometimes the kids would buy them weed in return. Che almost failed out of college his first semester—he got obsessed with making everything sound just right. He used his computer almost exclusively for ProTools and porn. In that order. Later he learned how to do just enough schoolwork to never be noticed in his classes.

The first demo they produced was for a kid named Ezekiel who rapped like Slick Rick. He was from London. Ezekiel used the demo to get gigs at the Village Underground and at CB's Gallery, and then he dropped out of school and moved back to England.

The second was for a whole band, consisting of a drummer, a lead guitarist, a bassist, three rappers, two female backup singers, and a girl who worked the turntables. That was a little more difficult. Che and Ty spent all spring working on five tracks for them, never asking for payment. When they finished one afternoon just before finals, they delivered nine burned copies of the tracks to the drummer, extending the disks to him as if they might crumble. "Hey, thanks a lot," said the drummer, and shut the door. They never heard from the band again except once—an e-mail telling them to come to a show they were doing at the Knitting Factory.

After that, Che and Ty drew up some contracts.

VII.

Jax Powers-Kline has never been more soaked. Her mascara is running down her cheeks and her hair—which she pays someone to blow straight every two days—has lapsed into a state of damp curliness. Despite her high heels, the cuffs of her pants have absorbed so much water that the wetness is creeping slowly toward her knees. The newspaper in her bag has become one mass, and its ink has smeared against the inner wall of the white purse.

And the kid sitting next to her won't stop talking.

"You want a napkin? I think I got one here," says Che, rooting around in his pocket. He produces a paper napkin with a large ketchup stain in its center. "Oh," he says. "Never mind."

Jax is looking for a mirror in her bag, bent away from Che.

"Yo, it's nasty out there, right? It's supposed to stop tonight, I think. That's what I heard, at least." Che drums the yellow plastic seat with his fingers. He's talking too loud. He still has the earpieces from his iPod in place. "You like Public Enemy?"

Jax has found a mirror and is examining her reflection in horror. She's not sure where to begin. She swipes under her eyes fruitlessly and then shuts the mirror.

"You want one of the headphone things?" Che removes one tiny—slightly waxy—speaker from his right ear and extends it.

"No."

Jax tells herself, as she does each time she is forced to ride the subway, that this subway ride will be the last.

"Elvis," raps Che, "was a hero to most, but he never meant shit to me."

VIII.

In New York, some nights are just great. Usually by accident. Che and Ty went to the Village Underground to see some band once, just an unknown hip-hop act that a friend told them about. They were eyeing the scene, drinking on the house because they knew the bartender. The band was weak and there weren't many girls. They wanted to leave. They were going to.

Then, across the room, there was a little stir. A man was walking from the entrance up to the stage. The band onstage quieted, consulted. Then one of the rappers walked up to the mic.

"Listen up," he said. He pointed in the direction of the man across the room. "Murs is in the house and he's gonna come on up here and entertain."

The room broke into noise. Che's jaw dropped. Murs was his hero. Ty nudged him. Onstage, Murs was greeting the band and checking the mic, and then he started rapping. Che and Ty pushed right to the front, right next to the stage.

They were there. So close. Last year, Che had seen Murs in a big room, packed to the walls with young men and the girls they'd brought along. The sound system had been shit; Che hadn't been able to hear a word. But tonight, every word seemed to be directed at him.

Che threw his fist in the air and jumped up and down with the crowd. He wanted it, wanted to be it, wanted to own it, wanted to make it. This was hip-hop. This was real.

IX.

The brakes of the train sing: one sustained high note, and then suddenly they aren't moving. Silence. The faces of fellow passengers turn up collectively toward the ceiling speakers, which crackle to life. A voice comes through them: "Ladies and gentlemen, we are being held by the train's dispatcher. We should be moving again shortly. We apologize for the unavoidable delay."

"No," says Jax Powers-Kline. She checks her watch. "No, no, no, no, no. No."

Che watches her out of the corner of his eye. "You late for something?" he asks.

"Oh, no, no, no," Jax is still saying. She rummages in her purse and pulls out a cell phone. She flips it open. No service. "Shit."

♮ ♮ ♮

After half an hour, the seated passengers are leaning their heads into their hands or against the wall. Some of the passengers who had been standing are sitting on the floor.

It's strange to be in a subway car without the noise of the motor and the wheels against the tracks. A man across from Che coughs, breaking the silence, and everyone looks at him. "Sorry," he says.

Che has given up talking to Jax, who has buried her head in her hands and is rocking slightly in her seat. He is listening instead to a J-Live track through his headphones. He doesn't realize that everyone else in the unusually quiet car is listening to it also.

The speakers sound and thirty heads jerk upward. "Ladies and gentleman," says a female voice, "there is a stalled train ahead of us." A collective groan. "The MTA is working to fix it. We will do our best to keep you updated."

Jax doesn't know whether to check her watch or not. She thinks she might be having a heart attack. The blood is pounding in her temples. She imagines the committee room where, right at this moment, the CEO of Titan and six board members are probably sitting in utter silence. She tries using mental telepathy to let them know where she is. She trained her secretary, Cynthia, to make up an excuse whenever Jax was late for anything, but Cynthia quit last month and she has not found a replacement, and her personal assistant, Mimi, is on vacation.

Jax checks the watch on her wrist and stifles a scream. Even if the train started moving right now, she would be twenty minutes late. And who really believes anyone who claims subway problems as an excuse for lateness?

Next to her, Che is muttering lines, oblivious that everyone in the car can hear him. "MCs out there, how deep does the underground get? Deep enough to set up the upset . . . with your dreams and aspirations of personal status in activation . . ."

A girl on the floor in front of him laughs out loud.

Jax can't take it anymore. She turns to face him. "Hey," she says. "Hey!"

Che pulls out an earphone and looks at her.

"I listen to that crap in your headphones all day long," says Jax. "Actually, I'm supposed to be listening to more of that crap right now. But I'm not there. The only fucking good thing about this train being stopped is *not* having to listen to the crap that I have to listen to all day. So if you don't mind, I would like you to do two things: turn down your headphones and then *stop singing along*. Okay?"

Che's mouth is open. His mind is turning. He pauses. He takes his headphones off.

"What do you do?" he says.

X.

Kendra has been walking past men with her head down since she can remember. It doesn't matter, though; they still call out. She's walking back from her internship at UNICEF. It's raining. The stupid subways aren't working. And the buses are packed.

"Hey, *mami*, where's your umbrella?" says a man who thinks Kendra looks a lot like that woman on the television. What's her name again? "You look good when you're wet, girl."

Kendra doesn't know why she doesn't ever say anything

back. What if she replied? What if she said, "Oh yeah? You wanna go out sometime?" What if she said, "Fuck you"?

She doesn't have a boyfriend. She's not sure why. She thinks boys are scared of her, but maybe she's just ugly or something. Fat? Kendra keeps her eyes on the pavement so she doesn't see herself in the glass of buildings she passes.

Thirty blocks to go.

XI.

Oh, shit, thinks Jax. Che is about to hand her a demo. His eyes are bright with excitement. This is usually what happens when somebody finds out where she works. "I've got a friend," they say. "Let me give you my CD," they say. She still doesn't know how to handle it. It always feels slightly unethical to take a CD she will never listen to. She imagines these people going home, feeling like their lives are about to change; waiting by the phone, by the computer; telling their families who they met, telling their friends; not letting themselves give up the hope that one day Jax will call them up and say, "I've got to sign you."

She never does. The CDs go into the garbage. Jax feels the weight of all the unsolicited demos she's ever received pressing into her skull. All that hope. Would it be better to tell them no right away? But the look in their eyes . . . it's already on the face of the boy sitting next to her.

"And the third track is my favorite," Che is saying. "These are all produced by me and my friend Ty. We've got this idea for the first track . . ."

Distantly, Jax remembers why she started working for Titan. Was there ever the thought that she might change something? Was such an idea possible?

The darkness of the subway tunnel has turned the window across from her into a mirror, and in it Jax sees her age. She's old enough to be the mother of the boy sitting next to her. In some places she might be his grandmother. Goddamnit.

"I'm so glad I had this with me," says Che earnestly. "I mean, I never carry it around, but it's like fate or something." He smiles. The passengers around him are pretending not to listen. Some of them have actually started talking to each other. The train has been stopped for almost an hour.

Jax looks at Che, looks down at the demo he's holding. It's just a blank CD. On it Che has written his name and number with a Sharpie. She wants to cry.

Jax opens her hand to it. "Thank you," she says. Maybe she'll listen to this one. Maybe she'll call Che tomorrow and tell him she wants to meet with him. She imagines it—his excitement palpable through the line, the way he might answer the phone with a tremble in his voice.

Abruptly, the train lurches forward. The hum of the engine. The screech of the wheels.

Jax closes her eyes. She's missed her meeting completely.

XII.

Che takes the subway stairs three at a time. He feels like a new man. This might be the start of something. It was destiny. He is grinning like a fool when he emerges onto the street and into the rain. And there, as if on cue, is Kendra. She's walking toward him. She is drenched, her arms crossed across her chest defensively, her brow furrowed. She looks great, thinks Che.

He's still high from meeting Jax and, in a burst of happy self-confidence, he waves to her. Kendra looks up, squints at him, and raises a hand.

They walk toward each other.

"Hi, Kendra," says Che.

"Hi, Che," says Kendra.

6.

TONY AND THE ATLAS STATUE

I.

Last night when Tony got home from work, there was a letter in his mailbox from his ex-wife. *Dear Tony*, it said, in Geri's neat handwriting. *I am going to be in New York from June 12 until June 15. Would you like to see me? I can meet you where you want. If yes, pls write back soon. I am fine. Kids are fine. Same address, as you will see on the outside of this envelope!* She had scratched something out there. *Geri.*

Tony said, "Jesus, Jesus," out loud in the hallway. He shut the door to his mailbox and went into his apartment.

Vanessa was inside, sitting on the couch in her underwear, eating Cheetos by tossing them into the air and catching them in her mouth. One after another. She was good at it.

Tony walked past her into the bedroom and shut the door. He sat on his bed and he read the letter again. He hadn't talked to Geri in seventeen years.

II.

At the Chelsea branch of Sound-Off Studios, there are three large practice rooms. They double as performance spaces for record label showcases. Each one is painted a different ugly color: bright purple, teal blue, orange. Tony spends most of his day in these rooms, setting up equipment or breaking down equipment for rehearsals. Doing sound.

There are tricks Tony knows about sound that come only with thirty years of working sound boards. Like how every member of a band wants to hear a different instrument loudest in the monitors. And how when they ask you to turn them up in the mix, you just nod and move your hand like you're doing it. Otherwise they'll just ask you to go louder and louder until the mix is cooked. Tony knows what will sound best. Most musicians can't tell the difference anyway from their places onstage.

♮ ♮ ♮

Tony checks his schedule as soon as he gets in for the day, usually around eleven. First up, a band of five young girls.

Hype Girlz. He's never heard of them. They must be new: one of the many acts who get some industry attention early on in their careers. Most fade away as quickly as they are noticed. A few make it.

He sets up five vocal mics—all they'll need, according to the chart. Easy enough. He checks them out.

"Test, test, one, *tssssoo, tsssooo*, three, four," he says. Then the door opens. A middle-aged man in a suit walks in, followed by five girls, most about thirteen or fourteen. They look ridiculous in their makeup and their tight clothes. The man walks up to Tony.

"Hey, buddy," he says. "Everything working?"

"Yeah," says Tony. Stupid question. A father, probably, he thinks. Record people don't wear suits.

"Dad," says the tallest girl. "Dad."

The man ignores her. He hands Tony a CD. "So here's what they're dancing to. We've got a big showcase coming up, don't we, girls?"

♮ ♯ ♮

A half hour later. The girls are singing along to a prerecorded soundtrack and doing their best to dance during instrumental breaks. The girl in the middle can't sing for shit, but she looks the best. Cutest. Best dancer. The girl on the far right has the best voice. Tony figures it out and cranks her up. He turns the middle girl down.

The man in the suit has assumed a position in the middle of the room, and he's standing there with one arm crossed over his middle and the other covering his eyes.

He has stopped the kids eight times so far. Tony can tell he's about to do it again.

Sure enough: "Wait! Wait! Wait!" He marches toward the stage. Tony stops the music. The five girls slump, shoulders hunched, arms dangling.

"*Daaaad,*" moans his daughter.

"Tia," he says to her, and his voice turns mean. "Get over here."

She straightens. "Get . . . over . . . here."

He waits while she walks toward him. He stares at her hard, as if he might slap her. "Pick up your feet when you dance," he says. "You're dragging everyone down."

The kid starts to cry. The other four girls have moved slowly toward one another for support.

Tia sits down on the edge of the stage and makes fists of her hands, wiping tears away like a much younger child. She takes short gasps. Her father turns around, smiles at Tony.

"I think we need a break here, guy. Five minutes?"

Tony stands there and stares at the wall. He thinks of Geri.

♮ ♮ ♮

Reagan died today. Tony finds out halfway down Fourteenth Street on his way home from work—a man hawking the late edition—and almost cries, there on the street, almost falls to his knees. Reagan in a cowboy hat, mouth parted just a bit as if to speak, there on the cover of the newspaper, and an old man yelling in Spanish-accented

English, "Reagan dead, Reagan died today, read it here!" Over and over again.

A memory hits him. Geri and Tony on a couch in their first apartment in Manhattan, a sixth-floor studio walk-up that felt like the jungle in the summer and Antarctica in the winter. They kept warm on that couch in January, and they watched the news each evening on a television that got reception only sometimes.

The day Ronald Reagan was inaugurated, they watched the ceremony on TV and then they had sex on the couch. Geri loved Reagan; he reminded her of her father. He was tall and thin like that, she said. He was friendly. So they had sex afterward; it wasn't right to do it while Reagan was on.

Their son was conceived. Tony thinks it's strange, what he remembers; but he knows that Jim was conceived on the day of Reagan's inauguration as surely as he knows the day that Jim was born.

He also remembers Geri saying "Congratulations, Ron!" and toasting the television with a beer; the two of them moving together, buried under piles and piles of blankets from secondhand stores; a certain pattern of light that used to show itself on the wall above the TV just as the sun was setting in the winter.

Tony buys a paper, folds it in half, tucks it under an armpit, and walks home.

♭ ♮ ♭

Now he lives in a slightly nicer apartment in Chelsea. It's still a walk-up, but Vanessa has decorated it so that it looks something like an airport: red plastic chairs, vinyl cushions, and three oddly placed blue dots on the wall opposite the door. There are three rooms. Four if you count the bathroom, and Tony does. It's a nice bathroom with a full tub and a wall that's all mirrors.

When he gets home, he checks the mail again, thinking maybe Geri has written a second letter, one that says, "Please ignore what I wrote—it wasn't meant for you. I put down the wrong name and address."

Instead he finds a few bills, a gossip magazine for Vanessa, and an ad for a gym opening up across the street.

Inside the apartment, Vanessa looks up guiltily. She is wearing an apron without any sense of irony, and she has set the table.

"I made dinner," she says; she sounds embarrassed about it. Tony laughs.

"What's funny?"

Vanessa is a cocktail waitress at a gentlemen's club in Times Square. Today a man told her that he would pay her five thousand dollars to live in his apartment for a week. She said no without thinking. "I've got a boyfriend." He probably wasn't serious anyway. But now she feels like she should get a reward for that from Tony. Does he know the offers she gets? Would he be jealous if he did?

"It's pasta," she says, and empties the noodles into a bowl, and sits down at the table. "Aren't you hungry? It's good."

"Yeah, starved," Tony lies. He's not hungry at all. He ate

a package of Hostess cupcakes late in the day. Then he ate
a bag of Doritos. And he's getting fat. But he sits down
across the small table from Vanessa, and smiles at her, and
eats the pasta that isn't very good after all. Lately she's
been looking tired.

♮ ♮ ♮

The next morning, feeling larger than ever, Tony decides
to join the new gym across the street. He has a few hours
before work; most bands won't rehearse before eleven or
twelve anyway. He digs around in the trash for the flyer he
brought in with the mail yesterday. It had mentioned some
discount. He uncrumples it and leaves, crossing Ninth Avenue with a spring in his step.

Inside, the gym is pulsing with techno music and with
bodies that are, on the whole, younger and much harder
than his. Recently, when Tony looks down, he has not been
able to see his toes. He notices this most in the shower.

A girl in a pink tank top is saying, "Hi, sir? Hello, sir?"

"Hi," says Tony. He walks toward her desk and extends
the piece of paper to her, smoothing it halfheartedly with
a fist. "I'm interested in joining."

The girl smiles. She wants to be encouraging. She's
probably twenty. Tony can't stand her already because he
suspects that she feels bad for him.

"I'm just gonna page Clarissa for you, 'kay? She'll get
you set up." She dials the black phone on her desk and
presses the earpiece to her shoulder, pursing her lips while

Tony paces casually around the small waiting area they have set up. Over his shoulder, Tony watches the girl as she speaks to Clarissa in a near-whisper.

"Yeah," he hears her say. "Yeah, he's . . ." Something inaudible. Tony's paranoia grows. He should just leave—he doesn't belong here.

Then Clarissa comes bouncing out of her office and Tony has the sudden urge to bolt, to hurl a chair in the path of would-be pursuers and make for the door.

It's only a glance at himself in one of the many mirrored walls—and the thought of seeing Geri—that keeps him there.

He still hasn't written back. But he might; he might.

III.

Jim was born nine months into Reagan's first term, but it wasn't until he had entered the first grade that his sister, Leila, was born. She was pink, and small, and full of snot for the first three months of her life. Jim's mother stuck a green suction ball syringe up each of her tiny nostrils twice a day. He liked watching.

Jim's father brought him to the hospital on the day that Leila was born. Jim wanted to look nice for his new sister, so he wore his bow tie around the nonexistent collar of a shirt that showed Superman flying across its front.

The hospital smelled like school, but sadder. Jim and his father walked together toward a room with an open door and inside it was a curtain and inside that were his mother and his grandmother and Leila, who wasn't Leila yet, and she was asleep in his mother's arms.

"Hi, honey," said his mother. "This is your sister."

"Go say hi to her," said his father. But Jim stayed back, his arms wrapped around Tony's leg. He watched the baby and felt shy.

♮ ♮ ♮

Jim is a father himself now. When his own daughter was born, a month ago today, he tried hard to remember the day of Leila's birth. He realized with a sudden ache that the memory stopped at that point, with his arms wrapped about his father's leg; he couldn't remember what Leila looked like, or what his mother looked like, or what he did next. That day is important to him for one reason: it is his last and best memory of his father. The strength of him, the width of his calf, the fabric of his pants. How Tony had reached down and placed one large hand on the back of Jim's head—not pushing him forward, just leaving it there. Just letting him be.

That's what Jim remembers of his father.

What Leila remembers: nothing. A black shape standing over her crib. Music. Nothing.

IV.

Clarissa is young and firm.

"Come on, Tony," she's saying. "You've done twenty

reps—five more aren't gonna kill you! Do five more for me, Tony!"

At the moment, Tony wants nothing more than to do five more bench presses for Clarissa. But his arms seem to have turned into Play-Doh.

"I can't," he mutters. The weights are sinking toward his chest. He panics and says it louder: "I can't!"

Clarissa heaves a disappointed sigh and casually returns the barbell to its original position.

" 'Nkay, you're done. Good job for today, Tony," she says. "Will I see you Wednesday, then?"

"Yes," says Tony. It's a lie. He'll never set foot in a gym again.

♮ ♮ ♮

Across the street, Vanessa is cleaning the apartment for perhaps the first time since she and Tony moved in together. Cooking dinner last night has inspired her. She thinks—in an abstract way—that maybe acting like Tony's wife will make Tony ask her to be his wife. If she let herself voice that hope too specifically, she'd only realize the impossibility of it. Right now it is a subconscious desire, this idea of marriage to Tony; it is far enough away from the forefront of her mind that it remains nothing but a sweet and unexamined feeling most of the time.

After washing the floor of the kitchen, Vanessa moves into the bedroom. She vacuums. She washes the window with water because she has no Windex. While looking for an old shirt to use as a dust rag, she opens the top drawer of Tony's dresser and sees a letter addressed to Tony in what looks like a woman's hand. It bears a recent postmark. She closes the drawer. She opens the drawer. She closes the drawer.

She opens the drawer, and takes the letter out, and reads it, and feels infinitely young, a child, an infant, a person incapable of self-care, and lies back on the bed, and cries like a widow.

V.

Leila: Tony's younger child, a teenage girl, small for her age, sitting in her room and staring out the window. She should be in a movie. She feels like she's in a movie much of the time. Imagines the camera scanning her face. Practices her thoughtful look in the mirror.

Sometimes she says her thoughts aloud when no one is around, as if she were the narrator in a movie of her life. Now, for example, she is saying, "If he knew, would he care? Would he care at all?" She's not sure who the "he" is, but the sentence sounds dramatic. Just right.

Over her mirror is a picture of her family—the only picture she has of herself and Jim and her mother all together. She can't remember who took it—a stranger, probably. They're in New York City outside the Carnegie Deli. They're much younger. Leila is wearing a ridiculous puff-sleeved party dress and holding an ice cream cone that has launched drips of white down her forearm. Jim is standing off to one side, the beginnings of adolescence turning down the corners of his mouth. Geri is looking past the camera somewhere and smiling. Vaguely, Leila recalls weekend trips to New York City, which her mother used to insist on annually. They have not been in a number of years. No explanation from Geri; they just stopped.

Her phone rings and she jumps. "Hello?"

It's her friend Anna, and she wants to know if Leila wants to go to a party tonight.

"Who's gonna be there?"

"Everyone," says Anna. Then adds, "Bobby will be."

"Oh. Cool. Yeah, maybe."

"Okay, I'll tell Bobby."

"You don't have to—I don't care."

Leila's lying. She does care that Bobby will be there, but it is because now she will have to think of exit plans and escape routes and excuses to leave the party. Anna and Leila and another friend attended a concert a few months ago that changed Leila. Since then, boys have lost their power for her; they've become predictable, all the same, all eager and lusting and slightly revolting. Bobby included. Her friends have worked hard to push the two of them together, not understanding that Leila can think of nothing but leaving when she's with him. Bobby himself—jockish, towheaded—seems totally oblivious to Leila's dismissal of his advances. He paws her hopefully sometimes. She moves away.

Leila walks to the mirror, watches her mouth as she

talks to Anna, and wonders what the soundtrack would be at this moment in a movie. Tommy Mays, she thinks instinctively, and then winces.

VI.

After the gym, Tony heads for work. He feels vaguely refreshed; more human, at least. The news at Sound-Off is that one of Titan's stars has rented rehearsal space for a week. Tommy Mays. Tony thinks: Leila is seventeen. Does Leila like Tommy Mays? Would Leila be excited? And then: Leila does not know me.

One of the kids who works the desk is excited. Tony walks past on his way to the bathroom, five minutes before Tommy and his band are scheduled to arrive. "So you're doing sound for Tommy Mays?" the kid says. Gregory. He's trying to play it cool.

"Yeah," says Tony. "How about that?"

"I, um," Gregory says, "was wondering—I mean, obviously, if you don't wanna you can just, like, tell me, but."

Tony stares. "What?"

"Oh—ha ha." Gregory has liked Tommy Mays ever since he was in middle school. He is in high school now and has been working at Sound-Off after school because his dad can't get a job. He has a poster up on his wall. In fact, he has a crush on Tommy Mays, but he won't admit it to anyone or to himself. Now, as he stands here behind the desk, asking Tony to get him an autograph seems impossible. Tony is going to know. He blushes.

"You want an autograph," says Tony. He's feeling kind.

"I mean, of course, if you don't—"

"I'll see what I can do," says Tony. He smiles on the way to the bathroom.

♭ ♮ ♭

Outside, Tommy Mays gets out of a car and stands on the street. His manager, Glen, who has been waiting for him on the sidewalk, takes a look at him and the smile drops from his face. Kai, Jeff, and Jordan are standing off to the side, smoking, looking surly.

"Are you?" asks Glen.

"Am I *what*. No."

"You are."

"A little," Tom admits. He laughs. Glen is furious.

"How much have you had?"

"Oh my *God*, Glen, iss not a big deal. Iss just rehearsal."

He heads for the door. Glen and the band follow. Tom tilts through the lobby and then catches himself at the desk. The boy behind it can't speak.

"Hello, friend," says Tom. "We have booked space here, I do believe." Glen scowls.

"Yes," says Gregory. He has rehearsed what he might say to Tommy Mays many times, but now here he is without words. Overcome by regret at a missed opportunity, he will go home tonight and make up a different story to tell his friends and family: He will falsely report that he was invited by Tommy Mays to watch rehearsal; he will pretend that Tommy Mays's drummer, Kai, chatted with him about the drum setup and then asked to hear him play; he will pretend that Kai told him he was a *sick* drummer.

Now he just says "Yes" again, and then Tony comes out of the bathroom, shakes hands with the band, says, "Right this way."

Gregory watches them walk down the hall, thinking about what Tommy Mays looked like onstage at every concert he has ever been to. Seventeen so far.

♮ ♯ ♮

Glen is practically carrying Tom as they walk behind Tony to the purple rehearsal room. Tom is tall and broad and sweating alcoholically and leaning on Glen, who is maybe half a foot shorter.

"There yet?" asks Tom. "We there yet?" Like a kid, thinks Tony.

Inside, Kai and Jordan and Jeff walk to their places onstage and glance at one another, uncertain of what to do. Jeff and Jordan plug in and start tuning. Glen walks Tom over to the stage and Tom plunks down there, despondent, feet swinging side to side. His fists find his chin and he assumes a childlike position. And stalls there. His eyes close and open slowly.

Tony looks at Glen for instruction.

"Tom," says Glen. "*Tom.*" He stands back, considers slapping him across the face, and decides against it.

"Forget it. He's gone," says Kai. He twirls a drumstick triumphantly. "Can we go?"

Suddenly Tommy Mays's eyes open wetly and he looks

right at Tony in his place behind the sound board. "You got kids?" he says.

Glen rolls his eyes. "Tom, you—"

Tom holds up a wavering hand and his chin trembles. "You got kids, man?"

"Yeah," says Tony. "I have two kids."

"Me too. I have two kids. Too."

Tom looks at Tony, and Tony looks at Tom, and for an instant each sees the other for what he is: a father, and each knows the other has failed in this role, and then they are sorry for each other and a little ashamed.

Then Tom passes back into senselessness as smoothly as he emerged from it, and Glen is helping him up from his place on the stage and apologizing for the wasted time and asking about refunds and Tony is showing them the door and thinking, I will write back to Geri tonight, I will write back to Geri tonight.

VII.

The apartment at night is still noisy. The complex was erected years ago in a part of New York that was first industrial and has recently become a hot spot of sorts; clubs line the street and at every hour they spit young people through their doors, fashionable young people who screech and scramble for cabs late into the night. Vanessa has gotten used to the noise, cannot sleep without it, in fact. But tonight it consumes her. Tony has not come to bed yet and it's one-thirty, and outside a girl is shouting, "Christopher! Chris! Chris!" and it sounds like the crow of a confused rooster.

♮ ♮ ♮

On the other side of the thin wall that separates the bedroom from the apartment, Tony is working out words and sentences. He hasn't done this since he was in school. He does not write letters. He does not write anything, really, so it is an unfamiliar feeling to him to place his pen on this paper and write the words *Dear Geri*. Next comes *I*. Next comes a blank sort of terror.

♮ ♮ ♮

When Tony was twelve he almost drowned. His stepfather took him to the beach at Coney Island. It was his first time to the ocean even though he grew up in New York. His mother worked most of the time and didn't have time for things like the beach. That summer, Tony discovered girls and the Velvet Underground. His stepfather hated his music and they fought over whether or not Lou Reed could sing. So it was supposed to be a treat for Tony to go to the beach at Coney Island; it was supposed to make up for his stepfather's terribly cruel decision to confiscate Tony's record collection for a week. But Tony could think of nothing he wanted to do less, in fact, than to spend a day with his stepfather—a large, loud, bearded man with a habit of calling Tony "Anthony" as if he had given him the name. Tony was a small, pale twelve-year-old who had neither the muscles nor the mustache that some of his peers had already sprouted.

It took him an hour to remove his shirt. At last, he summoned enough courage to sprint toward the ocean, his face burning at the idea of the millions of hand-shaded eyes that were undoubtedly trained on him. He wanted to plunge beneath the water quickly, to remove himself from sight, but as he moved forward the water disappeared before him like a retreating army. He advanced uncertainly.

What he remembers next is the yell of the crowd that had gathered about him. Then embarrassment. Overwhelming, unrelenting humiliation. There was a moment, though, when Tony hovered somewhere between death and life, and felt himself slip jarringly toward darkness; a time right between getting dragged up on the beach and getting the water beaten out of his lungs, when he was awake but not alive. Which is kind of what he felt like once again on the day he left New Jersey for New York, left his family for a walk-up apartment and endless time alone.

♮ ♮ ♮

He wants to write all this to Geri, but instead he writes—after many drafts:

> *Dear Geri,*
> *It would be nice to see you after all these years. I will*
> *meet you at the statue of Atlas at Rockefeller Center at*

*12 P.M. (noon) on June 13. I remember you liked that
statue once.*

Yours, Tony

He folds the paper and licks its envelope, then walks
out the door and slips it into the mail slot in the lobby.
Tony goes back inside, smiles, and feels something like the
presence of God more clearly than he has for many years.
He'll sleep on the couch tonight.

♮ ♮ ♮

In the bedroom, Vanessa has drifted into an uneasy and
dreamless sleep.

Outside, four children with trust funds are laughing at a
friend who has fallen to the ground and is vomiting up a
$190 bar tab.

VIII.

Two days later. Evening. A woman is walking uncertainly
from her car to her house. She touches her hair at the sight
of a letter showing its head over the edge of the mailbox.

"Oh," she says.

Anyone would guess that she is younger than her forty-
four years, standing there halfway between car and house,
one hand on her mouth and one holding a bag of gro-
ceries. Her lips are parted in indecision. She is small and
quick. She has red hair and freckles, which have faded

with time but still mark her from top to bottom as the mother of her son, who—to his chagrin—is similarly complexioned.

She walks forward and touches the letter, gingerly, as if it's hot. There is no return address.

"Oh," she says once more, and stands there on the front steps for a while, and then Leila opens the door.

"Mom?"

Geri turns the letter over in her hands and tucks it into the grocery bag. "Hi," she says.

Leila has dressed herself up: hair as straight as straw, jeans that show her hip bones, and the glittery eyeshadow that Geri once cautioned Leila against after seeing a 60 *Minutes* special on harmful cosmetics. "Glitter can blind," she had said. Leila just laughed.

"Where are you going?" asks Geri.

"To Anna's," her daughter tells her, shifty-eyed.

"Why are you all dressed up?"

"I'm *not* all dressed up, *Mom*." Then her voice turns nice—she has remembered her original intention. "Hey . . . can I have the keys?"

"Stay alive—don't drink and drive," says Geri, and Leila suppresses her urge to make a gagging sound. She hates it when her mother says things like that. Geri tosses her the keys and then she is gone.

She's changed, Geri thinks. Maybe two months ago Leila began to take herself away from her mother and to lose the safe distance she once had from her group of friends. Geri used to enjoy watching the intelligence in her daughter's eyes, the bemusement with which Leila observed high school politics, but recently it's almost as if she has thrown herself toward her friends to spite herself.

What happened? Geri wonders. Leila has lost some innocence. Geri sighs and supposes that it's a natural thing, and she walks into the house. The letter should be opened.

IX.

Jim does not know some of this, but he has inherited a great many things from Tony: his wide eyes, his prematurely balding head, a tendency toward terrible puns, and a record collection that saw Jim through high school. He had found the last in a closet a day after his thirteenth birthday; his mother had never elaborated on where the box of albums came from, but somehow Jim saw them at once as a present from his father. He played each one carefully, listening for words and notes that might let him into the life of a man he remembered less each year. The Beatles were a favorite, and the Rolling Stones, but it was the Velvet Underground that played steadily from the record player he set up in his room. For a while he created elaborate fantasies in which Lou Reed was actually his father—cool, brutal, drug-addled Lou Reed, standing on a street in Greenwich Village and longing for a glimpse of his lost son.

♮ ♮ ♮

Jim is driving now to visit his mother at her house in New Jersey. From the backseat, his daughter emits small infant sighs, and his wife says, "She needs a change soon."

Jim is a very young father. His wife is five years older than he is. He wakes up at night sometimes in a panic, for in his nightmares lately he has seen himself leaving them— his wife and daughter staring sadly at him as he drives away in a car that cannot be stopped.

He smiles now into the rearview mirror at the baby in her car seat, and he turns onto his childhood street. It is always as he remembers it.

When they get there, the kitchen door is open, so Jim walks through it first, followed by his wife and daughter. Geri is weeping at the kitchen table. She looks up and tries to laugh.

"Mom," says Jim, horrified.

Geri swipes at her eyes and tries to laugh. "Don't pay any attention."

Jim's wife smiles uncertainly and brings the baby to her mother-in-law for a kiss. Geri takes the infant and holds her, rocking slightly, her face streaked by makeup. Jim is holding back, still stuck in the doorway and still wounded by the sight of his crying mother—something he has not seen in years, not since Tony first left.

"Where's Leila?" he asks, to make things normal again.

X.

Leila is sitting on Anna's bed, long legs crossed, waiting for her friend to get dressed. Already, her body is wound up in anticipation of the alcohol that she will consume later tonight.

Anna is applying mascara in long strokes that end with a little flick of the wrist. "Bobby called," she says, and her eyes shift from her own reflection in the mirror to Leila's. "He wanted to know if you'd be there tonight. I told him maybe." She laughs.

Leila lies back on the bed. In her head, the movie narrator clicks on: "Why do we do this to ourselves? Why do we dress ourselves up?"

♮ ♮ ♮

The football team has persuaded a new student, recently immigrated from Russia, to have the party at his house while his parents are away. This is a favorite trick of theirs, to levy a chance at friendship with the most powerful group in the school in exchange for a night of unsupervised mayhem—and the total destruction of one's home, and the bitter enmity of one's parents. The Russian boy is running back and forth, snatching vases and pictures from the hands of drunken high school students, saying, "Please don't, please don't," to everyone he sees.

Leila is on a couch with Anna on one side of her and Bobby on the other. She feels bad for the Russian boy, but something in her chest won't let her act. She sits like a statue except to move Bobby's hand off her knee every now and then.

Someone throws a plastic cup at Bobby's head and it beans him between the eyes. Immediately he is up off the couch, enraged, a vein in his forehead frighteningly enlarged.

"Who the fuck was that? Who threw that?" He is shouting. He picks the cup off the floor and throws it at the wall. "That was so gay." Then Bobby leaves to locate the offending party.

Leila bursts into tears. Next to her, Anna is making out with a boy in their history class. She pauses to burble, "Leila, oh my God, are you *okay?*"

Leila turns away from her and nods. She has just enough alcohol in her system to cry without shame, and to realize clearly—to articulate for the first time—that she is terrified of men, that she is terrified of them and hates them with the same horrible force. She has been hurt by so many.

XI.

Tony is distracted at work. His boss notices and asks him about it, and he says that he's been having trouble sleeping. The excuse sounds lame even to Tony.

He is distracted by the thought of Geri coming. He has a frequent daydream that will not let him be. In it, he pictures Geri waiting by the statue of Atlas—her hair has grayed, perhaps, or maybe she dyes it—in the same dress that she used to wear in the summer when they first knew each other. She smiles when she sees him, and they kiss as if they have never been apart.

"I've missed you," says Tony. "I'm so sorry."

Or better: "I've never stopped loving you." Like in the movies.

Geri doesn't need to say anything. She just smiles, and sighs, and points to a car that she has parked on the avenue. Tony looks at her, incredulous, gesturing to himself as if to say, "Me?"

Geri nods. She takes his hand and they walk toward the car, and get into it, and Tony shuts the door behind him and then they are leaving New York City for good, the two of them, back to New Jersey to a small house and two children who are young and loving and who will welcome him home as their father. Leila and Jim have known all along that he is sorry. He doesn't even need to say it to them. He and Geri grow old together.

Then the daydream ends and he is staring at an orange wall, a teal wall, often a band manager.

♮ ♮ ♮

Last night, he made love to Vanessa for the first time in a month, and he thought of Geri the whole time. When he finished, Vanessa had said, "I love you" with more urgency than Tony had liked. It wasn't that they did not use the phrase; they had been saying it, when necessary, for years. It was that Vanessa's voice brought Tony back to the same cold place he had been trying to leave.

XII.

"Jim," says Geri. She's on the phone with him. It's seven P.M. on Friday, June 11. She has spent the day pacing and packing a small bag that she is not sure about yet. When she wrote to Tony, she had chosen the dates arbitrarily; June 12 to June 15 sounded casual, somehow, planned and responsible. But they were just words. She had no plan.

"Hey, Mom," says Jim. He senses something strangled in her voice.

"What are you doing tomorrow?"

♮ ♮ ♮

By evening's end, Geri has persuaded both her children to take a trip to New York City with her, just for the day, just for old time's sake. It's something that they used to do when Geri's kids were younger—mainly as an excuse for Geri to walk down the street looking up and down for Tony while pretending to take in the sights. She was never sure what she would have done if she had seen him there, and she wasn't sure if she even wanted to; it was just the thought of the chance that made her blood flow more smoothly through her system than it ever did in New Jersey.

Jim's wife will watch their baby for the day, and Jim and Leila will humor their mother by accompanying her to New York City. Both of them have been worried about her recently, and even Leila has managed to put aside her adolescent hostility for once and do as her mother wishes.

They will leave in the morning.

In bed, Geri remembers her walk-up apartment with Tony and smiles. They were so young. They were so pretty then, the two of them; walking down the street was a thrill, just the look on people's faces. When she got pregnant with Jim it was the same: she was just twenty-one and still so good-looking, and Tony was beaming with pride and fear, and when she got big they would see old people nod and approve and everything was right with the world. And Tony had never been stronger.

XIII.

On the other side of the Hudson River, Tony is standing by his window. He can see the lights of New Jersey if he stands at a certain angle to the building that partially obscures his view. A question is going off in his head like an alarm, an inner voice that has been with him since childhood, a sort of narrator he can't turn off.

He had thought Vanessa was asleep, but now she comes up behind him and holds him there, her arms wrapped around his ample waist.

"Hi," she says. Tony can see her face reflected in the window with his, and for a moment he wants to turn and kiss her, to hold her as if she were a child. Instead he brings her arms away from his waist and presses his lips to her forehead.

"Going to bed?" he asks.

She shakes her head. "You've left me," she says.

It is then that Tony looks behind her and sees her things packed neatly into a suitcase and three boxes, and then he looks in front of him and sees that she is wearing going-out clothes.

"I don't understand," says Tony. But he does; he understands.

"I'm not sorry," says Vanessa. "So I won't say it."

Tony is sorry, more sorry than he has been in a very long time. But he won't say it either. So Vanessa leaves, and the two of them will not see each other again, ever; in seven years they will come close to bumping into each other in a subway station, but they will miss by inches.

Tony watches Vanessa's back, and then watches as the door shuts behind her. That was me, he thinks. But I was wrong and she is right. He makes himself a cup of tea. He waits for morning and does not sleep.

XIV.

The next day, in a cab on his way from one meeting to another, Theo is riding down Fifth Avenue. He's on his cell phone.

"Yeah, taupe. The taupe," he is saying. "No, I—it *is* dope, but I'm saying *taupe*. I want the taupe one."

He taps the driver on the shoulder and gestures right. "Turn! Turn!" he mouths.

The driver rolls his eyes and slaps the wheel.

Then, to his right, Theo sees a man standing by the Atlas statue, a man—he squints—he recognizes as a sound tech from Sound-Off Studios. The poor guy looks terrible. He is pale, tired; he is dressed in a shirt that he has clearly outgrown. He has the stance of someone who has arrived at a party hours before it will really begin. Through traffic, through stopped cars and pedestrians, Theo can discern that the man by the Atlas statue is waiting for somebody or for something. He thinks briefly of an old movie he once saw—what was its name?

And who is this guy waiting for? Theo feels bad for him. He makes a wish for his well-being, and then the cab turns the corner and Theo loses sight of him.

"The taupe one is dope. Can we have it by Friday?"

XV.

Somewhere else, somewhere on the New Jersey Turnpike, a small disrupted family is driving toward their missing piece.

In the backseat, Leila leans her head on a hand and dreams of being filmed. She narrates internally: "The summer I was seventeen was the worst summer of my life." Leila thinks there is something more honest about movies than about real life. Things work out right in movies, most of the time.

In the passenger's seat, Jim has thoughts of dying in a crash and never being able to say goodbye to his wife and his child. "Careful," he says to his mother at every change of lane. He is not certain why he came today. He thinks it has something to do with the album he was listening to when she called. *The Velvet Underground and Nico*. He had been feeling romantic; he had been feeling like a lost boy, and he had a brief desire to be in the city that inspired Lou Reed. So here he is.

Next to him, his mother has turned the dial to an oldies station and she is smiling out on the road. Her children do not know this, but the song that has come on was popular the first summer she lived with Tony. So many memories, and her children know none of them. Is that right? They know nothing at all of their father. Geri has a sudden urge to tell them everything, to tell them where they are going, why they are going, to tell them why their father left—to tell them that she loves them, most of all. They are so young. She is so young. The three of them together. All so very young.

Geri turns the radio off and gazes for a while in the rearview mirror at Leila, who has leaned her head cinematically against the window in the backseat.

She turns to Jim. "I was almost your age when I had you," she says. And then: "Do you remember your father at all?"

Jim looks at her. It is the first time she has talked about Tony in years. He thinks of the day in the delivery room, his father's strong hand, his father's strong leg.

"No," he says. "I don't remember him."

In the backseat, Leila closes her eyes and smiles. "I do," she says.

Their exit appears like a beacon. Geri puts on the

blinker and they hurtle over the bridge toward Manhattan in their little car, the three of them together leaving New Jersey.

The three of them together. And they are all so broken-hearted. And they are all so very young.

7.

MIKE HAS
NEVER SEEN

I.

Mike R.'s mother called on Saturday to tell him that his first girlfriend had killed herself. Nora Cross.

"How?" he asked, and then regretted it deeply. It was an uncouth question, but she had caught him off guard.

"She shot herself in the head, Mikey. At her parents' house."

"Nora Cross," said Mike, and again for good measure: "Nora Cross." It had been years since he had spoken the name aloud.

"I know, dear," said his mother. Mike heard her drinking something on the other end of the telephone line.

Something with ice cubes, probably whiskey. "Her poor parents. The poor dears. Oh, Mike, it's just such a shame."

"Did she leave a note?"

"No," said Mike's mother, and then Mike marveled once more at the questions that sprang from his mouth unstoppably like sparks through a hearth grate. They were selfish. Predictable. Morbid.

He imagined, on the other end of the line, his mother sitting there in her kitchen, dabbing at red eyes with an edge of the tablecloth, her hair piled on her head to an astonishing height. The picture made him startle suddenly with grief, and he was relieved. He pretended the sadness came from Nora. When the lump in his throat started, he felt better.

"When's the funeral?" He was crying now, and sniffling audibly.

"Don't cry, honey," said Mike's mother. "It's next week sometime. The Cross family has been talking to funeral homes, but—" Her voice broke.

"What, Ma?"

"Mikey, they can't even have an open casket!"

Mike said he had to go and hung up the phone and then didn't know what to do next, so he put on Led Zeppelin IV and wished he could play like Jimmy Page—sloppy and careless and great. Next, he wondered how his mother knew whether or not Nora had left a note. Would such a thing appear in an obituary? Had there been an obituary?

Nora might have left a note. It might have gotten lost. Mike wondered how many suicide notes had been lost in history; how many questions unanswered; how many final wishes unfulfilled. He thought of Nora's note sitting next to an open window, being blown gracefully behind a desk, swept aside like a petal, like a feather. Perhaps it was lying where no one would think to look. Perhaps it was in the mail. Perhaps it was in the mail to him.

II.

Today Mike feels worse. Feigning illness, he has canceled the rehearsal that Titan scheduled a month ago for the Burn. The rest of the band will hate him. They're on shaky ground with the label as it is. Their first record came out last spring and has only done moderately well, but they're planning a tour based on Titan's prediction that it will help sales. Theo has been lobbying for them since he's signed them, but Mike gets the feeling that the rest of Titan couldn't give a shit about them. Theo has been out on a limb for them for the last year, and Mike likes Theo, so he feels bad.

And he's supposed to be the responsible one.

But now, prone on his unmade bed, his heart pounding with something unnatural, Mike thinks he might actually feel sick. He is hazy. The image of Nora Cross floats from his mind outward, forward, until she is before him in his room, roaming from eye to eye to eye. Nora Cross as he remembers her: sad, plump, blond. Eighteen-year-old Nora Cross, home from her first year at college for winter break and eating a candy cane and pointing out the Christmas lights on his childhood street (or on his wall now, on the wall of his little room) and saying, "They're nice this year," and then, "Mike, I miss you tons." Sucking on a candy cane, her full pink cheeks working at getting all the sweetness out of it. Nora Cross, her mittened hands clutching and catching at his and saying, "Mike? Mike?" like some desperate animal, like some round plaid animal. Here in his little room in New York.

"Why are you here?" asks Mike, but then his phone rings and he answers it.

A mistake. It is Jax Powers-Kline, and she is unhappy. He has never spoken to her on the phone before; he has seen her fleetingly at industry events and, of course, it was she who formalized the signing of the Burn.

"Is this Mike R.?" she asks.

"Yes," says Mike, and knows who it is immediately—Jax calls all the members of Titan's bands by their stage names. None of his friends use that name, except when distinguishing him from Mike G.

"Mike R.," says Jax sweetly, "I understand you're not feeling well."

"Yeah," says Mike. "I've got this cold."

"I'd like to clarify something for you," says Jax, and then tells him all the things he has done to hurt the band, the record, the label, and precisely what she will do to him if he misses another rehearsal, and while she is talking Mike closes his eyes and remembers being young enough to live at home in Rhode Island, and across the room Nora Cross has started crying, wiping her nose with her sleeve, just as she did the last day he saw her alive.

III.

On Wednesday, after speaking once more with his mother on the phone, Mike decides that he will go home for the funeral.

He has learned from her that the Cross family has arranged a closed-casket funeral for next Wednesday. Mike has never seen a dead person before. He is glad he will not have to yet.

He has also learned the following:

Nora Cross shot herself in the head while her family was out.

It was on her bed.

Her younger brother found her.

It was his gun.

His mother has always had a knack for finding things out. Like when Mike was twelve: he shoplifted two packages of Hostess Ding Dongs and a ruler with all the presidents on it from the White Hen Pantry just because he had been feeling too nice all day. His mother found out and didn't punish him but cried for a while and made him promise not to do it again.

He did do it again, the next day, but that was all. After that he was done with shoplifting.

IV.

Nora Cross was sleepy on the day she lost her virginity. " 'Losing your virginity,' " she had said to Mike. "An awful phrase." She had just turned seventeen, and she had always told herself that she would wait for seventeen—which seemed to her to be distant, an age that would never come. This she told herself at fourteen, when Mike asked her out. He was small and loud. She was large and sad and prone to fits of unstoppable nervous giggling in class, which caught her teachers off guard and made them frown at her. She was never laughing at anything, really. But once she started it was nearly impossible to stop.

By the time she was seventeen she had found a way to stop the giggling before it began: she would bite her tongue, literally—bite it between her front teeth and then her side teeth until it nearly bled. Her tongue, a pink snail between pebbles, a sea anemone gone soft, was something she took pride in. Nora Cross was proud of her tongue, and giggled, and sat large and blond in her seat in English class, and for these reasons Mike asked her out—because the prettiest girls wouldn't pay attention and the ugliest wouldn't talk.

And Nora lost her virginity at seventeen. Later she thought—though she hated the phrase—how appropriate it was, for it was a loss more than anything. It was giving something over, it was giving up some part of yourself to no one in particular. Not Mike; not anyone. It was opening a hole and making it deeper. It was filling yourself with space. Losing your virginity.

She was sleepy that day, nearly falling asleep in the warm basement of Mike's house in Rhode Island, nearly content on the couch, but she was seventeen, so when Mike began fumbling around and reached into a pocket and pulled out a condom that he had stolen from a stash his older brother kept in his car, Nora Cross felt that it was no longer in her power to say no, and she lost her virginity, and she never found it. It was gone after that.

♮ ♮ ♮

Nora Cross, sleepy, almost trusting, lost her virginity at seventeen.

V.

Mike's apartment is mainly a bedroom. There is a sink in the corner, which Nora Cross has found and is examining, touching the faucet and the basin and the handles with a wandering finger, running it over everything, just the way she used to.

Curious: she was always curious when Mike knew her.

Mike watches Nora Cross from his bed. He wonders what she's doing, but he is weak. He has not really left the house since he found out the news, except once to buy food for his cat, Maxie, and once to buy a paper, just to make sure the world had not blown apart during his stay in bed. Then yesterday he went out to buy the Natalie Merchant album that Nora Cross listened to compulsively in high school. She had given him a copy of it one Christmas because she loved it and she thought he would love it as well. It was her gift to him, so he listened to it and liked it warmly but not passionately, not the way she did, not enough to listen to it over and over again, the way she did.

She listened to it like breathing: each morning when she woke up, each evening while falling asleep.

Mike went out to buy it yesterday with the hope that it would tell him something about her that he didn't already know. It has been playing on repeat mode in his CD player for the better part of the last twenty-four hours, and he thinks he has some answers now, but he's not sure. It has made Nora happy anyway; it has her smiling. She is pleasant to have around the apartment. She sits on Mike's bed and soothes him. She looks at things as if they are endlessly interesting: pictures in frames on Mike's wall of Jimi Hendrix and Jimmy Page, positioned casually so it looks as if they are friends of his. Mike has been lying in bed, tossing from side to front to side to back like some animal on a slow-turning spit.

But he can do such things—he can fall into idleness for days. Mike has no job to worry about now. When the Burn got signed, he quit the temping job that he had acquired halfheartedly after college. He is twenty-four now and he feels pretty successful: he's a member of a Titan band, a band that opened for Tommy Mays's band, a band that gets recognized sometimes on the street.

The phone rings and Mike jumps, and then across the room Nora jumps and giggles nervously. It has been ringing off the hook, but he's been ignoring it. It's probably Siobhan. It's probably Mike's mother.

"Why don't you answer it, Nora?" asks Mike, but it's a joke. Nora falls into laughter once again. She has been laughing and laughing these days. When Mike knew her she only laughed in class.

Mike smiles; he considers and then rejects the idea of dragging himself out of bed to answer the phone, which has been ringing for nearly a minute. Mike has never had an answering machine. He doesn't believe in them. He is almost absurdly old fashioned about some things: no computer, no answering machine, no cell phone. He corresponds by mail. His manners are good. When the band got signed, Siobhan insisted that he needed to be easier to get in touch with. His one concession: a beeper, which still affords him the choice of whether or not to call back. It gives no one the opportunity to insist vocally on a returned call.

But the beeper has been uncharged on the counter for the past two days, and Mike has been turning over and over in bed and having dreams that are dark and dreary and eating almost nothing and drinking Orange Crush from a large plastic container and ignoring every phone call that has come his way.

Nora Cross wanders about the apartment; she comes and goes. She likes to disappear and reappear: first in the northeast corner, then at the foot of his bed, then by the stereo, nodding along with Natalie Merchant, mouthing the words that Mike has learned well in the last twenty-four hours. Her flickering existence is okay with Mike. It reminds him of being younger, the way children flicker in and out of each other's lives, the way they falter under pressure—like he did. He did that.

"Coward," says Mike. Though he is saying it to himself, Nora's face falls. He has always been able to make her cry.

VI.

Nora Cross lived on the water, in a small house with poles that suspended it over the ocean. The house supported the weight of her family. She had a mother and a father and a brother named Isaac.

Every autumn since they moved into the little house, the Cross family has watched the sky at sunset from their eastward-facing windows (it is nicer to watch the sky change without the glare of the sun in the west); they have watched the sunset over water reddened by refracted light. This autumn has been no different; it's just that first they had a daughter and then they did not. First there were four and now there are three.

Mr. and Mrs. Cross have not moved much this week. They still feel their daughter's presence in every corner of that house: in the basement, where she painted apples and jugs for art class in high school and, later, sketched stuffed animals with fruit or dice or holes for eyes and stuffing that strained and spewed from seams; in the kitchen, where once a week she baked a batch of cookies and then ate them more quickly than she should have; by the window in the living room, where she sat or reclined, catlike, for hours, arranging pillows on the floor when the sun came in and lit up the room brilliantly so it shone like copper, like mica.

Watching the sunset from their window, the three surviving members of the Cross family recall aloud the parts of Nora that hurt most to recall. It is a test for them; it is a game for them. Mrs. Cross says that Nora loved bright things. She loved weak things. She loved small things like ring boxes and seashells. Her bedroom was a very bad mess of green things and magazines. The number of trinkets that Nora owned was almost staggering. Here is the part where Mrs. Cross cries. Thinking of Nora's trinkets, she cries.

Isaac Cross, eighteen, puts a hand on his mother's back and tells his parents that he is going to write a song for Nora on his guitar. The Crosses tell him it is a lovely idea and remind one another that Nora always loved to hear her brother play.

VII.

"Nora, do you remember going to the prom with me?"

She nods. She is sitting on the floor in the only patch of sunlight that ever shows itself in the one-windowed apartment—around two in the afternoon on autumn days like this.

"Do you remember driving to Boston with me when we were seniors in high school?

"Do you remember watching a baseball game with me in the springtime, one April, one spring break? In a little park? A team we didn't know?"

Nora nods again. She seems upset today, thinks Mike. Her cheeks have lost their pinkness. She points to the CD player in the corner and suddenly Mike realizes it has been skipping for hours, maybe for days. Nora looks as though she might cry.

"Oh, Nora," says Mike. "Let me fix that for you." But he has not eaten anything in so long that he is almost too weak to get out of bed, and he tells himself he will rest for only a moment, just a moment more, and then he will fix the CD for Nora Cross. He puts his head back on the pillow. His bed is a mattress on the floor.

He drifts toward sleep while over the speaker comes the broken song: "I may know the word but not say it. I may know the word but not say it. I may know the I may know the I may know the I may I may I may I may I may know the word but not say it. I may know the I may know the truth I may I may know the truth but not face it I may know the truth but not face it face it I may know I may know I may know."

VIII.

When Mike went away to school, he thought of Nora as something static. They were apart for the first time and they spoke on the telephone all autumn. He knew he was not in love with Nora Cross anymore the night she called him crying because she missed him.

"I think about you with other girls," said Nora on that bewildering night. It was raining and cold. "I think about you wanting them. And touching them."

Mike heard her sniffling and it made him feel nothing. He said nothing.

"Mike?" said Nora. "Are you still there?"

♮ ♮ ♮

All fall, that first year at school, Mike had a recurring dream. In his dream he saw, one after another, all of the towns between his college in New York and hers in Rhode Island. All the little port towns that stood between them. He saw those towns lit up for Christmas, lit black against a red sky. He dreamed of their residents, lit up like the houses that kept them, residents who, like Nora, lived in houses on poles above water. The trust of those people! thought Mike. To live so. The innocence.

The dreams were unpleasantly long and complex. Sometimes he saw Nora in the midst of these towns, walking toward him, through them, over them, over poled houses and dim roads. Sometimes he saw her through windows: a Nora Cross in every house, a Nora Cross behind every tree, on every road. Always she was crying. Always, upon waking, he would shudder with guilt—and he had done nothing, really; he had no reason to feel guilty. He began to blame Nora for the dreams, and it ended them.

He came home that first rainy Christmas of college, and he went to Nora Cross, and he said, "It's over." Like someone in the movies. He could not think of his own line. Then he watched her cry on his childhood street for a while. Then he went home, and he did not see Nora Cross again.

IX.

On Tuesday, Mike wakes up and looks at himself. He has been lying in his bed for nearly a week. He can barely stand.

He goes to the refrigerator, half crawling. He opens a cup of yogurt and licks it in its container.

Then he remembers that the funeral is tomorrow. "I almost missed it, Nora," says Mike.

He calls his mother and leaves a message saying he will take a bus home tomorrow morning.

Later, he is haunted by the small details about Nora's death that seem most morbid to him. Why, he wonders, did she shoot herself on her bed? There is something sleepy about a death like that, something warm. He has pictured it many times over, each time a different way, each time a tragic ending to a tragic play. He is picturing it now, like this:

Nora's mouth would be open, but there is no mouth there. Just blood that has hardened over a cave of a face. She has slumped forward. She has almost fallen off the bed. There is blood on the wall behind her. Blood and brains. The door opens. Her brother cries out.

Or.

♮ ♮ ♮

Nora's eyes are open. Her face is drenched in sunlight. She has blown it to the side: the force of the bullet entering the bed, the bedsprings that pushed back. She was lying back on the bed when she did it, her knees bent so her feet touched the floor.

The door is open. From the hall her brother sees her and thinks she is daydreaming, so casually are her legs slung from the bed, so calmly is her arm draped across her waist. Then he sees the pistol, and then the blood, and then the blood, and then the eye that stares unblinkingly toward daylight. He cries out.

Or before.

Nora walks into the bedroom.

That's all Mike can see. A step. Five steps. From the doorway to the bed: steps that might have been retraced on a different afternoon, maybe.

Nora walks into the bedroom. That's all.

Or before everything.

X.

Nora at fourteen or fifteen. She and Mike are fumbling for each other on the couch in her parents' living room. Mike has an erection. With her small hand she reaches toward Mike's face. She stands and unbuttons her shirt. It's the first time Mike has seen breasts outside a magazine or a movie. She's young. Her breasts are small cones. Her stomach, an arc of flesh that she sucks in awkwardly, like a rescinded offer.

"You can touch me," she says.

But this all seems unholy now. Mike is ashamed. He looks at Nora across the room and she is frowning, sucking the candy cane, disapproving. She might be blushing, even. But it is difficult for him to think of anyone that he once knew naked as anything but naked. Nora crosses her legs and shakes her head at him.

"I'm sorry, Nora," says Mike, and he wishes he could think of a way to make it up to her. He wishes he could find

a way to make all sorts of things up to her: the time he was
going to take her to see a movie in tenth grade, a movie
they had talked about seeing for months before it came
out, and then went with Trevor King instead; the glass
pony that used to sit on her dresser, which he broke while
trying to throw it in the air and catch it in his hat, and
then hid behind her bureau; the terrible thing he said
to her once about her 'figure, the thing that had made
her cry and cry. He had only been joking, and he wants
to tell her that now, across his room, but she has turned
away from him and she is looking out the window, half
smiling, gazing dreamily toward daylight.

XI.

When Mike wakes up Wednesday, Nora is gone.

Mike looks everywhere in the apartment for her, but he
cannot find her.

"Nora Cross," he says. "Nora Cross."

He turns on Natalie Merchant but Natalie Merchant
does not make Nora appear. He closes his eyes and opens
them and still she is gone.

"Nora Cross."

She is not sitting at the foot of his bed; she is not sitting
on the kitchen counter; she is not lying on the floor in
sunlight; she is not there at all.

♮ ♮ ♮

When it's time to leave, Mike wanders into the hallway and down the stairs of his fifth-floor walk-up. He is wearing a suit. It hangs on him like a tent—he is very thin today. He is not bringing a suitcase to Rhode Island. In his right hand is his wallet. In his left, an apple.

There is no one in the small lobby of his building. It echoes when he walks through it, sending back to him the sound of the rustling fabric of his suit, the sound of his own footsteps. Mike opens the door and it is lovely outside, warm for autumn, bright and warm. Then he turns around. He walks back inside. He opens his mailbox.

Inside it, propped informally against the left wall, is a letter in a pink envelope.

8.

ABRAHAM AND
PACIFICA

I.

Abraham Kline, on the occasion of the eightieth birthday
of his wife, Pacifica, decides to invite a small group of old
friends and well-wishers to their home in Brooklyn Heights.
For many years, the Powers-Kline brownstone has served
as headquarters for Brooklyn's intellectual and financial
aristocracy. It has been in Abraham's family for three gen-
erations; his grandfather bought it when Brooklyn Heights
was first becoming a suburb of busy Manhattan. It is old

and graceful: dark wood frames the three-paneled window at the front of the sitting room; the ceilings and the doors are high and detailed, customary in Victorian architecture; charmingly, a laughing jade Buddha sits on the mantelpiece (Pacifica Powers, since visiting China as a young girl with her widower father, has always considered herself a bit of an expert on Asia, so, when she and Abraham moved into this home forty-five years ago, she decorated it in bright shades of red and green and gold; she often sighs over the fading of these colors, and over Abraham's insistence, when they were young enough to travel, upon traveling exclusively in North America and Europe). But despite its grandeur, the Powers-Kline brownstone is always warm, and the Powers-Klines themselves, it is almost universally agreed, are unparalleled conversationalists, well schooled in art and the history of Brooklyn.

On Thursday, Pacifica leads a tour of old brownstones in her neighborhood. Biannually, the Powers-Klines visit the Green-Wood Cemetery to pay their respects to friends, family, and unrelated soldiers—Abraham is himself a veteran of the Second World War—and to indulge Pacifica's rather eccentric passion for tombstone rubbings. Over the years she has acquired a large collection, the best of which she frames and places on the already-cluttered wall of the front hallway; she is especially fond of finding stones marked "Powers" or "Roth," her mother's maiden name, and inventing or imagining some family tie. Often, she closes her eyes as she stands by a grave and thinks of the bones beneath her feet and secretly clacks her teeth together so that she feels close to a skeleton herself—but she

only ever acts on this impulse when she is certain that
Abraham has wandered off someplace, perhaps to meditate on some other gravesite, on some particular tree or
monument, as he often does.

II.

"Monkey," says Pacifica, on the morning of her eightieth
birthday. It is her special name for Abraham—one that
has become effortless to her over its many years of use, so
that although Abraham, with his cane and his faded velvet bow ties, is in fact very far from possessing any kind of
apelike vigor, the name suits him as well as his own. "Today I am eighty."

Abraham has been reading his paper in an old armchair
that faces the three-paneled window. It overlooks the street,
and for a moment Abraham looks down at the young
nanny who is pushing a carriage while holding her young
charge by his hand. She is lovely and her hair is being blown
about her face in an enchanting way—the way Pacifica's
used to, when her hair was long and dark. She wears it
short now, and it has been silver for two decades. "Oh,
you're very old, Pacifica," says Abraham. "I think it might
be time to take a mistress."

♮ ♮ ♮

He has already begun to plan the day's dinner. Maris, their
housekeeper, will arrive in time to put in three racks of

lamb. The guests will arrive at seven for cocktails and hors d'oeuvres: among them, the candied pralines that Pacifica's cousin sends each year for her birthday; miniature quiche lorraines, made by Maris yesterday evening; an assortment of table crackers that the Powers-Klines seem to accumulate in great quantities, no matter how many dinners they host; and—Abraham's face lights up at the thought—a magnificent Gouda brought back from their most recent excursion to Murray's Cheese Shop on Bleecker Street. It is here that the Powers-Klines signed up for a course in cheese making and tasting, two of Abraham's many ardent passions.

Hors d'oeuvres hour at the Powers-Kline brownstone is always accompanied by the bottles of excellent wine their guests bring. And tonight, thinks Abraham, will be no different, for among the invited there are several connoisseurs. Abraham knows that the Blandes will bring a bottle from their favorite vineyard in the South of France, for they have just returned after a winter abroad at their home in Nice. Arthur and Naomi Plassey have a son in California, and they will bring a fruity red wine from the West Coast. Others will bring what they have selected from stores in Manhattan or a borough, and Abraham's mouth waters at the idea of a glass of his favorite merlot with the Gouda that sits provocatively on the kitchen counter.

He straightens his bow tie with pleasure. Tonight, he thinks, will make Pacifica happy; and making his wife happy has been his chiefest goal for as long as he can recall.

III.

Upon reaching her office building, Jax Powers-Kline takes the elevator to the top floor and glares at the new secretary as she walks to her door. This girl is the fourth since Cynthia left: a little incompetent mouse of a girl who wears braces—braces, thinks Jax, at her age—and a perpetually shocked expression. For these reasons, Jax would love to fire her, but it would just mean hiring someone else, having to train someone all over again. She's sick of it.

"Good morning," says the new girl, and Jax stares.

"I have a message for you," says the new girl. "From your father."

IV.

There has always been something childlike in the aspect of Pacifica Powers, and it is upon this quality that Abraham now meditates. He is supposed to be reading as Pacifica sleeps in the sitting room, her head on one end of the sofa, her mouth ungracefully open, her stockinged feet tucked into the crevice between an end cushion and the upholstered arm. This is her midafternoon nap. Light from the three-paneled window strikes her cheek and makes Abraham recall a time, many years ago, when he and Pacifica stayed for a weekend on the coast of northern Maine. It was summer and the light was as it is now: warm, memorial, specific—as if created to emphasize all of Pacifica's loveliest parts: then, the dark hair that pooled about her face on an unmade bed; now, the white of her brow, the warmth of her cheek.

Abraham is moved. I am fond and foolish, he thinks, and scolds himself for the tears that come more easily than they used to. He looks down at his book, checks his watch to distract himself, and sees that Maris is overdue. The lamb, he thinks. The lamb will not be done.

Maris buzzes. Pacifica awakes, her left cheek reddened by the fabric of the sofa.

"I had a dream about you," she says to Abraham. "You were wearing your green sweater, and you had to swim across the Hudson." She thinks for a moment. "I don't know why."

"Perhaps you were on the other side," says Abraham, dashingly, he hopes.

"No," says Pacifica, who is not yet fully awake. "I think it had something to do with Reagan—or Gorbachev." She rests her head once more on the arm of the sofa. "Yes, I think it was Gorbachev: I remember his birthmark."

Abraham walks from the room, turns down the hall, and sees Maris's stocky outline through the wavering glass of the front door. He assumes his gravest face and opens the door and says, "Maris, you're late."

Maris knows he's not serious. She and Abraham have been friends for years. She is short and dark. She was slight when she was younger, but the years have widened her and compressed her slightly, so she stands bent despite her relative youth. Her hair is graying at the temples. It just reaches her shoulders and Abraham has never seen her without two tortoiseshell combs in it, one on either side of her broad face. She has a son named Che, who does not know his father. Maris does not know him either, any-more. He was a mildly famous Jamaican reggae singer who claimed to have taught Bob Marley everything he knew. Maris didn't believe him, but she tells Che this and Che tells his friends this because it sounds romantic. Some-times he lies and says his father was Jimmy Cliff, because that's who he wishes his father was. Che is musical, so Maris figures that part of what his father said might have been true—Maris herself is tone-deaf and rhythmless and likes Diana Ross and the Supremes because her older sis-ters played their records over and over again.

When Che was applying to college, Abraham called the president of NYU, with whom he plays chess each Wednesday evening. Che now studies music at Tisch; he is finishing a rap opera he has tentatively named *Diva: The Barbra Streisand Story.*

Now Maris thrusts a bouquet of flowers into Abraham's hands and says, "I was picking these up." They're violets. Violets are Pacifica's favorite.

It is warm inside, and Maris makes small huffing noises as she enters the house and takes her coat off. "Hoo," she says.

"After you, Maris," says Abraham, and places a gentle hand on her back. The two of them walk toward the kitchen, where the racks of lamb sit heavily on the lowest, widest shelf of the refrigerator. Maris has not told Abra-ham this, but she has never cooked a rack of lamb before— does not, in fact, even know what part of the lamb the rack is, though she has some shocking ideas—and she is terrified. She has hatched a plan to extract the information from *The Joy of Cooking*, which is tucked in a drawer in the kitchen, once Abraham has left the room.

In the sitting room, Pacifica sits up and stretches. How does it feel to be eighty? she asks herself.

She doesn't know. In her mind, she is still watching her husband swim across the Hudson in his green sweater, being chased by Reagan or Gorbachev.

V.

Jax Powers-Kline, suddenly confronted with the embarrassing task of either admitting to her father that she has forgotten her mother's birthday or clearing her evening of long-standing plans, stares at the Elvis cutout in her office.

"I haven't heard from you since I left a message last week," Abraham is saying. "Guests are coming at seven. Maris is cooking rack of lamb."

(Maris, in the kitchen, has just discovered that someone has moved *The Joy of Cooking*. Refusing to panic, she picks up the phone to dial her son, Che. "Get on the Internet," she tells him. "I need to make rack of lamb.")

"Of course, Daddy," says Jax. "I'll be there."

Abraham knows his daughter has made plans already. He does not know when Jax changed, exactly, but he fondly remembers a time when he and Pacifica called her Jacqueline: before she left for Harvard and became Jax, before she began wearing orange velvet blazers and calling everybody "babe." Once, in Brooklyn for dinner, she called

Pacifica "darling" to her face. Her mother had recoiled in distaste, and Abraham hadn't known what to say, so he asked Jax how work was going.

"Fabu," she had said, and had taken a sip of wine unenthusiastically.

That was six months ago. They haven't seen each other since. When Jax left after dinner, Pacifica and Abraham talked late into the night. Abraham put on a record of Joan Sutherland and Pavarotti singing *Turandot*—always a comfort to his wife—and poured a glass of wine for Pacifica. She looked dazed; she pulled at memories of her daughter as an infant, at four, at fourteen.

Together, they mused at the fact that they were old when they had her. Abraham had come home from the war with two convictions: that he would marry Pacifica, and that they would not have children—for Abraham could not bear the knowledge that his children would someday die. He was young and deeply hurt by what he had seen abroad; he trembles still at times, remembering the deaths of friends and, more distressingly for Abraham, the deaths of enemies. He still does not speak of his service.

Despite his insistence that the world did not deserve a new generation to populate it, Abraham was also the one to insist, when Jax was conceived accidentally in a Parisian hotel, that Pacifica keep the baby. She was forty then. Their rapidly increasing wealth could have made it possible, even in the 1960s, for the Powers-Klines to arrange a discreet and safe termination of the pregnancy. But Abraham said no, and said that the baby's name would be Jacques, after the bellboy at the hotel—Jacqueline for a girl. Perhaps his years since the war had given him a gentler idea of the world; perhaps his age had presented him with a vision of his dotage that he did not wish to see. Jax was born because of his insistence on her birth, and since then she has changed, and changed, and pulled away.

For Pacifica, there is no fate worse than having a daughter who does not care for people, who sees people as means to an end. It is Pacifica's great mission in life to be kind, to elicit reciprocal kindness in others; and she cannot deny the knowledge—the realization hit her stunningly one day, like a comet—that her daughter has lost her compassion.

"It sounds great," says Jax to her father. She scans the ceiling, thinking of ways to cancel between now and then. "What can I bring?"

VI.

Maris is sweating. She has turned the oven to 325 degrees, as instructed. She has taken the racks of lamb from their place in the fridge and put them in a roasting pan, where they sit staring at her, daring her to make her next move.

"You there, Ma?" asks Che. "Ma?"

"I'm here. What next?" She gives the racks of lamb her look of death.

"It says you have to slit them and put garlic in them."

"How much garlic?"

"Doesn't say."

"Of course it says."

"Doesn't say," says Che.

"How many slits?"

"Doesn't say."

Maris, exasperated, walks to the left of the pan, paces back to the right. The truth is that Maris is a good cook; she is a very good cook, but she is also a know-it-all. So when Abraham informed her that racks of lamb were on the menu, she had said instinctively that she loved rack of lamb—even referencing a fictitious rack of lamb that she had fictitiously prepared last week. A bit over the top, she now realizes; a bit unnecessary.

She examines the meat from all angles. It is red and dripping. Selecting a large sharp knife from the block on the counter of the Powers-Klines' generously proportioned kitchen, Maris stands at arm's length from the meat and brandishes the knife like a sword.

"I'm gonna do it, Che," says Maris.

"Do it, Ma," says Che. In his dorm room, he is leaning back on a wooden chair in front of his computer, dressed in his boxer shorts and a shirt that says PHATTY DRUMS. He closes his eyes, imagining his mother exactly as she is— one arm clutching the cordless phone, one arm extended, legs braced, face twisted in concentration.

With a sudden lunge, Maris spears the first rack. She touches bone and slices downward. She yanks the knife back out. She is crazy with the recklessness of her actions; she always has a plan when she cooks, and the spontaneity, the lack of method in this preparation, is giving her a thrill.

"I did the first one!" says Maris. Once again assuming her fencing position, she turns on the second.

VII.

Once, when Jax was Jacqueline, her mother did something very kind. When Jax remembers it now, she thinks it might be her best time with Pacifica, who was always very kind but rarely impulsive.

Morning came to Jacqueline's bedroom in the great brownstone early because of her eastern-facing window. So it was that on the first nice day of each year, she woke to sun that seemed endlessly, impossibly bright and warm.

They had said it would be nice out on the evening news the night before. Jacqueline woke up and saw they were right, first, and then saw her mother sitting on the end of her bed.

"Good morning," said Pacifica.

"Good morning," said Jacqueline. She felt she was on unfamiliar territory—the territory of TV sitcoms or after-school specials; the territory of her friends with mothers who insisted on being called "Annie" or "Sharon," never "Mom" or, worse, "Mother," as she had been taught to call her own. Pacifica had never before, in her daughter's memory, sat on her bed.

She was thirteen. She was miserable in school. Her teachers called her "bright" and "polite." Steve Garron called her fat. Jacqueline called herself nothing; she read quite a bit and drew quite a bit and did things like taking out books on tarot cards and learning how to read her own fortune. Every weekend, her parents took her to a museum of her choice. Most of the time it was the Met. Occasionally she would ask to be taken to the Children's Museum, just to prove something about herself to Pacifica and Abraham, something about their expectations of her. For the same reason, she insisted on reading the entire Nancy Drew series, though she didn't even like them that much. She simply got satisfaction from seeing the look on Pacifica's face when, at the bookstore, Jacqueline would shake her head at Edith Wharton and choose yet another yellow-bound Nancy Drew book, a pretty sketch of its clever heroine splashed across the front.

When Jacqueline woke to find Pacifica sitting on the end of her bed, she wondered what was wrong.

"What would you like to do today?" asked Pacifica.

"It's a school day," said Jacqueline. "I have school."

Pacifica was gazing out the window, and Jacqueline reconsidered. "I would like to bake cookies with you," she said. She had done it once with her friend Marie's mother. It had been thrilling: Marie's mother wore an apron with a kitten on it, and she had let them lick the spoons.

"Would you like to come out for a drive?" Pacifica asked, as if she hadn't heard her daughter at all. "It's so lovely outside."

♮ ♯ ♮

At the Green-Wood Cemetery, Pacifica showed Jacqueline how to look for "Powers" and "Roth" and her father's name, "Kline." She produced a bag with charcoal in it, and some paper from her large leather purse.

"Here," Pacifica said, handing these things to her daughter. "When you see a grave you like, hold the paper over it like this"—she demonstrated—"and rub the charcoal across it."

Jacqueline watched as letters emerged smoothly across the page. ISABELLA WARD, they spelled. BELOVED WIFE AND MOTHER.

Together, they scanned the expanse of graves for names that bore some meaning for them. Jacqueline had never been to a cemetery before, though she knew her parents went when she was in school sometimes. It frightened her and excited her at once. Pacifica seemed intent on exploring the farthest reaches of the cemetery.

"How do you remember where you've been before?" asked her daughter.

"I don't try to," said Pacifica. She passed her hand along the top of a grave and touched the damp earth before it. It had rained the night before, and Jacqueline imagined the very drops of water that hung on the blades of grass she touched working their way down through the earth, down toward the coffins, down toward the terrible fullness or the terrible emptiness of the coffins.

Pacifica knelt as if in prayer, and closed her eyes. "I'll be buried here too someday," she said to Jacqueline. "And so will your father, and we'll be buried together."

She paused then, and looked at Jax. "You may be buried here too, if you'd like. We've arranged a family plot." She said it as if it were a gift, and smiled generously, and Jacqueline knew it was the only way her mother knew how to make her daughter a part of the love she felt for Abraham.

That day, Jacqueline allowed herself to say what she

had felt since she was born: that her parents loved each other better than they loved her. That she was their gift to each other and nothing more.

VIII.

The kitchen is smoky and Maris is fanning the air with a dishtowel, aiming her flapping in the general direction of the open window. The stove is open and the racks of lamb are burned black on the outside and exploding with juice in the middle.

When the buzzer goes, she nearly faints. The guests are arriving, and she has no racks of lamb, and she has not even begun the mousse she had intended to make for dessert. She grabs the portable phone and dials Che's number.

"Help!" she begins, and Che puts down the joint he has just rolled and pulls on a pair of jeans—which he has never washed, despite owning them for perhaps a year— over his boxers.

"What's up?" he asks.

♭ ♮ ♭

Outside the Powers-Kline brownstone, a small group has gathered. The Plasseys and the Harcourts have arrived at the same time, clutching bottles of wine. Waiting for Abraham to open the door, they regard each other with the easy familiarity that their many mutual social engagements have afforded them.

"I always say this house is the loveliest in Brooklyn," whispers Naomi Plassey, who rarely raises her voice. It is one of her many affectations; she thinks it brings people toward her, that it is more distinguished to speak in low tones. Tonight, as always, she wears a white gardenia tucked behind her right ear. Once, after a lengthy dinner and the consumption of six glasses of wine, Abraham had asked her about it.

"I do it because of Billie," Naomi had whispered, and she cast a languishing glance to her left.

Naomi Plassey has always eagerly striven for the bohemianism that eludes her; the gardenia sits above her ear as awkwardly as it would on a politician or a garbageman. The child of soap magnates, Naomi has claimed jazz vocalists as her one eccentricity, the way the very wealthy decide that a charity or a child or a country will be the reason for their otherwise effortless existence. For Naomi, this cause is Billie Holiday, and tonight she hums "Strange Fruit" darkly while her husband makes small talk with the Harcourts.

♮ ♮ ♮

On the other side of the door, Abraham descends the grand staircase. Its banisters are dark mahogany, worn along the top by the touch of many hands and many trips up and down.

He has left Pacifica to her dressing table. He has always loved to spy on his wife preparing herself for evenings out. He likes to sit on the bed as a child might and watch Pacifica lay out her brushes and bottles methodically. She always combs her hair first. In Abraham's mind, he can see her when her hair was long—she would comb it until it shone and then twist it up off her neck, pinning it in brilliant ways that seemed to defy gravity. Now she combs it a few times through and then moves on to her face. She adds color to white cheeks. She removes her glasses and brushes across her eyelids with brown powder.

Tonight, Pacifica takes special care not to smudge the mascara she applies to her sparse eyelashes. She darkens her brows with a pencil and dabs at her lips with a lovely pearlish pink and then she is finished, and downstairs she can hear Abraham opening the door and welcoming the guests.

Pacifica stands. She is wearing one of her best outfits: loose black pants that end just shy of the green satin slippers that were brought to her as a gift by Bing Li, the wife of their tailor on Atlantic Avenue. She has been Pacifica's friend since she moved here from China twenty years ago and Pacifica, eager to discuss her impressions of China with anyone, offered to teach her English.

Over the pants, Pacifica wears a sort of tunic. It is plum, beaded with a design of climbing flowers. In any sort of light, the beads shimmer and flash, lending Pacifica an air of prismatic gracefulness. Her earrings are small mother-of-pearl disks that hang just below her jawbone. She feels lovely, and smiles at herself in the mirror, and thinks that she does not, after all, look bad for eighty.

♮ ♮ ♮

"Welcome," says Abraham, receiving the bottles of wine delightedly. "Pacifica will be down in a moment."

♮ ♮ ♮

The Plasseys and the Harcourts and the Blandes and Georgina Thompson, widowed five years ago, are all seated in the Powers-Klines' living room. Naomi Plassey wrinkles her nose slightly at the smell of smoke and thinks with hope that perhaps something has gone wrong with dinner— something that rarely happens at these affairs. She looks around the room. There is a fire in the fireplace, which runs nearly constantly from October through April. It is kindled every hour by the housekeeper, Maris, when she is there, and by Abraham when she is not. It throws heat and light and the mustiness of a more rural place into the room, and throughout the house itself, so that inside the Powers-Kline brownstone there is a feeling at once of the country or a farmhouse or any cozy place. It is only the decor that places the home as a child of New York.

Though Naomi Plassey has been here many times, she never tires of taking in the rooms in this home. Here in the living room there is a stately photograph of Abraham, Pacifica, and their daughter, done in black and white, taken perhaps twenty-five years ago; their daughter must have been fifteen, thinks Naomi. It was taken on Shelter Island, where the Powers-Klines summer. In the photograph, a brown-haired, bespectacled Abraham stares straight at the camera, his arms wrapped about his wife. Pacifica looks down and to the left—a shame, thinks Abraham, who loves her eyes—and she might be looking at the water, or she might be looking at the sand. Their daughter stands to their right, one hand placed tentatively on her father's shoulder, the only one smiling in the portrait. One might describe it as serious but for her.

Naomi is contemplating the photograph when two things happen simultaneously.

"Hello!" says Pacifica, descending the stairs like a dancer.

"Hello," says Jax, coming in through the door, left unlatched by the Blandes, and locking eyes with her mother. She too holds a bottle of wine in her hands. "Happy birthday, Mother."

IX.

Che's joviality and general good-naturedness have helped him to win an astounding number of allies in New York over the span of his short life. One of his close friends from high school is at culinary school and owes Che for two eighths of weed he borrowed more than a month ago, for which he still has not paid. He readily agrees to see what he can do upon receiving Che's phone call. Che meets him outside the French Culinary Institute and runs down the steps of the N/R stop at Canal Street, a package under his arm. On the train, he pretends not to know where the smell of meat is coming from, looking at the ceiling as the passengers around him edge away. Despite the plastic that surrounds the cooked racks of lamb, a small spot of grease has worked its way through the paper bag and onto his cotton jacket.

He taps his foot impatiently, waiting for Brooklyn Heights.

X.

Maris emerges from the kitchen with her quiche lorraines, some table crackers, and the Gouda.

"Maris!" proclaims Abraham, who is already on his third glass of wine. "Maris, everybody," he says.

"Hello," comes the awkward murmured response.

Maris bends toward Abraham and whispers something to him. He nods in understanding, says, "Yes, that's fine then."

Maris retreats into the kitchen and the room lapses back into conversation. Georgina Thompson, who has always been a flirt, tosses her head back with laughter at something Fred Harcourt is telling her. Abraham and Pacifica gaze into each other's eyes from across the room, as they have done so many times—each conversing with someone else, each focused on no one but the other. Pacifica begins to enjoy herself. She is discussing Ellen Mills, the newest soprano at the Met. Pacifica has always secretly liked her birthday, for Abraham has always made sure to make her feel special. Her friends are here and she is eighty. She glances at her daughter, who sits unsmiling in a corner, speaking to no one.

Then there is a ringing. Jax's cell phone is going off, emitting a shrill high-pitched version of "La Cucaracha." Jax pauses, considering her options. It could be a client. It could be Tommy Mays, who has been missing in action since last week and is scheduled to be on Letterman in two days.

"Excuse me," she says, and walks from the room, her mother's glare on her back. Naomi Plassey covers her mouth and shakes her head unsubtly, and Pacifica's attention is diverted from her anger with her daughter to her disgust with Naomi.

"Busy, is she?" asks Fred Harcourt, helping himself to a generous slice of the Gouda and placing it, crackerless, on his tongue. There is silence in the room, and a record of *Carmen*, playing in the background, skips a few beats to emphasize it. All around Pacifica, her guests eye her with measured pity.

"Yes, well," says Pacifica.

Suddenly, she is overwhelmed. I must help her, thinks Pacifica. I must help my daughter; I must save her from herself. She has a sudden impulse to take her daughter upstairs and sit her on her childhood bed and stroke her hair, as she remembers doing. From the hallway she can hear Jax's voice as she talks on her cell phone, but it is not her voice, not really; it is the voice of an unscrupulous woman, of an inhumane woman.

"I don't care, I don't care!" Jax is saying—nearly shouting.

The silence in the living room is deafening.

"Will you excuse me?" says Pacifica, and rises unsteadily

from her chair and walks into the hallway. She takes the phone from her daughter's right hand and holds it uncertainly for a few measured beats—the tinny voice inside it repeating a confused "Hello? Jax?"—and then shuts it with a resounding click.

XI.

Maris cannot postpone the dinner any longer. She calls everyone in to the table, praying that Che arrives with the racks of lamb before the guests have finished their soup.

Maris has arranged the table beautifully. As a centerpiece, white candles frame a pot of ivy. The silverware has been polished so it shines. Abraham has instructed her to use their ancestral china, and he is pleased as he seats himself at one end of the long table. On the runner by the wall, Maris has placed her bouquet of violets and a large tureen of white bean soup. She serves the soup now, as slowly as possible.

"Thank you," each guest murmurs in turn. Then Maris walks away and stands in the kitchen, the burnt racks of lamb glaring at her from the garbage, and waits for the buzzer to signify Che's arrival.

♮ ♮ ♮

The guests have almost cleared their bowls when the buzzer goes off. "I'll get it," says Jax. She is wounded from her earlier conversation with her mother and has been searching for an excuse to leave the table.

In the kitchen, Maris starts and then runs for the door, but the Powers-Klines' daughter has gotten there first. Maris has met Jax only a very few times; she is rarely there in the evenings, which is when Jax visits, on the rare occasions that she does. Maris stands back and lets Jax turn the handle.

Jax opens the door and sees a young man.

♮ ♭ ♮

Che walks in the door and stops. "I know you," says Che. "I'm Che? I sat next to you on the subway? When it stalled one time? I gave you my demo?"

Jax remembers and is moved, inexplicably, forcefully. She takes in a breath and holds it.

"Did you listen to it? Did you get a chance to listen to it? This is crazy; this is a sign," says Che, his voice cracking with excitement.

Jax is very tired. She drops onto the bench in the hallway, a bench made of dark wood with a large mirror behind it. In the mirror, her back looks small and fragile, like the back of a much older woman. As it so often does, her head finds her hands.

Maris is confused. "Che," she says. "Leave her alone." She reaches out for the package of meat, and Che extends it to her absently.

"I can't believe this, man," he says.

"Che," says his mother. "Come in here with me to the kitchen."

Jax looks up and smiles at Maris. "No, please," she says. "Sit down next to me, Che." She is almost whispering. "Sit down right here." She pats the dark wood of the bench, and Che obliges. "I want to tell you something."

♮ ♮ ♮

Through the open double doors that lead from the foyer into the dining room, Pacifica Powers watches her daughter speaking with Maris's son and her heart is lighter than it has been in many years. She cannot hear what Jax is saying, but in her aspect there is real concern. Che is nodding; his right foot is tapping the ground to whichever rhythm is in his head at the moment. Pacifica sees the two of them laugh and feels like laughing herself—feels like hearing a good joke, or being as carefree as she used to be sometimes when she was very young.

At the other end of the table, Abraham sits with his back to the hallway. He sees his wife and his hands tremble. She looks very beautiful by candlelight, and her face has softened. If he knew she was looking at her daughter! Her daughter, who is more and more the image of Pacifica. He thinks his wife is remembering something about him and herself, as he does so often; perhaps remembering the bed-and-breakfast in Maine, or the boulangerie in Paris, or Abraham's homecoming from the war—all memories of their life together before their daughter, all the memories most cherished by Abraham. He tries to catch his wife's eye, but he can't. Her gaze is fixed and loving, and Abraham wonders that she does not see him there at the end of the table at which they've eaten so many meals together. She is distant and blooming with warmth, and he wants to touch her face, to stroke the outline of her jaw with a trembling finger, but she will not look his way.

♮ ♮ ♮

When Maris emerges from the kitchen with the racks of lamb on a silver platter, she raises her gaze to the hallway and sees her son speaking with the Powers-Klines' daughter.

She can hear Che laughing, a clear low manly laugh that she barely recognizes above the din of conversation that fills the dining room.

In her head she sends him a message: You are all that I have in the world. She wishes that Jax would leave him alone. After all, she thinks, he's only a child.

9.

GREGORY GETS A KISS

I.

"You're my horse!" says Jilly, who is clinging like a koala to the left foot of her brother. "Dad. Dad. Daddy."

Gregory looks down at Jilly. She is nearly hysterical with joy, her small face alight with heat, her yellow hair hopelessly snarled, beginning to form a lock at the back of her head.

"You're my horse!" she says again, and grins aggressively, and buries her face in the leg of Gregory's pants. "Go!"

"Jilly, get off," says Gregory. He gives his leg a small shake and his sister shrieks with laughter.

"Dad. Daddy, Daddy, Dad!"

"Why are you saying 'Dad,' Jilly?" asks Gregory.

"You're my horse named Daddy," says Jilly. "Hi, Daddy!"
She collapses once again into yelps of joy, and Gregory
seizes the opportunity to pry her thin limbs from his own.
He runs toward his room, which was once a walk-in closet
and can hold exactly one twin bed. The door does not
open all the way. He turns sideways to enter, then shuts the
door behind him and says hello with his eyes to Tommy
Mays. The poster has lived on the back of Gregory's door
since his family moved to Manhattan three years ago. In
California, Tommy Mays had lived on the wall, but the
walls of his room here are so close together that to deco-
rate them at all seems impractical, ridiculous.

Gregory lies back on the bed. He reaches behind his
head and feels for the small stereo on his windowsill, presses
Play. Tommy Mays is the only thing he really listens to
anymore.

On the other side of his door, Jilly is livid, betrayed.

"Gregory? You're my horse!" she wails, her fists in balls
by her sides. "My horse, my horse. Daddy." She bangs on
the door once, a bit afraid of her own bravery, and there is
no response. Then Jilly knows she has lost, and she walks
solemnly down the hall to where her mother is reading in
the common room, which includes a kitchen area and a
table for four.

"Gregory has gone into his room again," says Jilly, and
her mother, Helen—who remembers childhood more compassionately than most women her age—puts down her
book and offers her lap to Jilly. Her daughter climbs into it

with dignity and settles back against Helen and lets out a great sigh.

Jilly always accepts defeat gracefully. For this reason, for many others, she will one day become a successful local politician in suburban Pennsylvania, losing twice to an incumbent and then winning the mayoral election by a landslide after a third campaign.

For now, her thumb finds her mouth and she turns her head toward her mother's shoulder.

"Silly Jilly," says Helen. "Poor Jilly."

♮ ♮ ♮

Gregory feels a pleasant sense of guilt at shutting out his sister. He has a plan and he is mulling it over on his bed. It is nice inside his room: tiny and absurd. It is a perfect place to hatch the sort of plan he is hatching.

He is sixteen and hopelessly confused. Since meeting Tommy Mays, three things have changed: his after-school job at Sound-Off has taken on a new significance for him, as he watches the door every moment and expects that Tommy Mays will walk in again, the way he did last time, as if he were human, as if it were natural; he has become quieter in school, has become easily distracted; and he has become preoccupied with sex.

The third change has been the most difficult for Gregory, since his preoccupation with sex does not happen to coincide with an increase in sexual activity, or really any sexual activity at all. Gregory cringes when he thinks about how he is sixteen years old and has never kissed anyone, girl or boy. Certainly he knows by now that he has no interest in kissing girls, but at least if a girl wanted to kiss him it would confirm something for Gregory about his own desirability. He has friends. He has many male friends with glasses or acne or too-short pants who are similarly undesirable. But recently it seems that even they have achieved a fumbling feeling-up at some party, a terrible sloppy kiss on some street corner. Gregory cannot imagine telling his friends that these things do not interest him—that his dreams are not of Heather Hall at school, or of actresses or models, but of Tommy Mays. He wakes often to a vision of Tommy Mays undressing him, kissing his eyes, his mouth. He wakes and nearly cries out in frustration. Wakes and wonders if he will ever meet a boy.

He aches for physical contact. Every nerve in his sixteen-year-old self buzzes for it—he has turned brushes with his peers in the hall into meaningful events in his life. There was the time that Ryan Mulligan ran a hand across his back in lab—the possibility that it had been intentional thrills Gregory to his bones. There was the time that Mr. Adams, very young and handsome, leaned over his desk so close that Gregory could feel the teacher's breath on his ear. Gregory is swimming in thoughts like these, but acting on them has always seemed impossible, like shrinking in height seems impossible, like breathing underwater.

He still pretends for his friends. He wants to kiss a girl for their sake, because they have such high hopes for him. When Gregory and his friends get together outside school, his friends talk about the best-looking girls at Stuyvesant and look at him encouragingly, for really Gregory is not bad to look at, though his body on the bed seems impossibly thin, and his feet, huge and distant, turn out awkwardly against the wall.

When lying down, Gregory himself nearly spans the length of his room. To him this seems preposterous. Just a year ago he was almost graceful, still childish like Jilly, still able to run without looking giraffelike and ungainly. Now he ducks his head as a habit when walking. He is six-three. He has very little facial hair. He has even features and a slender face that always looks worried because his eyebrows turn up a little near the bridge of his nose. His lips are full and pale. Yes: he is just a boy still, a very tall boy.

Now Gregory checks his watch and shrugs with a little thrill of pleasure. At last, he has a plan.

II.

David comes home with a surprise for his son. He is carrying a large box and Jilly greets him at the door.

"Hi," she says. "Dad."

Helen appears with her book, and her glasses have fallen down on her nose.

"What in the world," says Helen.

Gregory hears his father, opens the door to his room. He sees what his father is holding—sees the writing on the outside of the box—and feels terrible and ashamed. "Silent Drums," it says.

His father looks up at him like a child waiting to be praised. Gregory feels sick. In the box, he knows, is the electronic drum set he has been coveting since they moved to New York. He cannot have a real set in their small apartment. It would not fit, for one thing; it would disturb the neighbors. Since he got the part-time job at Sound-Off last year, he has been playing their sets on his breaks. But not having a set at home has been the worst part of the move for Gregory.

But David has been unemployed. He has not worked in a year.

Now he watches Gregory expectantly, still in the doorway with the big cardboard box. The drums cost more than a thousand dollars. Gregory knows.

"A late birthday present, Gregie," says David, using Gregory's childhood nickname. His eyes are hopeful. Lately his son has been acting strange. "Set it up with me?"

"Dad," begins Gregory.

"How could you," Helen whispers. "David."

Jilly observes her family. Her small body is tense. She walks to her father, puts an arm around his leg. She cannot see his face above the box.

"I'll help you," says Jilly.

At this moment, Gregory hates his family with a passion that only a sixteen-year-old could muster. He looks at his father reproachfully and retreats into his room. If he could slam the door, he would. But he can't, so he throws himself on the bed and pounds his pillow instead.

He hears his mother and his father as they speak in low tones. He hears Jilly singing one of her Jilly songs, this one about a brave soldier who goes off to war and leaves behind a series of pets. Each pet gets a verse.

"Sneakers, oh Sneakers, oh Sneakers, my cat," sings Jilly through the door.

Then Gregory falls asleep.

III.

As usual, he dreams about Tommy Mays. In his dream, Tommy Mays is performing onstage, but the stage is a small one, perhaps four feet from the ground. Gregory is near the stage. He can reach out and touch Tommy Mays. He reaches out and touches Tommy Mays, and then he starts to cry.

"Oh, Tommy," he says.

Tommy Mays leans down and he is still singing but he kneels at the edge of the stage and his face looks like the face of God, and with his God-like hand he traces the place on Gregory's face where a tear has left its trail. All the while singing.

♮ ♮ ♮

When Gregory wakes, it is dark outside. Again he checks his watch. It is eight P.M. and he is already running behind the schedule he has created for himself. He looks down at himself and changes from his wrinkled shirt into a less wrinkled shirt. He walks out of his room and into the bathroom, where he examines his face in the light and picks at a pimple on the end of his chin.

Then out of the bathroom and into the common space in the house, where the rest of his family is gathered: his father in an armchair before the television, not really watching; his mother reading her book, her back deliberately to David; Jilly on the floor playing with an army doll that once belonged to Gregory.

"I'm going to Tim's," says Gregory. He has a messenger bag slung across his torso. "For a science project."

His father will not look at him. "Goodbye, Gregie," he says, his face blue in the light of the television.

"Bye, Gregory," says his mother. "Careful on the subway. Don't be past ten-thirty."

Only Jilly knows he is lying. "Bye, Daddy the horse," she says.

IV.

Somewhere else in New York, Tom is putting his daughters, Clara and Alice, to bed. He has not had a drink in a week. He feels real; he feels scared. Camilla enters the dim, sweet room and gazes at him and their daughters, already older than she can believe.

"Oh, Tom," she says.

Tom smiles and feels blessed. Camilla is wearing a red dress that she has not been able to wear since before her last pregnancy. They are going on a date.

V.

On the subway, Gregory examines the identification he has bought with one whole paycheck from Sound-Off. Seventy-five dollars for the ID of a twenty-four-year-old named Henry Muller, which strikes Gregory as an odd name for a young man: it's more like a lawyer's name, like the name of a famous prospector during the gold rush. Henry does not look like Gregory. He is dark where Gregory is fair; Henry is thin-lipped and smiling tightly.

And Henry is five-ten. Gregory is not sure how that will work. But the boy at school who sold it to him had said that it didn't matter. "It's a real ID," he had said. "That's all they care about."

It was probably stolen. Gregory feels momentarily upset at the illicitness of the whole affair. He's really very honest, and he hopes that Henry didn't have too much trouble replacing the ID that Gregory now holds in his fluttering hands.

♮ ♮ ♮

He is alone as he approaches the club. He heard about it from two boys who were joking that they had walked by it one night around this time, had seen men going into it singly and leaving in pairs.

In the doorway there is a young man who is taller than Gregory and perhaps twice as broad. Gregory nearly turns around and leaves, feeling the falseness of the ID burning a hole in his pocket. But he has locked eyes with the bouncer and feels now that he must proceed. He affects confidence and reaches for the door handle—a trick he heard about from a senior boy at his school.

"Don't pull out an ID until they ask for it, and then look surprised," the boy had said. "Act like you own the place."

But when the bouncer places a massive hand on Gregory's shoulder and says, "ID," Gregory's expression registers not as surprise, but as terror. He produces Henry Muller's identification and looks to the left, the way Henry did for the picture.

The bouncer looks at him and smiles. He was Gregory's age not very long ago. He went to high school in the suburbs of Madison, Wisconsin. He waited to come out until he moved to New York two years ago, and when he did it was like taking a particularly deep breath of air after being underwater.

"How old are you?" he asks Gregory.

"I'm twenty-four," says Gregory. He wonders what twenty-four-year-old Henry Muller is doing these days.

"Go ahead," says the bouncer.

VI.

In Gregory's mind, the inside of the bar had been sleek, something like the interior of a particularly dark hotel lobby.

On entering, his eyes adjust to the dim light and he is shocked by the barrenness of the place. The long bar is on the right, beaten and brown. Five stools line it sparsely, and behind it is a bartender who looks alarmingly like a teacher Gregory had in California. To his left, there are three booths; above them on the wall, Christmas lights that run in a blinking line toward the back of the narrow room. A framed painting of a penis hangs on the back wall, lit dramatically by three spotlights. The whole place reeks of beer and of something Gregory cannot quite identify. He imagines it must be sex.

Gregory feels ashamed. He stares at the floor. He wants to lean against a wall in the dark corner by the door, but a coatrack occupies the space he covets. Briefly, he considers hiding behind it and then abandons the idea.

He came here to meet a boy. You wanted this, he thinks. He cannot now turn around. Gregory forces himself to look up, to meet the eyes of the three other people in the bar. Two are a couple: older men who are laughing and wearing matching denim jackets. Gregory imagines their laughter might be at his expense. He can only hear some of what they are saying:

"They just don't know . . . a joke! A joke! I know . . . dear God," says one.

Gregory suddenly realizes that he has been standing near the door for perhaps thirty seconds and he goes over to the bar, careful to turn his back to the bartender so that the bartender will not speak to him.

It is then that he notices the man to his right. He is low to the earth and he moves effortlessly and quickly toward Gregory, so quickly that Gregory is afraid and his whole body jerks in reaction. Then the man stops beside him, and he's smiling.

"Warm in here," he says, but makes no move to uncloak himself.

Gregory takes him in. "Yes, warm," he says.

The man could be twenty-five and he could be forty. His hair falls in childlike curls to his ears, which are tiny and delicate, like the ears of a young boy. His coat is fashionable: It is made of fine cotton and it hits at the hip, its zipper set left of center. Its wearer has turned up the collar at the back and out at the sides, as if protecting himself from a particularly strong wind. The coat is black and impeccably clean.

Everything about this man is clean, thinks Gregory. Even his smell. To Gregory, he smells new, like a department store. He wonders briefly if the coat is newly bought, or—Gregory's eyebrows furrow at the thought—stolen.

The man notices Gregory's expression and smiles more broadly, and Gregory sees in horror that one of his teeth is missing: a side one, a large one. So incongruous is the missing tooth with the man's clothing that Gregory wonders if the tooth was knocked out tonight—if the man even knows it is missing. Next to the man with the black coat and the missing tooth, Gregory feels out of control, chaotic, as if his life is not his anymore.

The man is very polite: "May I buy you a drink?" he asks.

Gregory pauses, completely unsure of what sort of drink he would ask for, were he to accept.

"Soda? Water? Juice?" asks the man, smiling still, complicit. And Gregory falters. It's a joke, he thinks. It must be a joke.

"A drink for you?" the man asks again, more urgently, and Gregory thinks of his father, David, and what David orders at their infrequent trips to restaurants. Brooklyn Lager, mostly. Occasionally a margarita if they go to a Mexican place. But then Gregory wonders if these drinks are too fatherly. Desperate, he summons the only other drink he can think of, and spits out the name of it.

"A cosmopolitan," Gregory says. His voice falters. "Thank you."

The man laughs. The empty space in his mouth lends him the air of a jack-o'-lantern; and like a jack-o'-lantern, his skin is orange, his eyes lit from within by an anticipation that terrifies Gregory and thrills him at once.

The man in the black coat catches the bartender's eye. "A Brooklyn Lager, please," he says. "And the lady will have a cosmopolitan." He winks at Gregory, turns to him so that his knee touches Gregory's. Gregory closes his eyes for one beat longer than a blink.

"I love this song," says the man. It's "Just Like Heaven," by the Cure. Gregory likes it too, but he feels speechless and slightly shocked that he has anything at all in common with this stranger, who has made fists of his hands and is now making strange little dancing movements. His weight shifts from left to right with little relation to the beat of the song. He stops when he sees Gregory is not dancing.

"I bet you're in college," says the man. He places a finger over his own two lips, raises his eyes to Gregory's appraisingly. "You look like a college boy to me."

"I am," says Gregory. He tries to lean his elbow on the

bar and misses, instead planting an unsteady hand on the stool next to him.

"What's your name?"

"Henry," says Gregory.

"Does anyone call you Hank?" The man reaches for Gregory's sleeve and fingers it at Gregory's elbow. "I like that name. Hank."

"Yes," says Gregory. "Yes, most of my friends call me Hank."

VII.

Outside, the air is warmer than Gregory imagined. It is eleven-thirty P.M. and three cosmopolitans swim sickeningly in his stomach. Gregory is sure that by now his mother has called Tim's mother, maybe even called the police. He does not know why he won't go home. The man takes his hand and Gregory is shocked at the feeling: holding hands with a man on the street. He is wise and sophisticated; he is a man of the world. Holding hands with a man on the street. Another couple passes them and the woman smiles at Gregory approvingly. She nods to them, but the man she is with looks at Gregory a bit too long.

The man in the black coat walks one step in front of Gregory, leading him a bit, refusing to look at him.

"Almost there," he says at intervals.

Gregory allows himself to imagine that the man is Tommy Mays and feels better. Tommy Mays, who would not call him "Hank"; Tommy Mays, who would know that he was lying about his name, about his age. Tommy Mays, who would take his hand gently and walk beside him, perhaps placing a hand on his back or about his shoulders.

Gregory looks up at the man in the black coat and feels sick for himself.

♮ ♮ ♮

He wishes he were home with Jilly and Helen and David, who are probably watching the television in their small common room. Jilly might be sleeping, her soft blond baby hair flush on the lap of their mother. Jilly! thinks Gregory, and feels a sudden rage toward the man in the dark coat, for every part of Gregory knows that the quiet place toward which they are walking is no place for boys like him. Still, Gregory will follow him, and walk with him hand in hand while Gregory's gut reviles and his heart races in indignation. He thinks of his sister, thinks, But I am not so much older than Jilly at all! He should know; the man in the black coat should know these things and be ashamed.

The man tightens his sweaty grip on Gregory's hand. "Almost there, Hank," he says. Gone is the look of anticipation in his eyes from earlier, replaced by nervousness, by a gaze fixed distantly, frankly upon the sidewalk, and he will not look at Gregory. He quickens his pace.

Gregory begins to feel ridiculous. He towers over this man. He feels the meaninglessness of his size as sharply as he feels that he is clumsy and great, that there is no one in the world as huge as he.

VIII.

The restaurant is crowded when Tom and Camilla arrive, even though it's late. This is a restaurant that is crowded from six until closing, every night of the week.

"Somewhere else, Tom," says Camilla. She feels awkward next to her husband: plain-looking. Especially in crowds like this one. Every eye is drawn to Tom, and immediately afterward to Camilla, appraisingly, she thinks. If she could do so without embarrassing Tom, she would bury her head in the back of Tom's jacket like a child, press her face into it and pretend that she was reciprocally invisible to the people she could not see. She would wait for slow, spidery colors to make their way across her corneas, as she has done since she was young and liked to press her small fists into her eyes.

Instead, she looks at the host from over Tom's shoulder. The host sees Tom and smiles ingratiatingly. Tom looks past the crowd of people who alternately stare and pretend not to stare. He motions with his hand: *Two.*

And the host motions back: *This way.*

Camilla is familiar with this exchange, for it happens wherever they go. It is nearly universal, this sort of special treatment for Tom, and Camilla thinks to herself how it is really not good for him. It makes him too unsure of himself.

Tom takes her hand and begins to lead the way through the crowd, and Camilla begins to follow and she looks at the faces of the people who stare at her now, more than at Tom, imagines they are going to whisper about her long after she has left: "She was so ordinary-looking," they'll say. "That makes me like him more," the woman in the green dress will say. "It takes a good man to keep a wife like that when fame and fortune come his way."

"I bet he cheats on her," the skinny one over there will say. "They all cheat." She will take an overly long sip from the martini she clutches in her long thin fingers.

Camilla can hear all of these words before they are spoken, and she stares at Tom's heels as he leads her by the hand, following the earnest host to some table reserved for people like Tom.

Then Camilla, who is never prone to outbursts, decides suddenly to make a stand. She stops where she is, removes her hand from Tom's, forcing Tom to stop also and forcing him to look at her. The host keeps walking toward the table across the room, unaware that he has lost his guests, thinking about the impression of Tommy Mays he will perform later for his actor friends. It will include Tom's habit of bringing his shoulders toward his ears when he speaks; it will also include his inability to look strangers directly in the eye.

"Somewhere else," Camilla is saying to Tom. "Let's go somewhere else."

"I don't understand what the problem is," says Tom.

"They were here first," says his wife, motioning with her eyes to the dozens of eyes that observe her in turn.

Tom half laughs. "They don't mind."

"Please, please," says Camilla. "Please, let's go somewhere else."

IX.

Gregory is numb with disillusionment. He has never been drunk before, not even close. His face feels hot and his stomach groans in disapproval. The man in the dark coat will not slow down. Gregory is nearly stumbling to keep up with him, and then he realizes something terrible: he is going to vomit.

Vomiting, for Gregory, is always marked by a split-second decision. It is hard for Gregory to decide whether to alert the people around him of his imminent regurgitation or to simply throw up. In this instance, he has no choice; the man will not turn around, and Gregory feels unable to speak. He stops and drops the man's hand.

The man turns around, annoyed. "What is . . ." he says, and that's all he says, for he sees that Gregory has turned green. The man pulls at the collar of his jacket, rocks back on his heels. He looks like he's deciding whether to just leave, and he glances up and down the street.

They have stopped in front of a restaurant, one with large windows and a large glass door, and Gregory leans against the clear front of the building, only half-aware that the restaurant is crowded with people who are now gazing at his back. Gregory doubles over, puts his hands on his knees. He spits at the ground.

Tom and Camilla walk out.

Gregory, from his position, can only see the ground, and distantly he hears a man's voice coming through in waves: "Don't care . . . it's not a very . . . it's you. It's you."

Gregory vomits. He feels ashamed, drunk. He wants to be with Jilly and David and Helen. The Silent Drums are waiting for him at home. He can play them in his room. It was nice of his father to get them for him, so nice of David to get them. He wants to say thank you. He never said thank you.

A moment later, he feels a hand on his back. He pulls away, imagining that it is the hand of the man in the black jacket, a hand that might be scaly or diseased. He is repulsed by the thought of the man in the black coat—his missing tooth, his boyish curls. He stops himself from lashing out, but straightens quickly and then almost cries out when he sees that the man in the black coat is nowhere in sight. That the hand belongs to Tommy Mays.

"You okay, guy?" says Tom. He is surprised at how young the boy is: his position had looked, to Tom, like an old man's. The boy is well dressed, looks like a tourist, maybe. Maybe he is lost.

Gregory wipes his mouth and his eyes.

"Okay?" asks Tommy again. "You should get in a cab and go home."

Gregory remembers his dream and wonders if it was a premonition. He waits for it: Tommy Mays is going to reach toward him and touch his face. Tommy Mays is going to touch his ear, the top of his ear. Tommy Mays is going to place a gentle, firm hand on the back of Gregory's neck, and he will bring Gregory's face to his, and he will lower Gregory's head, and he will kiss his eyes and his mouth. He waits.

"I'm going to get a cab for you," says Tom. He walks to

the curb and hails a cab. The kid looks vaguely familiar to him. He wonders if they've met.

Then a cab stops and Tom beckons to Gregory, who pushes off from the wall and walks crookedly toward Tommy Mays.

Tom places a hand on his back, and Gregory imagines that he can feel it burning him through his shirt, and makes a wish to remember that touch always. Then Tom takes out a fifty-dollar bill and hands it to the cabdriver.

"Take him wherever he wants to go," says Tom. He leans into the backseat again.

Gregory's mouth hangs open a bit in wonder. Tommy Mays's face is warm, and older than Gregory expected. In the light from the roof of the cab, Gregory can see small wrinkles around his eyes.

"Good luck," says Tommy Mays. He shuts the door, pats the roof of the cab twice, and trots toward the sidewalk. Gregory looks after him, feeling the place on his back that was touched by Tommy Mays. He sees Tommy Mays place an arm about the waist of a woman who Gregory thinks is very beautiful, and he doesn't even mind. The woman turns around to look at him, says something to Tommy Mays. She smiles at him. They walk down the sidewalk.

"Where am I taking you?" asks the cabdriver.

X.

At Gregory's apartment, everyone is up, even Jilly. She is sitting silently on the floor, her small face drawn in worry.

Her parents have forgotten to monitor their own troubles in front of her, as they often do. She has not been put to bed because Helen and David have other things on their mind. It is quarter of twelve and their older child is not yet home. Normally they are fairly lenient about curfews; they know that the trains can be delayed, that sometimes they can break down. But Gregory was supposed to be home more than an hour ago.

"I called Tim's apartment again," says Helen. "Still no answer." She paces ineffectively about the tiny kitchen. "Gregory's not answering his cell phone."

She widens her pacing circle, stepping over the large cardboard box of drums that lies like a carcass before the front door.

"I think maybe we should call the police," she says, and then wonders if she has become a hysterical mother, a psychotic mother—the kind of mother her own was.

David gazes at his wife and considers the odds that his son is, in fact, in danger. He doesn't believe that he is. David believes deeply that his son is angry with him, that he is avoiding him because of the drums that are sitting there on the floor. He wonders if he will ever get a job again. It seems impossible in New York. Maybe they will have to move back to California. He shakes himself, pulls himself back to the present, and looks at his wife, who is now crouched on the floor next to Jilly.

"The police?" says Jilly. "The real police?"

David stands and stretches. "Gregory's just growing up," he says. "Wait an hour more."

10.

THOREAU'S
PEN

I.

He has finished his training. He is a reporter, and here is a pad of paper in his left hand, a reporter's pad with a spiral binding at the top, and here is a portable tape recorder in his right. He holds up his pen to the dim light inside South-paw and thinks about how the pen is the tool of his trade, his noble and respected trade. It is like a needle to a seam-stress, like a baton to a conductor. This pen is a particu-larly nice one that his parents gave him last year when he graduated from the Columbia School of Journalism: smooth and dapper and pleasantly fat, it is unquestionably a reporter's pen. It is marbled and brown, with gold trimmings and a gold clip close to its stem that holds the pen nicely in place when he tucks it into his front shirt pocket. The tip of the pen lives inside its body until he turns the base, and then it emerges into the world like the head of a turtle. The pen writes gracefully, gratifyingly, in a smooth black line that is not thick enough to bleed through a page and is not too thin to be easily read.

Thoreau D'Hemecourt is here at the Brooklyn club to write about a band, the first of many pieces he will complete for his new employer, *NY, NY*. It's a start-up magazine, he knows, not nearly as prestigious as working for the *Times* or (someday! someday!) *The New Yorker*. Some of his classmates got hired at these establishments straight from J school. But here, now, he convinces himself that he is lucky; while Therese Kriegel and Leo Greene are probably doing slave work for their fancy titles—covering weddings or something, answering e-mails, even—he is out in the field. He crafts his own assignments. He writes his own stories. He answers to himself. And, of course, to his editor, Marie. Still.

NY, NY is small yet, with a circulation of just under ten thousand. Most of their sales come from the magazine stands around New York. This gives Thoreau hope. He has fantasies of taking the pub over, of coming up with something that will make the magazine take off. What this might be, he cannot quite imagine, but standing here he feels a surge of inspiration—the kind of creative pulse that he has felt at intervals throughout his life for as long as he can remember. It is something he cannot quite describe: the feeling is one of boundless capacity for accomplishment of an attention-getting kind, of a praiseworthy kind. The kind of accomplishment that makes people really think of you as somebody different, somebody with a great deal of talent. An artist. Thoreau wants to be an artist. He is an arts writer, he thinks; his reporting should be as artistic as possible. Sentences form before him in the air. Phrases compose themselves almost by accident. The band has not even taken the stage, and already he knows something of what he will write. He is impressed.

With his beautiful pen he writes down whatever comes to him. *Drums like cannon fire*, he writes. *The lead guitarist [insert name!] plays with a kind of intensity that merits notice. He is fervent, nearly reverent. His instrument seems almost to be an extension of himself.* Then: *The Burn is so young and pretty that it would not be a surprise to see its members on MTV someday: their clothes are ideally unkempt, their faces even-featured, and their skin flawless.* He pauses, hopes that these statements are true enough to work in his story. He likes them a great deal. He looks up at his surroundings, feeling that he is on a roll, craving further inspiration.

Southpaw is quickly becoming crowded with people who look very much alike to Thoreau. Most in their twenties. Some in their thirties. Thoreau himself has done his best to predict what the audience will be wearing, to blend into the crowd, as a true reporter should. He has dressed down in khakis and a plain black T-shirt, trading his standard Italian leather loafers for a pair of old sneakers. Still, he wonders if his distinguished wire-rimmed glasses give him away as an outsider, as someone with an important reason to be there.

Everyone else is wearing T-shirts too. Thoreau feels good about this. Most of the men wear T-shirts with writing on them of one kind or another (he should have worn his Rolling Stones T-shirt—he knew it!) and Converse All Stars. Most of the women wear some variant on the same theme, usually with a feminine touch: a pair of chandelier earrings, a patterned skirt. Thoreau is just beginning to describe the crowd when the curtain opens and the crowd surges away from the bar, away from the pool table on the upper level, toward the front of the midsize room. Thoreau is left behind. Indignant, he pushes his way closer, and then realizes he cannot possibly make notes with his elbows pressed as they are to his side. Also, it's too dark to see his pad of paper.

Defeated, he retreats backward through the crowd and sits on a stool at the bar, resigning himself to watching the show from there, to use the dim brassy light from behind the bar. The band is still tuning and he makes a note of this giddily: they are inexperienced. A more practiced band would have waited to open the curtain until they were totally ready. Or is it the fault of Southpaw? Either way, he thinks, it's a sign of their youth. And then he knows what the angle of the piece will be. Young bands—the trend of young bands. Why is it that bands have to be young? Why don't old bands get signed? Interesting. Very.

Then the lights point to the stage and the Burn is illuminated. They begin to play and the crowd cheers.

He is disappointed to see that the lead singer (what was her name? Shauna?) is not, in fact, flawlessly pretty. She could lose a few pounds, and her face looks more tired than perfect. Disappointed, he draws one line through his description of the band as "pretty," leaving "young" in place. He supposes that her face is still even-featured enough, and her skin is not bad. He leaves the last half of his sentence alone.

He listens carefully, decides that yes, the drums do sound like cannon fire. Yes, the lead guitarist is intense enough. He is relieved. Now all he has to do is find out his name. And confirm that the lead singer's name is Shauna.

He could easily look it up online once he's home, but he prefers to have the information now—it is important, he thinks, to have names for the subjects of a piece. Names tell a great deal about an individual. His own, for example: Thoreau D'Hemecourt. He loves his name. At the time of his birth, his mother had been reading *Walden* and had discovered in herself a great affinity for the concept of the Oversoul. Yes, his mother had been something of a bohemian; though her fifties have finally brought her to dress a bit more conservatively, Thoreau can remember his extreme embarrassment, as a grade-schooler, when she picked him up from school one day wearing a long skirt, a sports bra, and a T-shirt that she had cut off just below her ample bosom. Her navel was set deeply in a stomach that was too plump for her fashion sense, and her coarse black hair fell to her waist—it was always much longer than the hair of any of his friends' mothers.

Most embarrassing of all: Meredith, the precocious

fourth-grader who had stolen Thoreau's heart two years earlier with her astounding ability to recite the alphabet backward, had pointed at his mother when she emerged from her car across the street. "Her stomach!" she had said to Thoreau. "Look at that stomach!"

For a moment, Thoreau considered laughing with the beautiful Meredith, who had hair that was sleek and blond, the opposite of his mother's. He considered walking home, pretending that he had not seen his mother there across the street, standing in front of her blue VW bug. Instead, little Thoreau gurgled something unintelligible to Meredith—"Goodbye" had been his intention—and walked toward his mother, eyes down, and begged her to get into the car. He was silent all the way home.

"D'Hemecourt" comes from his father: a mathematician and a professor, the son of French immigrants, who lacked social grace but never lacked for opinions. Fortunately for Thoreau, his parents' views, political and otherwise, tended to align. Had they not, Thoreau's childhood memories might not have been of games like "dictionary" around the dining room table after dinner, of happy but bashful participation in weekend festivals put on by the Society for Creative Anachronism. Thoreau used to marvel sometimes at the humiliation that would surely ensue at school had anybody planted in his classroom a picture of him in his medieval costume. Certainly, Thoreau was different from his classmates. He grew up trying desperately to be as like to his peers as he could be, but his parents felt always like anchors of strangeness in his life—no matter how close he came to normalcy, his parents were there, pulling him enthusiastically away from acceptance. Perhaps this explains why Thoreau is more politically conservative than his parents; why he avoids poetry but embraces journalism; why his wardrobe is expensive and made from unpatterned, very-high-quality material; why he believes in knowing about things like wine and geography and, yes, pens.

Perhaps it is for this reason also that he feels a thrill now at blending in so nicely with this crowd. He did his research well. He may not know as much about music as the average member of this audience—cannot pull from memory the names of obscure early-nineties hard-core bands, or name every album by the Sex Pistols or the Clash or whomever these people like at the moment—but Thoreau is quite certain that he is a much better writer than any of them. He feels satisfied: he is going to be an unbiased arts writer. He can be a naive listener. If music sounds good, then it is good, he thinks. He feels no need to engage in the kind of name-dropping that he has read in other music reviews.

He turns to the young man next to him. "What's the lead singer's name?"

"Siobhan O'Hara," says Hugh. He's about to say something pert about his sister, but then he notices the guy's pen and paper. A reporter. A sudden benevolent impulse takes him over. "Isn't she great?" For good measure: "This is my favorite band."

Thoreau shrugs. "Yeah," he says, writing *Chevonne O'Hara?* on his reporter's pad with his beautiful pen. Actually, this kind of music doesn't appeal to him very much at all, or perhaps it is the noise in the club—he wishes he had brought earplugs. He can barely hear his own thoughts, and he certainly can't have a conversation with the young man next to him, though he'd like to. Always important to get the crowd's opinion, he thinks. He makes a note to do it after the show.

Then he thinks about her name. Chevonne? What kind of name is that for a young girl? Strange. Very.

He focuses on the music. The noise inside the club makes it hard to hear what the lead singer is singing, but he thinks it sounds like "Save our souls, save our souls." Thoreau rolls his eyes. How trite.

II.

This is a good crowd. This is a crowd that makes Mike like playing again. They are rapt and respectful, enthusiastic and energetic. There is a girl in the front who is making eyes at him, and he plays a game with himself: how long can he hold her gaze? He is a nervous person by nature and eye contact makes him uncomfortable. But this is a test. Over the length of a measure? Yes. Over the length of an eight-bar solo? Yes. Over the length of a song? No.

The girl, who is there with another girl who might be her sister, is a brazen girl, a girl who would jump on a bar and dance. A girl who gets drunk, Mike imagines. She is slight and catlike. Big eyes.

Mike is afraid of women recently. It's nice to flirt from onstage. He knows it's safer than flirting in person. From onstage, he feels held down, anchored to something. He feels that his feet are pulled reassuringly toward earth; when offstage, he feels he might float off someplace like a helium balloon. He cannot, therefore, speak with women. What would they think, should he find himself suddenly launched into space?

The girl with the big eyes smiles at him, and for the first time since Nora Cross killed herself, Mike considers talking to a girl after the show. The odds are in his favor. He does not fear rejection; he can fairly guarantee that this girl would be interested, would be nice to him, at least. Here she is making eyes at him from the audience. Looking up at him. Yes, he decides; he will find her after the show. He'll say something ridiculous like "I noticed you in the audience. I like your shirt." He laughs to himself at the thought and then remembers that he is onstage, that he's in the middle of a song. It's a song they've played hundreds of times and he doesn't really need to pay much attention to it and then suddenly he's afraid that he's getting burned out already. That being onstage no longer holds his interest the way it did once. That soon he will be waiting to get offstage, or that playing will become as dull as any other job.

Southpaw is the smallest club they've played in more than a year. They have not been commercially successful. After opening for Tommy Mays, their album came out and sort of flopped. They tried to tour on their own, but the clubs Titan booked them into were too large. They were only ever half full. The Burn and Theo have high hopes for their next album, which they've been working on, due in the spring, but in the meantime it is refreshing to play to a packed house in their hometown.

He tries to focus on this feeling, to enjoy the show. Soon, though, his eyes find the girl with the big eyes once again and he is thinking to himself now that a girl like that has had a lot of sex. A lot of sex with a lot of different people. Sex in strange positions—the kind of sex he has no desire for. Mike is really very uncreative, when it comes to sex, and he has always felt a bit uneasy and defensive when asked to experiment: as if he is being told, "I'm bored with you." This is a girl who would like to have sex with him upside down. In a swing. Something like that. She would fool around behind his back with other men. Other women, even. She's very pretty. She's very small. Mike wants to put her in his pocket. No: he wants to forget she exists.

He looks down at his guitar and turns his mind back to Siobhan and the band. Katia, the drummer, drops a beat and fumbles her way back to a semblance of the original rhythm. The mistake is small enough that Mike feels quite sure that no one in the audience noticed, and Mike feels a sudden thrill at being on the inside of things, for once in his life. He and his bandmates catch eyes, smile a little at the error. They're having a good time. Mike G. is jumping on the fourth beat of every other measure. Pete is stomping his feet. Siobhan is melting forward, into the microphone, into the crowd, bending her knees, swooning along with her words. Mike thinks to himself that he feels real affection for them. They're like family. He loves them. He doesn't need to talk to the girl in the audience, who certainly has had too much sex, who would certainly leave him for someone else anyway. All he needs is his band.

The girl with big eyes wonders if Mike will come into the audience after the show. She's excited by the attention he's paid her. She'd like to meet him. She'd like to shake his hand. She's been listening to the Burn since a friend gave her their CD a year ago.

She's very young. She's had sex with one person, and she called it making love. It was her boyfriend. They broke up last month.

She will get married in four years. She will not ever be unfaithful.

III.

Thoreau writes:

It is not common to hear music that is immediately appealing, that seems at all musical *upon a first listen, and the Burn's music is no exception. One can imagine liking their songs after a few intensive study sessions, headphones on, eyes closed. But last night's show at Southpaw revealed not much more to this reporter than a dedicated local fan base and a distinct lack of stage presence.*

He is pleased. Then he considers the way the Burn looks onstage and momentarily thinks of amending his description, for the members of the Burn do indeed have a scrappy sort of stage presence: each player does something different at a given time, the bassist swinging his head about erratically, the dueling guitarists jumping into the air occasionally or staring into the space of the room. The lead singer too has an appeal that Thoreau cannot deny, and he regrets his first impression of her; for despite her unfashionably full arms, her almost motherly bosom, she is supple and moves well and gracefully, and Thoreau is stirred by her.

But he likes his sentence a great deal, the rhythm of it: *Last night's show at Southpaw revealed not much more to this reporter than a dedicated fan base and a distinct lack of stage presence.* He angles his head at the stage and thinks, Yes, their stage presence might be described as lacking. Yes, they are inexperienced. They have no sense of choreography or timing but move as spastically as puppies.

He likes that thought. He writes it down. *Onstage, the Burn come off as puppies: eager to please, overly energetic, a bit skittish.* Perfect.

But he knows that there is a moroseness too, and Thoreau feels suddenly uneasy at his inability to describe it in words. He looks again at the lead singer and imagines that she has suffered in her life.

He would like to touch her.

He imagines that many people would like to touch her. To be touched by her.

Look at me, he finds himself saying to her. See me. Without thinking, he stands up from the stool and tucks the pad and paper into his pocket. He is compelled to move toward the stage, and he does so as if in a trance. He pushes his way into the mass of audience members, suddenly desperate to reach the stage, to hang his fingers over the edge of it, put his chin to the place near where the girl's feet are planted.

"Hey," says a young man in a collared shirt who suddenly finds Thoreau's elbow in his side. But nothing can stop Thoreau, who is tall and quite good at making space for himself. He keeps moving until he gets quite close. Still, he is not where he wants to be, not yet directly in front of the stage.

He is just behind a girl who barely reaches his chest. She's there with her friend or her sister. They are both small and fragile-looking, but Thoreau knows that he must be closer. Recklessly, he pushes between them to the stage and does as he has imagined: places his fingers over the edge of it, looks timidly up into the face of the lead singer.

A shock washes over him. But she is so lovely: her eyebrows furrowed together, gorgeous beads of sweat forming on her upper lip and brow. He is consumed by lust. Thoreau has always prided himself on his ability to suppress his own desires—he is very rational. He does not lust. He does not whine for what he cannot have.

Until now. Look at me, he says again to her. See me.

And then he feels a tap on his shoulder. He turns, annoyed at the interruption.

One of the two small girls is staring angrily at him. Her large gray eyes flash with indignation. She says something to him, but he cannot hear above the band.

"What?" he asks.

"You're very rude," the girl shouts, and her friend nods emphatically. "You hurt my friend's shoulder."

She takes her friend's hand, motions to her: *Come on.* The two of them turn from Thoreau and walk back toward the bar, and the crowd closes in quickly behind them.

IV.

Mike sees the girl with big eyes leaving and his heart sinks a bit. Despite his resolution not to speak with her after the show, he had been enjoying her attention and he thought she was making him play better. He had been showing off for her.

And maybe he would have talked to her after all. He might have changed his mind.

Now he'll never know her name.

V.

Thoreau, in a fit of shame, looks rapturously at the lead singer and feels certain both that he cannot now write a piece about her, having fallen in love with her, and that he is not worthy of her love, having pushed small helpless girls out of his way to be close to her.

He will have to tell his editor, Marie, that he cannot complete his first assignment. Perhaps he is not cut out to be an arts writer. Perhaps he should write for the real estate section. He feels foolish in his carefully conceived outfit, and he misses his Italian leather loafers. The sneakers he wears make him feel childish, powerless.

He leaves before the show is over. On the street outside it is quiet but for the muted sounds of the band inside. He scuffs his feet as he walks toward the subway, wondering if tonight was a triumph or a defeat, wondering about the lead singer and what her name means, where it comes from.

On the subway, he reaches into his back pocket and notices that his new pen is no longer there.

II.

TIA,
A TERRIBLE
DANCER

I.

Being the fattest member of a girl band is not fair. Tia thinks this as she looks at herself in the mirror of the rehearsal space they've been renting by the week for the past three months.

She's not fat, really: the other four girls are just smaller. There always has to be a fat one. She's it. She's the tallest and the widest. When her father ordered pants for them from Dance Depot, sparkly pants that stretched tight across their bottoms, hung loose to their calves, and zipped up the side, three of the other girls had to get theirs tailored because the smallest size was too big. Linette fit into the smallest size. And Tia wore a size eight. They have not yet worn the costumes in public, and Tia dreads the day that she must.

It would be okay with her to be the big one if she had the best voice, but she doesn't. Ravenne does. Ravenne sounds like Christina Aguilera, and that's why Tia's dad said she could be in the band, even though she has the wrong kind of nose. Tia has a pretty nose. It's her one vanity. It slopes; it upturns slightly. A nice nose.

"Again," says her father, whose name is Paul. He hits the CD player and the song starts up—the same song they have been singing for the last week. Tia is so sick of it she almost groans out loud. But she knows what her father would say.

"Isn't it, isn't it, isn't it over now?" This is what they are supposed to be singing in five-part harmony. But they aren't singing at all, because this is a dancing rehearsal only: the kind that Tia hates. Her father hired a choreographer to create a dance for them, and a dance coach who would rehearse them through it. Tia is definitely the worst dancer. Mainly because she does everything she can do to avoid jiggling, and this puts her at a disadvantage. It gives her a robotic look, a stiffness that the other girls don't have.

If she looked at her father, she would see him glaring at her, perhaps mouthing, "Pick up your feet!" So she rarely does. Instead, she looks at herself in the mirror, and then at the other girls, and thinks for the thousandth time that they must talk about her fatness when she is not there, because it is so obvious. She sticks out. Her breasts are bigger than theirs. Her hips are bigger than theirs.

Tia plays a game with herself. It's called "What's Wrong with That Girl?" She plays it now and thinks about her bandmates. She already knows that Ravenne has an ugly nose. But also, her lower half is wider than her upper half. She would look better if her shoulders were wider. They're too small for her frame. And Janelle's blond hair is the wrong kind of blond. It's too yellow, not white enough. It looks really fake. She should get a better dye job, thinks Tia. Linette is pretty, but she's old. Tia's father has decided to say that Linette is fifteen, but she's really twenty. She looks older too: a little more ashamed of her outfit, maybe. A little more subdued when she's dancing.

Then Tia looks at Kira and despairs. Kira is perfect. Really perfect. Her thighs don't touch in the middle between her legs. Her stomach is cut, almost concave. Her neck is slender and graceful and her eyes are the most striking part about her: they're bright blue. Also, she's the best dancer. But she can't sing, thinks Tia, and is comforted briefly before her gaze falls once more upon herself, distant and huge, in the mirror before them.

II.

Their story, the story that Tia's father Paul has decided to put together when pitching them to labels, is that they sang together in a church choir from the time they could talk. Even though only Tia and Janelle have known each other since they were little. The others Tia's father found by putting an ad in the paper. "Female singers and dancers wanted for girl band," the ad said. "Ages 12–18. Industry attention." Which was also a lie. Paul had met one record executive in his life, and it was an accident, and they did not talk about Tia or about bands or anything at all. The exec was a friend of his wife's friend. But meeting him, and seeing an episode of *Oprah* about obsessive stage dads, had given Paul the idea. He hated his job as a car salesman. Tia was not a good student. She liked to sing.

And Paul was always impulsive.

♭ ♮ ♭

Now the band is together, and they have been for a year. They have been rehearsing at Sound-Off with full sound once a month—Sound-Off is expensive—and at a dance studio in the Bronx three nights a week. The girls are all from Queens, except for Linette, who is a student at Brooklyn College. But they got a fantastic rate at this dance studio, and so Paul picks four of them up in a van before every rehearsal, and Linette takes the subway and meets them, and then afterward she goes home on her own and Paul drops the other four girls off. It works nicely. He likes picking them up—likes their parents to have limited involvement in the enterprise. It's his idea, his creation. He made it clear to all the parents, before offering their daughters a place in the group, that he was in charge, that he had final say over everything. It was, he said, the only way he could make the band work. The only way to get them a chance.

Now, looking at the five of them preparing for what will be their most important audition to date, he feels that he was right all along. It's ten in the morning. At four this afternoon, the girls have been invited to the office of Theo Brigham, an A&R man at Titan Records. They will perform for him personally. Paul imagines telling this story in the past tense on VH1's *Driven*. Imagines Theo Brigham himself being interviewed. "I was blown out of the water," he will say. "I knew these girls had it."

III.

"You look scared!" says Paul to his daughter, who does, in fact, look scared—for she has noticed that her father's gaze is on her. "If you look scared now, what will you be like this afternoon?"

The girls keep dancing, and Tia does her best to smile and look relaxed.

"Tia!" says Paul. "I'm talking to you."

"She doesn't look scared to me," Janelle volunteers.

"I'm not scared," says Tia. And imagines meeting Theo Brigham, imagines an infinitely blond man with very white sharp teeth and very piercing blue eyes, a supremely tall man who smells like cologne and sits on a stack of record contracts as high as a chair. Her knees nearly give out beneath her. She thinks her father may be right. She does get scared quite easily. She lacks the showmanship of the other girls. Her movements betray a distinct lack of sass, of pizzazz, of—Tia cringes at the thought—sex. She's only fourteen. But Janelle is her age, and the other girls aren't much older, and already they know how to move so that people think of sex, of what they must be like in bed. It's all a game.

"Look at Kira," says Paul.

Tia looks at Kira in the mirror, watches her face change with the words of the song, watches her flip her hair and slap her hips at appropriate moments.

She tries to imitate Kira. Tries very hard to imitate Kira.

"Smile," says Paul. "Look like you're having fun, Tia!"

Having fun. Having fun. I'm having fun, thinks Tia. Then the song ends, with a thunderous "Isn't it over now?" Yes, thinks Tia. Thank God.

Paul pauses before speaking, as he always does, as if considering the most effective way to convey the very important thought in his head to the rest of the world. The girls relax gradually out of the poses they strike at the song's conclusion. They are breathing hard. Tia worries, not for the first time, about singing while she is dancing—she can do each separately fairly well, but together is more difficult.

"Terrible," her father says at last.

IV.

Paul has read all the right books on the music business. He knows that it is very difficult for a band to make it. He knows that in order to attain success, a group must have an image, one that is easy to remember. The group must be different from other groups so that people will take notice of the group, not confuse the group with other groups. Most of all, the band must be attractive and visually appealing, easily marketable.

In this case, Paul thinks he has found the right way to promote the girls. He has named them Hype Girlz. He has commissioned a song for them from a fairly prominent songwriter who has had other hits. The song is catchy and sassy—it's about dumping a boy. This is the vision he has for Hype Girlz: girls with attitude. The comeback of grrl power. It hasn't been done since the Spice Girls. Paul thinks the public is ready for more of the same, but with an edgy, current twist. Hype Girlz are tougher than Spice Girls. They'll dump you and then they'll kick your ass.

This was how he described the girls to Theo Brigham when he finally got a phone meeting with him. Theo had heard of Hype Girlz—Paul's aggressive, guerrilla-style campaigning has been hard to ignore—but had been dubious about the public's need for another girl band.

"We've filled that niche," he had said. "Girl groups are notorious for being one-hit wonders. Look at Dream, look at 3LW."

Paul, desperate to keep Theo on the phone, had promised he would change his mind if he saw them in person.

"Just one chance," he had said over and over again. "That's all I'm asking for."

So Theo transferred him to the new secretary, who penciled Hype Girlz in for today at four. Then he hung up the phone, preparing to disappoint this group, as he does most groups; hoping, as he always does, that these girls would be different. He has been desperate to sign someone. Once again, Jax has been on his back.

Once Paul got off the phone, he ordered costumes for the girls. He remembered being younger, in his twenties (he is almost forty now) and wondering what he was meant to do with his life. He feels fairly certain that this is it. He feels proud of himself for the first time in a good while. He knows he is accomplishing something.

V.

The Hype Girlz run the dance a few more times, and then it is time for a break before their vocal warm-up. Tia sits in a corner with a water bottle. It gets hot in the studio. Janelle comes over and sits facing Tia.

"Hi," she says.

Tia offers her a drink from her bottle.

"I'm okay," says Janelle. She tucks her yellow-blond hair behind her ears and thinks a minute.

"Are you nervous?" she asks Tia.

"No," says Tia. "Are you?"

"No," says Janelle.

The girls sit in silence until their vocal coach arrives.

"Here we go, Hype Girlz," says Paul. "Vocal warm-ups. Then we hit the road."

♮ ♮ ♮

Paul has decided that for the big audition the Hype Girlz should sing their song a cappella. He read once that Jessica Simpson did that and it worked. So each time they sing, they do it unaccompanied. Their vocal coach, Ilsa, gives them a note and then they break into song. They are decent. Some are better than others. Ravenne's voice shines through the other girls' voices: Ilsa has given her the melody. The others sing with her at times and in harmony at times. Ravenne also has the only solo of the song—the bridge, which goes like this: "If I can't make you want me then we're better off apart / I was wrong to give you my love when I knew you'd break my heart." Ravenne really sells this part: she ends on a high note that seems to last forever while the other girls come back in on the verse. It works. It's a good song for them.

♮ ♮ ♮

An hour passes, and once again the girls are sitting in a corner of the studio. Paul is outside on his cell phone, speaking with the stylist, who is late to do hair and makeup for the girls before they drive to the Titan building.

"Just get here as soon as you can," Paul is saying. "I'm not sure you understand how important this is."

Inside, the girls can see his expression and they know

how tense he is. They are silent, the five of them, each thinking something separate about what the afternoon holds. Ravenne passes her bottle of water to Linette, who takes it without saying anything.

"Do you think we'll be on MTV?" says Janelle.

No one answers.

♭ ♮ ♭

When Georgia, the stylist, finally arrives, they have thirty minutes before they're scheduled to leave in the van.

"Let's see what we're working with," says Georgia, inspecting them in turn.

"Pretty eyes," she says to Kira. She starts with her. When she is finished, Kira looks like she was born to be on television: her eyes are outlined in smoky black eyeliner and her black hair is pulled back from her face into five spikes that look like a crown on her head.

Georgia does each of the girls in turn, and leaves Tia for last. It is two minutes before three P.M.

"We've gotta go," says Paul, walking into the room from outside with an armful of outfits on hangers. He has been on his cell phone again.

"She hasn't done me yet, Dad," says Tia, who wants desperately now to get her hair and makeup done. She looks at the other girls, who are looking at themselves in the large mirrors in the dance studio. Each has a different hairstyle. Tia's hair is straight and she is wearing a headband. She looks like a little girl. A little chubby girl. The others look like stars.

"You look great, Tia," says Paul. "Traffic is bad. We have to go now. Get your clothes on." He hands each outfit to its owner and shoos them into the bathroom to change.

The injustice of this event will haunt Tia for most of her life—even when she is old enough to realize its triviality, even when she has children of her own and knows how children exaggerate slights, how they can be unabashedly indignant on their own behalf. It is something about her father's tone. Something about the look of pity and understanding on Georgia's face.

Now she does not dare complain but heads into the bathroom of the studio to change into her outfit with the other girls.

In the bathroom, Kira immediately strips down to her bra and underwear. She looks at herself in the mirror as she talks to Ravenne.

"You always get that 'boy, it's over' from the chorus," she says. "I always miss it." She brushes at something invisible on her abdomen, stretches her arms languorously toward the ceiling. "Maybe I just won't sing that note."

Ravenne shrugs and pulls up the black pants. They look good on her despite her larger lower half.

"I don't know why we all have to wear the same pants," says Ravenne. "I hate these pants." She glances over her shoulder at her reflection. "Ew."

Tia hates changing in front of anyone. She takes off her socks one at a time, turns awkwardly toward the wall and gets her shirt ready to pull off, gathering it upward with one hand while she readies its replacement in the other. Then she pulls it fast over her head and fumbles with the new one until it is in place. She turns back toward the other girls and is disappointed to see that all four of them are fully dressed. Each wears the same black pants and tops of varying colors and cuts. They are standing together and talking, and Tia thinks that now there is nothing to distract them. She must change her pants, and they will watch her from behind and maybe laugh.

Resigned, she faces the wall once more. She lays the monstrous black pants on the chair in front of her and slowly removes her old pair, her face burning at the thought of what she must look like from behind. She wonders if anyone is looking and imagines that they all must be, even though they're hiding it by talking about today's audition, chattering nervously and teasing one another.

She lifts the pants from the chair and pulls them on one leg at a time, realizing in horror that they are tighter than they were the last time she tried them on—a good two months ago. In fact, they feel too tight altogether. She tries to zip them up the side, but the zipper won't come up. Rage and grief fill her. She gathers the material at her waist and pulls it together and tugs and tugs, but it will not budge. She stops and breathes heavily for a moment, wondering what she should do. Behind her, the other girls have fallen silent, and she knows without a doubt that four pairs of eyes are on her. She fights with the lump in her throat.

"Need some help?" asks Kira.

"No," says Tia, who would rather staple the pants to her skin than have thin and lovely Kira help her pull the zipper up over the flesh of her hip.

She tries again, and struggles against the tears that feel as though they might burst out of her at any moment. She knows she cannot talk or they will come. And then, at last, at last, the zipper moves an inch, and then an inch more, and she sucks her stomach in to her spine, and then the whole thing is up and she pats her face and exhales and turns to face her band and sees her own reflection instead and nearly cries out in anguish.

A large roll of flesh falls over the waist of the hateful black pants. Her salmon-colored shirt, ripped fashionably at the shoulders and up the sides, looks stretched and uncomfortable. Her hair hangs limply by the sides of her head, held back by the childish headband. She takes the headband off and sees that her hair still bears its impression, so she puts it back on. She wears no makeup, and she has three pimples on her forehead. She noticed them this morning before driving to the studio and had felt relieved that they would be getting their makeup done before their audition. Now they stand out in contrast to the perfect-looking skin of her heavily made up bandmates.

She does not want to go. She wants to lock herself in a bathroom stall and cry.

The other four girls watch her curiously—each secretly feels grateful that she is not Tia, or built like Tia, or wearing a headband like Tia's.

Then a knock on the door comes, and through it they hear Paul.

"Let's hit the road!" he says.

Tia, too shocked by her own appearance to think, follows her bandmates out of the bathroom and into the van.

"This is it," says Paul, and pulls out into the road, heading toward Manhattan.

In the farthest-back seat, Tia leans her head against the window and dreads the audition with a force she has not felt before.

VI.

The thinness of some women. Every time she visits Manhattan, Tia sees so much of it that her eyes hurt, that her heart nearly skips a beat with jealousy when a woman walks by and Tia can see her bones beneath her skin. That is what she wants: to see her own bones when she looks in the mirror. She has seen it on MTV, on the girls in the sorts of bands that she is supposed to be in. She likes it when she can see their hip bones like ledges above low-slung pants or skirts. She likes very thin upper arms, the kind you could fit your hand around. Most of all, Tia likes knobby knees: slender knees and slender calves below them and slender thighs above them. She wishes her own knees were knobby. A boy in her fifth-grade class once told Tia that her knees looked like bowling balls, and Tia felt as if a terrible secret had been exposed to the world. She often struggles with this feeling: knowing herself that she is fat and wondering if others will notice it too or if she is hiding it well. When she is feeling confident about her looks, she thinks to herself that today she is hiding her fat well.

She thinks she has a pretty face, but then accuses herself of vanity—perhaps even self-deception. What do people think of me? she asks herself throughout the day. And imagines the worst.

Everyone in the van is silent. From the backseat, Tia divides the women she sees on the street into three categories: thin and pretty, thin and ugly, and fat. She feels guilty about doing it, but it has become a compulsion. She feels especially bad about placing women into the second category, for these, she feels, are hopeless. But she does it compassionately, and often she likes these women and the fat women best: trusts them more, thinks they must be better people, somehow.

But how she envies the thin and pretty ones! The ones who turn heads with their loveliness, turn the heads of men who scare Tia with disloyalty toward their wives or girlfriends. Here is a scene that Tia hates: A man and a woman sit together. They are eating at a restaurant. They are on a bench in a park. They are sitting on a stoop. A different woman walks by—a thin and pretty one, one with knobby knees and ledges for hip bones and a lovely face and good fashion sense, and maybe it's raining and her shirt has gotten wet, but unintentionally, carelessly, for this woman is never what Tia calls slutty (slutty women Tia places into a separate category altogether and disdains with all her might)—and then the man's head turns, or his head stays deliberately in place and his eyes turn, and all the while he is talking to his wife or his girlfriend, who notices the woman too, and she thinks, That woman is prettier and thinner than I am, and her husband or boyfriend thinks, That woman is thinner and prettier than you are, and I would like to have sex with her. Tia has created this scene in her head countless times, and she imag-ines she has witnessed it countless times, and she has never had a boyfriend but she thinks that she could never abide having one whose head would turn for thin and pretty women.

VII.

They arrive at the Titan building as silent as they were when they left the studio. It looms above them; it is pre-posterously high. Even Paul seems frightened, and Tia, whose rage at her appearance has not yet subsided, feels a guilty sort of pleasure at her own father's fear. She wants him to fail. She wants to revel in his failure, for making her wear the pants he has made her wear, for denying her the thrill of having her makeup done. For allowing her to be the ugliest member of the band he has put together.

As instructed, they take the elevator up to the top floor. The doors close behind them and Tia sees with chagrin that these too are mirrored. And that she is indeed larger by far than all four of her bandmates. She catches her fa-ther's eye in the reflection and looks away.

♮ ♮ ♮

Paul is surprised at his inability to speak. His mouth has turned dry and papery. He can barely think, and yet the need to speak overwhelms him: he needs to show the girls that he is in control, that their audition will be okay. He looks about him for inspiration and says the first thing he can think of, turning to his daughter.

"Your pants look a little tight," he says to Tia in the silent elevator. "Guess we should have gotten the bigger size."

In Paul's mind, he is making conversation. He cannot know what he has said, cannot know the wrongness of it— he cannot possibly know what he has done. He turns back toward the doors, relieved that he has successfully completed a sentence. He congratulates himself on the nonchalance of the statement. The girls must know now that he is not at all nervous, and that they shouldn't be either. It's just an audition, he reminds himself. There will be others. He smiles a bit. Breathe, he tells himself. Relax.

♮ ♮ ♮

Tia's smallish body shakes with the sort of rage one cannot ever fully accommodate. It fills her. It is disturbingly wide and long. In her sparkling pants, she feels she looks like a show elephant, a circus elephant dressed to look human. She wishes fervently for retaliation—for some means of revenge. Later in life, Tia will not speak to her father, and for the first time she has a glimpse of this future. Its inevitability does not surprise her, and neither does it subdue her hot and hellish rage. She wants to hurt him with something dull, like a bowling ball. She wants to drop a bowling ball on his head. She imagines it: the release of the ball from some second- or third-story window, the sickening double thud of ball meeting head and head meeting pavement. Would the bone crack? Would there be a dent?

The doors open.

They face a desk with a secretary behind it.

"Welcome to Titan," says the secretary. "You're here to see Theo?"

"Yes," says Paul. He is slowly regaining confidence.

♮ ♮ ♮

In the waiting room, there is a ficus plant that looks underwatered.

The girls sit like small ducks on the chairs provided them. They catch glimpses, through his half-open door, of a man they assume must be Theo Brigham. He is pacing while talking on a headset. His hands move rapidly, illustrating whatever it is he is discussing (guns? It looks as though he is aiming at something), now and then finding the bridge of his nose and pinching it tight.

He looks much younger than the man Tia had imagined, and much slighter. Much less blond. She wonders briefly about his personal life. Wonders if he is the sort of man who would cheat on his wife or his girlfriend. If he likes pretty girls. Her eyes shift to Kira, who sits straight in her chair, her legs crossed and then uncrossed and then crossed again. Will Kira be the reason they get signed?

Will I be the reason we don't? Tia asks herself.

Through the door, Theo Brigham looks annoyed as he takes off the headset he has been wearing.

♮ ♮ ♮

He sits on his desk for a moment, collecting his thoughts, preparing himself for the next item on his agenda: meeting with a girl band. What is their name? he asks himself. All he can think of is "Spice Girls."

He can see them in the lobby, five young girls sitting silently in the chairs the secretary has offered them. They are all wearing similar outfits and similar expressions: expressions of utter fear. Next to them, a tall black man in a suit is checking his watch compulsively. The situation isn't promising. Theo considers just shutting his door, maybe even calling his secretary from inside his office and telling her to cancel their appointment. But he really has nothing scheduled for the next hour, and he figures that it would be a good deed to give them a shot—something the girls can tell their friends about. He takes in a deep breath, smiles, and walks to the door to invite them in.

♮ ♮ ♮

He comes forward into the lobby.

"Paul, hey," he says.

"Good afternoon, Mr. Brigham," says her father, and Tia holds back a shudder. It was, she knows, the wrong thing to say. Exactly the wrong tone. Just as her father is wearing a suit and Theo Brigham is wearing jeans and a T-shirt.

And he looks like he's twenty-five. Her father is older than him.

It's all wrong.

Everything is wrong.

♮ ♮ ♮

Paul is shaking with nerves. He recalls baseball tryouts as a boy, wonders if the girls feel now as he did then. Imagines that they must be even more nervous.

Paul is experiencing a new emotion: protectiveness. He feels these girls are his, and he feels a difficult sort of love for them. Certainly he loves his daughter, Tia, as all fathers love their daughters: worries for her, wants the best for her. But this is something different. It's as if these girls are an artwork that he has created, an artwork that he may not be ready to unveil. He wonders if it isn't too late to reschedule, to squeeze in a few more rehearsals. Kira always hits the same wrong note halfway through the chorus. Janelle has been turning the wrong way for their big finish.

And Tia still looks like she wants to disappear when she's dancing.

But Theo Brigham leads them into his office and Paul knows that the audition must happen now if it is ever going to happen. He tries to make himself breathe slowly and calmly.

♮ ♮ ♮

"Have a seat," says Theo. He gestures to a small sofa, to two chairs next to it. Ravenne and Kira and Linette sit on the sofa. Tia and Janelle take the chairs. Paul, uncertain of where he is expected to sit, hovers tentatively by Tia's chair. Then Theo turns to him.

"If you wouldn't mind, Paul," he says, walking to the door and pulling it open.

Paul thinks he must be kidding. He smiles.

"I like to work alone with the artists," says Theo, and waits.

Paul cannot comprehend. He arranged this meeting. He drove the girls here. He has worked and waited a year for this moment. His was the phone call that got through to Theo Brigham, young Theo Brigham, A&R man for Titan, now standing by his office door and all but commanding Paul to leave.

"Mr. Brigham," says Paul, straightening his spine. His daughter gives him an imploring look; the other girls wait and wonder what might happen next. And then Paul thinks better of what he is about to say. What good would it do, after all? To insist on seeing the audition. To defy the man who may hold the key to the Hype Girlz' success. It would hurt their chances. Better to cooperate.

"Certainly," says Paul, and walks with dignity to the door, and hears, behind him, Tia's sigh of relief. Theo shuts the door. Then they are alone with Theo Brigham. He sits on his desk, facing them.

"So," he says. "Why are you here?"

In the lobby, Paul paces to and fro. He circles a ficus tree by the window three times.

The secretary looks at him and says, "Would you care to have a seat?"

"No," says Paul. He walks to the window and looks out at the tall buildings surrounding Titan.

"Please have a seat," says the secretary, who is concerned that Jax Powers-Kline—due to return imminently from lunch at Da Silvano—will criticize her for her failure to keep the guests appeased and orderly. She tries again: "Can I get you anything to drink?"

"Got any vodka?" asks Paul. It's his bad attempt at a joke, but the secretary doesn't understand—she smiles uncertainly and shakes her head.

"Coffee?" she asks.

♮ ♯ ♮

Facing Theo Brigham, Tia feels suddenly and surprisingly relaxed. This man is not like men she has feared before. He has none of the fierce single-mindedness of her father. He is many-minded; his hands find projects of their own to complete as he is talking to them. He is reserved—he is aware of his actions, meticulous about them—but he is sweeter than her father, somehow.

Tia looks at her bandmates. No one is speaking. Next to her, Janelle glances at the door wistfully, willing Paul to come back in.

"Anyone?" asks Theo. "Why are you here today?" He

can see most of the girls are terrified. With the exception of one, they look young, quite young: this is a good thing. They are all passably pretty. The one on the right needs to lose weight. The one in the middle, with her bright blue eyes, is strikingly good-looking. She'd be the face of the band, the one to put up close on the album covers. The one to go on *TRL*. Theo's mind works this way: in terms of product. He leaps ahead to their TV appearances. They could put the oldest one in pigtails, make her look younger. How old did the father say they were? Fourteen? Fourteen is a good age. Fourteen-year-old girls are album buyers, product buyers. They watch MTV. They believe what you tell them.

These girls are nervous. Nervousness is good too. These girls haven't learned to be difficult yet, to be spoiled, like the kids who have been in the business since they could talk. Theo has met kids who refuse to speak without a lawyer present. He has met kids who demand cappuccinos upon entrance. These girls wouldn't dare: they wouldn't ask to go to the bathroom. Theo likes these qualities in artists. Obedience. A little bit of fear. But how long would it last? Fame is potent. Fame changes things. Theo has seen it.

♭ ♮ ♭

Tia looks once more down the row of her bandmates. Even Kira is silent—Kira, who flirts, who never shuts up. None of them has ever been asked to speak before. Paul has always done their talking for them: to local newspapers, to voice coaches.

Theo tries one more time: "Are you here to sing for me?" he coaxes.

"Yes," Tia ventures. "We're here to sing you a song."

Janelle looks at her gratefully.

"Do you have a backing track?" asks Theo.

"No," says Tia. She is feeling brave. She cannot let her father down. "We're singing a cappella."

"Well!" says Theo. "That's good. That's great." He waits. He is surprised: most pop artists require backing tracks; many require backing vocals. Many cannot sing at all.

The girls wait. Four of them look at Tia, who stands uncertainly. She is not sure how she has become the leader, but she likes her new role. Never before has she felt more powerful.

"Come on," she hisses behind her at the other four. Reluctantly, Kira stands, and then Janelle, and then Ravenne and Linette. Then Tia realizes that the pitch pipe is in her father's pocket and that her father is outside the office. She looks about desperately and then sees a keyboard in the corner of Theo's office.

"Can I?" she asks Theo.

"Please," he says.

♮ ♮ ♮

Paul is sitting down by the ficus tree when, on the other side of the door, he hears the girls begin to sing. His body tenses perceptibly. He sits up, leans forward. It takes all his willpower to stop himself from rushing to Theo's office door and pressing his ear to it.

The secretary returns with a cup of coffee.

"I forgot to ask about milk and sugar," she says.

"Shhhhh," says Paul, pressing a finger to his lips. "That's them," he whispers. "That's my daughter."

"Oh," whispers the secretary, confused. "Okay." She places the coffee on the table in front of Paul, backs away from him slowly, and returns to her desk.

Paul can hear only faint strains of music, but he thinks to himself that the girls are really very good, that their training has paid off. He wishes he could be in there with them. He wants to see them; it feels as if he is missing the ninth inning of a close baseball game. He wonders how Tia is doing.

And then something goes wrong: the song has only just started, and they go silent.

♮ ♮ ♮

"Stop," says Theo. He cannot hear them: they are dancing and singing a cappella, and the song is lost. "Stop dancing, Okay? Just sing."

Tia is relieved. She had been on the verge of breathlessness before Theo's command, and the song had just started.

Enjoying her new role as leader, Tia turns to the other girls. "Ready?" she asks. The other four nod, and once more Tia walks to the keyboard and plays a C.

They break into song: "Isn't it, isn't it, isn't it over now?"

Since she isn't thinking about her dance moves, Tia is able to focus on the song. She makes sure to hit the note she always sings flat. She smiles at Ravenne when Ravenne takes her solo on the bridge. Even Kira hits her note on "boy, it's over." More than anything, though, there is an excitement to their singing that Tia can feel, and she feels certain that Theo Brigham must feel it too. She feels proud of her bandmates—even proud of herself.

When they finish, Theo is smiling.

"That was great," he says.

♮ ♮ ♮

It was. Theo is delighted. They are actually good. He appreciates this band for the smallest things: something as simple as being able to find a C on a keyboard. Something as simple as graciousness, humility: Theo is touched and relieved, somehow, that he can still recognize these qualities in others and appreciate them.

It has been so long since he has been interested in the well-being of the bands he sees every day; this one is different. He likes them and he thinks others will like them. They are likable.

He wants them. He opens the door.

♮ ♮ ♮

Outside the office, Tia's father sits on a bench in the lobby. He has worn his best suit: a dark one with pinstripes. It fits him nicely through the shoulders. For a moment, seeing her father through the door, Tia lets herself imagine what it would be like to be him, and she lets herself feel bad for disappointing him, for being too fat, for being a terrible dancer. For being the only child. Now, for the first time, she has done as her father hoped she would do, and she has never felt worse.

My life is over, she thinks, and gazes sadly out the window of the office to the street below, at the thin and lovely women of New York City—some of whom have husbands and boyfriends who have forgotten their loveliness—and remembers, distantly, distantly, a song her father used to sing when she was younger. It was a lullaby. It was the only song she's ever heard him sing.

12.

JEFFREY THE GREAT

I.

She was too young, Jeff thinks, waking up once again beside someone he does not know. Too young, too young. Again. The hotel room is littered with clothes and magazines. Things come into focus in quick succession: the dizzying abstract print on the wall above the television; the flowers that came with the room, beginning now to wilt; his Strat, out of its case and propped up against the wall (bad! thinks Jeff, knowing he should care for his instruments better). The room itself is dim, the air inside it stale. The curtains are drawn across the wall-to-wall windows that look out over a parking lot in Colorado. Beyond the parking lot are mountains. Beyond the mountains is the state west of Colorado, which Jeff tries now to think of but cannot.

He can barely bring himself to look to his right. When he does he sees a bare shoulder and a brown ponytail. The rest of the girl is turned away from him, under the hotel bedspread. An old girlfriend once told him never to touch hotel bedspreads. "People have sex on them!" she had said, laughing. "You think anyone washes those things?" This had given Jeff pause. But I have sex on them, he had thought. I am that person. Still, he avoided them after that, and he wants now to pull the bedspread away from the girl's face—but more than that, he wants to avoid waking her up while he decides upon a course of action.

He tries to remember last night. They played at Red Rocks. Tom has his wife and kids with him on this tour, so they went back to the hotel early, right after the show ended. Kai, Jeff, and Jordan had hung out backstage after the show. All three of them had been drinking since before the show started. Jeff had a thermos of bourbon and Coke onstage with him. When he drinks he gets rowdy. He remembers telling one of the security guys to find them girls, remembers the guy coming back with four or five of them, all of them friends. What happened next?

The girl stirs a bit but does not turn over. Jeff holds his breath and then slowly, slowly sits up. He swings first his left foot, then his right, over the side of the bed. He tip-toes to the window and pulls one edge of the floor-length drape back the tiniest bit. Outside it is broad daylight. It might be noon. He holds his wrist up to the light and sees by his watch that it is eleven-thirty. What now? He looks back at the bed, at the girl in it. He has been in this situation before. He is constantly in this situation, and he never seems to improve at it. Sometimes, if he is feeling particularly cowardly, he simply leaves, packing up so quietly that he barely breathes, camping out in Jordan or Kai's room until the bus is nearly pulling out of the parking lot, then sprinting.

But he just doesn't feel like doing that today. He is feeling generous. Maybe even tender. He pulls open the shade a tiny bit, enough to see by, and walks over to the other side of the bed. He sits down on it. The girl is still asleep. If he squints at her, he can believe that she's twenty. She has a lovely profile: a nose that is strong and slightly convex; full lips; dark, well-formed brow. Tiny shell-like ears. Brown smooth hair pulled back in a rubber band. He almost wants to touch her neck: it looks so soft, and a blue vein runs the length of it, pulsing minutely. Against his will, Jeff's mind flashes forward over the years and he imagines having a relationship with this one; marrying her; having kids. Like Tom. Jeff admires Tom for his family. He is nearly in love with Camilla, and when no one is looking he likes to make googly faces at their daughters and watch their baby faces break into smiles.

The girl turns onto her back.

"Hey," says Jeff, very quietly, so as not to frighten her. "Good morning."

Then something terrible happens: the girl's hand comes up from beneath the blanket and she rubs her eyes, taking in a sleepy breath and holding it, blinking in the dim light.

"Mom?" she says.

Crap, thinks Jeff. *Mom?*

Suddenly the girl is very awake, sitting up, clutching at the blanket, pulling it over herself and terribly embarrassed. "Oh, God," she says. "Hi. Good morning."

"Good morning," Jeff says again, dumbly. "How are you today?"

"Um, fine," says the girl. "Can I use your phone?"

"Sure, of course. Of course." Jeff stands up and gets the phone from the other bed table, brings it around to her, and holds it out stiffly. "I'm just gonna—" He makes a lame pointing motion with his right hand and the girl nods, pressing the receiver into her shoulder with her ear, dialing the phone shakily.

Jeff backs out of the room and shuts the door behind him. Realizes next that his key is still inside. Runs down the hall, his heart hammering, and pounds on Jordan's door. He will hide until it is time to leave. Maybe he can pay a maid to pack up his things for him.

II.

This is the last leg of their tour. They will go home to New York in a week, Tommy Mays and his band and his family. Tom and Camilla have their own bus. Tom asked her abruptly one day, not long before they were to leave, if she didn't think the girls were old enough to come along this time. She had said she agreed. With the girls along, it was impossible not to have a bus to themselves, and the band has been selling records, so Titan was happy to oblige. They are waiting in the lobby of the hotel for the roadies to load up and for the drivers to be ready to go.

Alice is walking now but still cannot talk. In this way she is the opposite of her sister, Clara, who spoke early and often and now has a vocabulary that belies her three years on earth. Already, though, Alice has taken over: she is in charge, the force of the two.

"Bah. Bah. Bah," says Alice, standing with her hands on the knees of her mother, bouncing up and down on her baby toes.

" 'Papa'?" says Camilla hopefully. "Is that your papa, Alice?"

"Bah!" says Alice, looking cross.

Tom scoops her up and is then accosted by two high-schoolers who want his autograph.

"We saw you guys last night!" says one girl, nearly shouting. "Oh my God, you guys were awesome!"

Her friend nods in solemn agreement. Tom hands Alice to Camilla, signing the backs of the receipts the girls have proffered.

"Thanks," says Tom, and still the fans stare at him, not wanting to leave.

"Bah! Bah!" says Alice insistently, and Clara says imperiously, "Use words, Alice," which she herself is often told midtantrum.

Out of the corner of his eye, Tom sees a figure slinking

along the wall from the elevator into the lobby. He turns to see Jeff scanning the lobby nervously before coming over to them.

"Hi," says Jeff, shifty-eyed, feigning nonchalance. "We're leaving now, right?"

"They went to find a gas station. Filling up the buses," says Tom, tossing Alice up in the air, thrilling her so she shrieks happily.

"Cool," says Jeff, swearing in his mind. Can he hide behind a plant? He opts instead to walk outside and find a tree to stand near, so he can duck behind it if he sees the girl from this morning. "See you guys out there."

The two fans have watched this whole exchange as if it were a movie. Finally they take the hint and leave. "You were awesome," the one girl says one last time, with conviction, over her shoulder. "Awesome."

"Thank you," says Tom.

"Bye," says Camilla.

"Bus," says Alice, toddling quickly after the girls.

Camilla runs after her and picks her up. "What did you say, Alice?"

"Bus," says Alice, and yawns.

III.

Jeff, Kai, and Jordan sit on the bus behind Tom and his family's bus as they drive south. They have two nights before they are scheduled to appear in Austin, Texas, Jeff's hometown. Over the course of the next two and a half days, they will fight about who is using all the goddamn paper towels; switch beds because Kai is taller than Jordan and demands the longer one; sing along with an entire Tom Petty album, pointing and laughing when they catch Jeff clumsily mouthing words he does not know; stop at three truck stops, four roadside diners, and one Radio Shack (Kai has misplaced his cell phone charger); blow twenty-seven spitballs and nearly three hundred bubbles with the supersize pack of watermelon Bubble Yum chewing gum that Jordan will delightedly buy at one of the truck stops; cruelly quiz Junior, their old and unmarried driver, about his love life; develop a system of racing one another to the fore and aft of the bus at red lights; silence themselves suddenly at Kai's confession that he does not like the Beatles, and then worry the issue to pieces for the rest of the drive.

Jeff feels as he always does, approaching Austin: a sense of regret and mild amazement, a sort of marveling at his life. He has not told his family he would be in town, though they may have seen it in the papers—Jeff's father and younger sister follow the band, keep a little scrapbook in the family's living room with press clippings and advertisements—for he does not like to know that they are in the audience. It's an agreement they've worked out. He feels he cannot be himself (his unself, his stage self, he thinks sometimes) onstage if he knows his parents and his little sister are around. He leaves ten tickets and backstage passes for them and their guests at the box office, and they know to check there. After the show he will call them and invite them backstage if they are there—and they always are. They have not yet missed an Austin show. His sister, Celeste, brings a friend or two, though she does not like to play up his fame and is quiet and very rational herself.

As Jeff's superstition about his family is his one folly, the scrapbook is hers: she likes to feel close to her brother, likes to imagine that she knows where he is and what he is doing on a given day. She checks the Tommy Mays Web site with some frequency, keeping track of their tour, reading the guestbook and the discussion boards and seeing what everyone has to say about her big brother Jeff. She is especially amused by the postings of girls her own age who proclaim their undying love for him. She is fifteen, but wise. Today, as her brother and his band make their way toward Austin in two imposing black buses, she is baking cookies for her brother and debating with herself about whether bringing cookies for a band is too cute. She is, after all, a feminist, and has recently cut short and dyed black her fine hair, which used to hang down her back in a shiny brown sheet. In the end, she decides that baking cookies for a loved one is not entirely incompatible with feminism, and besides, they are Jeff's favorite—chocolate chocolate chip—and she knows he will take them from her hands gratefully and gobble them up until he is sick.

IV.

They turn off the highway toward Austin in the early hours of the morning, when it is still dark. Jeff wakes with a flutter of excitement in his gut. He can smell Austin even in the air of the bus. He can see it in the red light that crosses the ceiling. Jordan and Kai are still asleep: he can hear their heavy solemn breathing, and spends these moments thinking of all he has done wrong in the last year. It has been a bad one for Jeff. The girls—mostly the girls. He has had two dreams about the girl who woke up in his bed most recently, she of the ponytail and bare shoulder. "Mom?" she had said. It echoes in his ears: it was so innocent, so casual and unaffected. *Mom?* He had wished in that moment to be her mother, to see her waking up in a childish bedroom, frosted with pink; to touch the vein in her neck innocently, as a mother would.

"Fuck," he says aloud, very quietly. He often has the compulsion to curse aloud to relieve tension. "Shit."

His mind flashes over the other girls he has slept with this year, and stops, as it always does, at one he wishes most he could forget, the one he met almost a year ago in New Jersey: the one who cried.

"Fuck," he says again, a bit louder, and Jordan, across the bus, flops over in his sleep. "Goddamn it all to hell."

He feels like Humbert Humbert. He can remember reading *Lolita* in high school, in the English class instructed by young Ms. Murphy, who taught the relatively racy book against the wishes of the PTA because she loved it for its writing. He remembers feeling disgusted with both its protagonist and with Nabokov himself. He could not see it as satire; he simply felt the impulse to rescue young Lolita from the clutch of the snobbish narrator. But I am no better than he is, thinks Jeff. He remembers Ms. Murphy at the head of the classroom, probing her students for their reactions: "Who likes Humbert? Who likes Charlotte Haze? Who likes Lolita?" He had raised his hand quite high when asked about Charlotte Haze, whom he pitied for her cluelessness and for whom he felt endless empathy.

"But Jeffrey," Ms. Murphy had said, "are we meant to like her?" He had shrugged. He had liked Ms. Murphy. She was young (how old, in retrospect? twenty-five? thirty?) when he had her, and had very blond hair, and touched her lower lip when she spoke, and called him "Jeffrey" as a rule. She was unmarried then. At one point she had been Jeff's favorite teacher. He had never liked English— at sixteen or seventeen, he was already interested nearly exclusively in music—but for Ms. Murphy he read voraciously, neglecting his other homework. He read everything she told him to, and though he was too shy to join the large and doting group of students who stayed after for extra help, and too susceptible to peer pressure to participate in the drama club Ms. Murphy advised, he found other ways to show her he appreciated her. He did not, for example, sleep in her class the way he did in others. With a sturdy and delinquent student who had called her a bitch in class, he had nearly gotten into a fistfight, reports of which had surely made their way back to lovely Ms. Murphy (he hoped). Just before graduation, he had written her a love note, and had carried it with him beneath his graduation robes, envisioning himself thrusting it into Ms. Murphy's hands just before they left and never seeing her again. Fortunately or unfortunately, he had not seen Ms. Murphy at all, as she had caught a cold and was bedridden on the day of the ceremony.

♮ ♮ ♮

Just as the bus pulls up to the hotel, Jeff has a brief burst of inspiration. He checks his watch. It is five A.M. I will call Ms. Murphy, he thinks, halfway into the morning. It is a Saturday. She will be up, perhaps grading papers. She will be sitting at home, wherever that is, perhaps petting a cat, perhaps grading papers. She will be holding a cup of tea in her hands—she always had one in class, the little paper dangling off the end of its string distractingly—and when I call she will get up to answer the phone, sending the cat and the papers flying. I will invite her to coffee, thinks Jeff, because I am uncertain about whether she drinks. Or maybe we should go someplace with coffee and drinks. Yes: "for coffee or a drink," Jeff will say. He can ask the hotel staff for a recommendation. Surely she will have heard about him through the grapevine of students at his high school. Surely, because Celeste goes there now. Maybe she even likes his music! But this seems unlikely to Jeff. He wants urgently to call Celeste and ask her about Ms. Murphy, but he is superstitious by nature and refuses to break the tradition he has of speaking to his family only after his shows. He is in agony. He wishes for the clock to speed up, but they are signing in to the hotel now and it is only five-fifteen A.M. He will sleep for a few hours in his hotel bed, making sure to turn down the bedspread first.

♮ ♮ ♮

When he wakes up again, it is noon.

"Shit," says Jeff. "Fucker."

He sees a yellow phone book on a shelf below the bed-side table. It is from 2002. He flips to the white pages and runs a finger down the names, dismayed at the hugeness of the "Murphy" section. For a dreadful moment, he thinks he has forgotten Ms. Murphy's first name, but it comes to him quickly: Marguerite. A lovely old-fashioned name. Marguerite Murphy. And there she is, between Margaret and Mitchell Murphy. He looks up, out the window. Their call for sound check is at four o'clock. He will have time to see her.

He dials the number with a trembling finger. Hangs up before it rings. Tries again and lets it ring this time.

A woman answers the telephone. "Hello?"

Jeff pauses, frozen by the familiarity of her voice.

"Hello?" she says again.

"Ms. Murphy?" says Jeff.

Silence. He can hear her breathing. Then: "Jeffrey?"

"Yes," says Jeff. "How did you know it was me?"

"I never forget my students," says Ms. Murphy.

"Oh," says Jeff, fighting his impulse to curse. *Fucker*, he mouths. *Fuck!*

"Jeffrey?" says Ms. Murphy. "Are you there?"

"Sure, I'm here," he says. "Ms. Murphy, I'm in town, and I was wondering: would you like to get a drink?"

A pause.

"I mean, coffee?" says Jeff. "Do you have a minute to get coffee with me?"

"Ms. Redding," says Ms. Murphy.

"I'm sorry?"

"I'm Ms. Redding now, Jeffrey," says Ms. Murphy. "I got married, you see. But you can call me Marguerite now, anyway." She laughs her trilling laugh.

"Marguerite," says Jeff. "Congratulations, Marguerite."

"Thank you."

"Would you like to get coffee?"

V.

They meet at an artsy little café near his old high school. Jeff gets there first and sits fidgeting in his chair, an old leather one that smells like cigarettes, though smoking is not allowed in the restaurant and probably has not been for years. The restaurant is warm inside and crowded with people, but no one notices him. He is relieved. He scans right and left out the corners of his eyes, facing straight ahead. Perhaps he should get a newspaper. Will she recognize him after such a long time? He does not think he has changed much, and she recognized his voice, after all. He sees a newspaper to his right, abandoned on a table. He stands to retrieve it and in that instant sees Ms. Murphy as she walks through the door, a folder tucked under her arm, in jeans and a plain blue crew neck shirt. He has never seen her wearing jeans before. He is perplexed.

She notices him before he can wave, and makes her way

toward his table. Jeff is still standing, half bent over from his attempt to retrieve the newspaper, and he wishes he weren't: she takes an uncomfortably long time to arrive at his table, and he feels silly and stiff-armed. When she finally does, she places her folder on the table.

"Well!" she says. "Look at you."

"Hello," says Jeff, avoiding her name altogether. He sits back down abruptly, gesturing to the chair across from him. Should he have kissed her on the cheek? Shaken her hand?

Her hair has grown longer and hangs down her back wholesomely in a braid, like a shining stalk of corn or a vine. She sits and cups her hands beneath her chin: *Here is the church, and here is the steeple.*

"How are you doing?" Jeff asks.

"I'm doing quite well, thank you," says Ms. Murphy. "I love my students this year. They're bright and inspired. Like you," she says.

"Who's your husband?" asks Jeff, pointing to the small ring on her left hand.

"Hyland Redding," says Ms. Murphy. "He's an artist."

"Cool," says Jeff, suddenly wishing with all his might that he had not had this idea. Ms. Murphy has grown, if anything, more attractive since Jeff had her in high school: small and alluring laugh lines make their way from the corners of her eyes to the tops of her round pink cheeks; her breasts, in the blue crew neck shirt, have taken on a warm fullness; in her ears are tiny gold earrings shaped like stars. Over the phone, she gave no sign that she knew anything about his band, about his career, but he wishes now that she did know, and racks his brain for ways to bring up the topic casually.

"What can I get you to drink? I love this song," says Jeff, in one breath. He does not even know what strange song is playing in the little café, but he wants them to talk about music.

"Nana Mouskouri," says Ms. Murphy, sighing approvingly. "I like her too."

A waitress stops at their table and takes Ms. Murphy's order: a cup of Earl Grey tea. Jeff asks for a second Belgian beer.

"Where are you living these days?" asks Ms. Murphy, at the same time as Jeff says, "What are you doing tonight?"

"I'm grading, I think. Hyland is away visiting friends," says Ms. Murphy, looking down at the folder between them ruefully. Jeff surmises that it is full of student papers. He is filled with sudden hope: Hyland Redding is away.

"Would you like to come to a concert?" says Jeff. But however, he wonders, however will I tell her it is mine? And that it will be huge and populated by screaming sixteen-year-old girls? He is disgusted, suddenly, with his life. Here is Ms. Murphy and she is married. He should be married to a woman like Ms. Murphy. He vows immediately never to have another one-night stand. He has vowed this before, unsuccessfully, but he means it now.

Ms. Murphy looks at him closely. "I'd love to come to your concert, Jeffrey," she says. "Half of my students will be there too!"

♮ ♯ ♭

Thirty minutes later, the two of them say goodbye.

VI.

Celeste, in her way, is burning the cookies. She has forgotten about them and now they are burning in the oven. She is on the phone.

"Yes," she is saying, "it's tonight."

On the other end of the phone is a fifteen-year-old boy who loves Celeste. Kenneth Wang.

"I'd love to come," says Kenneth. He doesn't really like music, but he likes Celeste. He likes her hair, the way she cut it short. He shares her interest in French poetry and, like Celeste, is passionately liberal. He thinks of Celeste as a beacon of intellect and beauty in their stereotypical high school. She thinks of him as her friend Kenneth Wang, who is funny, who wears suit jackets and ties and blue jeans to school because he likes to look older than his age, a bit like a movie producer (Kenneth loves film) or a graduate student.

"Crap," says Celeste, "my cookies!"

"What?" says Kenneth Wang. "Celeste?" But there is no one there.

The cookies are black on the bottom but fine on the top. Celeste decides that she can salvage them and gets out a plate and a knife. One by one, she saws the bottom off each cookie and places it on the plate, thinking all the while of her big brother Jeff and how she will be glad to see him. She remembers him before he got famous, of course. She is much younger than he is, so to her he always seemed famous, in a way, as much-older siblings do. A bit legendary, as if he got to everything first, as if he set some path from which diverging is prohibited. But Celeste has diverged from her brother's path, and she is surprisingly adult in most of her manners. Every time Jeff sees her—two or three or four times a year—he is surprised by her ability with language. He never had her way with words, and he envies her for it, the way she envies him for his music. But only a little bit. They are brother and sister.

"Dad!" calls Celeste, from the kitchen. Her father is reading a book in their small living room. "Dad, Kenneth is coming with us tonight!"

"Okay," says her father. He has his camera around his neck. He has his wallet and his cell phone in his pocket, and a light jacket on the back of his chair. He is ready, and it is only three-thirty.

VII.

In the flourescent light of the backstage area, Tom and Camilla sit quietly with the girls, who have fallen asleep on a white leather couch. Tom taps a little rhythm on his knee with his left hand, his head resting on the wall behind him. He is waiting for his sound check call. He can hear the techs now:

"New York Giants," comes an echoing voice from the stage. "New England P-p-patriots. S-s-san Francisco F-f-forty-Niners."

Camilla has learned in all her years with Tom that to initiate conversation with him before his shows is usually fruitless. His responses are mostly monosyllabic; his look is faraway. But today he seems different. He is looking at her intently, smiling a bit.

"Remember when we played at the Bowery Ballroom for the first time?" says Tom suddenly, wanting her to share with him a moment from their past, wanting her to re-member him in his youth. Camilla does remember: Tom was playing then with Jeff and a different drummer and bassist. It was maybe six years ago. The first time Tom had headlined a show in a big New York venue. He had gotten too drunk and had played sloppily, cringing when he heard a recording of the show the next day.

But she feigns forgetfulness. "When?" she says. She does not know why she is pretending this way. Perhaps so that he does not think she keeps track of every show, so that he remembers that once she had a life of her own, away from him, away from his music. They were just dating then, and Camilla remembers being afraid of what would happen in the greenroom, in the backstage area, after the show, be-fore the show. She did not possess then the resigned secu-rity that comes with marriage. She had not yet made the decision she has since made: never to worry about Tom's faithfulness. She trusts their marriage now, yes, but more than that, she feels secure as the mother of his children.

"My God, it was years ago, years ago!" says Tom, laughing. Then he is called from the room by a trembling boy of eighteen who wears the green and blue uniform assigned to him by the arena, and he leaves Camilla with Clara and Alice, who breathe slowly and collectively, their round tummies rising and falling together. They are sisters.

VIII.

Sometime between the sound check and the show, Jeff heads for the bathroom and locks the door behind him. He needs a quiet moment to think, and Jordan and Kai have designated one room for themselves, and Tom and Camilla and their daughters are being a happy family in another, and acned teenagers in uniform roam the halls backstage. He is sweating. He has an upset stomach from some Chinese food he ate for dinner. He is looking at himself in the mirror in the bathroom and imagining Ms. Murphy naked. But she is married to Hyland Redding! he says to himself. An artist; she married an artist.

"You disgust me," he says to his reflection, suddenly remembering the girl who cried. He does not deserve a woman like Ms. Murphy, who is married anyway and certainly would not have him. But oh, to reach beneath her blue crew neck with a greedy hand. Oh, to touch her golden braid.

"Hello, Marguerite," he says aloud. "I love you. Come away with me." He pauses. "On a tour bus. With two of my friends. This is Jordan; this is Kai. We can share the top bunk."

He hangs his head in despair. Marguerite Murphy, grading papers in an armchair, with cats. If they were married, he would bring her tea if she wanted, or rub her feet. Anything she wanted. He would play his guitar for her. If she wanted.

He checks his watch. He has been in the bathroom for an hour, but no one has come looking for him. They are consumed by their own lives, he thinks, and they do not care about mine. Jordan and Kai have always been better friends with each other than with him. Tom and Camilla and their girls are a family. He has no one.

IX.

Celeste and Kenneth Wang sit in the backseat of the Toyota Corolla that Celeste's father drives. Beside him, her mother lowers the eye shade and looks in the little mirror, applying lipstick.

"I hope you brought your camera, Bob," she says. "I think you forgot it last time."

"Of course I brought it," says Celeste's father, giving the camera around his neck a reassuring pat.

Celeste looks at Kenneth and rolls her eyes. He smiles because he can think of nothing to say, no witty remark that would be unheard by her parents. How he wants to be witty around Celeste, to impress her with his dry sense of humor, with his intellect. Often this desire manifests itself in unsummoned lectures about this or that Asian filmmaker, this or that politician. Celeste endures these because she thinks Kenneth Wang is funny, most of the time, and because he occasionally helps her with her history homework. Celeste has no head for history, prefers fiction over nonfiction, cannot keep track of dates. Kenneth, contrarily, has an astounding ability to memorize facts.

"Almost there!" says Celeste's mother brightly. "I just hope we're not late."

"We are nearly one hour early, Joanne," says Celeste's father.

X.

Jeff walks onstage with a fluttering in his heart that threatens to fell him. He wonders for a moment if his heart has stopped completely, and then comes the thud-thud that tells him he is still alive. The crowd is no bigger than any other; they are no louder; the lights are no brighter. He lifts his Strat from its stand, not even bothering to make eye contact with his guitar tech, breaking routine. Usually, he likes to look into the wings and get a reassuring nod from Jerry the tech: *All set, pal.*

Tonight he is mono-visioned and insane with fear. Somewhere in this crowd, he thinks, is Ms. Murphy. He has left a ticket for her along with the usual ten tickets for his family at the ticket booth. Somewhere in this crowd is Ms. Murphy, and here I am onstage and her eyes are on me, he thinks. He cannot remember how he usually moves: intense thought precedes every twitch, every step, every note.

Sometime during their first song, Tom looks back at

him over his left shoulder and arches an eyebrow. Jeff pretends not to see him. He knows he is not on his game tonight, but he prays that his sloppiness will go unnoticed by the laypeople in the audience. This is one of his tricks. *No one will notice, no one will care*, he repeats to himself. A mantra.

By the third song, he regains his stride suddenly and unexpectedly and is relieved to find that his fingers work again. He begins to have fun. He struts a little. He is glad that Ms. Murphy is here to see him like this, a rock star in front of his fans, a god among men. It is a very powerful feeling. He makes a point tonight of marching to the front of the stage, to its very precipice, and peering through the blinding spotlight at the crowd. His toes touch the air beyond the stage. A girl in the front row screams and reaches for him, but metal bars keep her about four feet away. She slams an angry fist against them. Through the glare of the spot, she looks possessed, feral.

Jeff has no microphone; only Jordan lends backup vocals to Tom's strong clear songs. He realizes suddenly that he can say anything out loud and no one will hear, ever; he cannot even hear himself. He tests this theory:

"I am Jeff," he says, in the middle of a guitar solo, wondering next why he would say "I am Jeff," of all things.

"Ms. Murphy, are you out there?" he tries. "Ms. Murphy!" He is shouting now.

Turning around, he suddenly he realizes that his face is being projected on the large screen above the stage as he yells. He must look insane.

XI.

The backstage area glows an unearthly red. Jeff walks into the greenroom, sweating, unkempt, his bandmates behind him. The concrete walls and white leather couches, the folding tables loaded with all the food they request on their rider, remind Jeff of every other greenroom he has ever seen.

"Good show, men," says Tom, throwing himself onto a couch violently.

"Dudemeister," says Kai. He slaps Jeff on the back. "Who's here to see you tonight, Jeffrey?"

"No one," says Jeff.

"Liar," says Kai, "We're in Austin. I bet your moms is coming."

Jordan whistles. "I like when Jeff's mom comes," he announces, and Jeff is too tired to tell him to fuck off.

Camilla comes in next with the girls.

"Babies, babies, baby alert," says Kai. "Watch your mouth, Jordan."

"Watch your own mouth," mutters Jordan, who had been fumbling in his pocket for a lighter and a smoke until the door opened.

"Good show, men," says Camilla, and Jeff is secretly thrilled at being let inside their marriage for an instant. They share a language, like his parents do. He wonders if Ms. Murphy and Hyland Redding share a language, if they say things at the same time and then turn to each other fondly, laughing; if they call each other simultaneously from across town, across country, and leave each other mirrored voice mails.

He sits up straight at the thought of Ms. Murphy. Now is the time after shows when the guards begin to let people backstage, the lucky few with hot pink passes slung about their necks.

Jeff stands abruptly and walks across the room to fix himself a drink. His usual is a bourbon and Coke. He has specific ideas about what constitutes bourbon, which he will recite if prompted. His bourbon is Maker's Mark. He likes three ice cubes in a highball glass. He takes a sip of the dark liquid gratefully, quickly, hoping to finish before Ms. Murphy arrives.

The door opens and Jeff turns around, his right hand automatically going around behind his back with the bourbon. But it is only three girls, youngish, and Jeff does not know who they are. Neither do Jordan or Kai, apparently, but they say hello nonetheless and invite them to sit down.

Next comes an old friend of Tom and Camilla's.

"Annie!" shouts Camilla, and Tom stands to give the woman a kiss on the cheek. "My God, Annie, you haven't even met the girls!"

Annie laughs in disbelief at the sight of Clara and Alice, who eye her shyly from their places on the couch. "I can't decide who they look like," she says.

"Each other," says Tom, and everyone laughs—an exclusive laugh, a hearty exclusive laugh. Jeff chuckles a little too, quietly, wanting to be part of it all.

Once again the door opens, but it is only Jerry the

guitar tech, who comes in carrying Jeff's Strat in its case and marches it over to Jeff.

"All set, pal," he says.

XII.

Kenneth, Celeste, and Celeste's parents wait patiently in the line to get backstage. At the door is a large man with a walkie-talkie.

"Anyone without a pink pass, leave now," he says. Nobody moves. He points at a girl halfway back. "You," he says. "Where's your pass?"

"I lost it," says the girl. "I had one, though, seriously."

The guard shakes his head back and forth slowly, definitely. "You're not getting back there, hon," he says. "Not tonight."

"Please," says the girl. "You don't understand. They're expecting me backstage."

Celeste feels terribly embarrassed for her family, suddenly, and wishes with all her might that she were not in this line with these people. She misses her brother Jeff, and she holds her bag of cookies (which the guards at the gate almost did not let her bring) ashamedly. It was a stupid idea to bring cookies. Her parents are silent, and she tries hard to think of something to say to Kenneth, who is trying hard to think of something to say to her.

"Glad we've got these," says Kenneth, fingering his pink pass. It is exactly the wrong thing to say.

"I'm not," says Celeste. "I hate them." She takes hers off

and for a split second considers handing it to the girl without the pass. But the guard is approaching the girl now, and
she has started crying—humiliatingly, childishly—and the
guard actually picks her up by her armpits and carries her
down the aisle away from the line.

"No," the girl is saying. Celeste can hear her. "I had
one! I lost it!"

In her peripheral vision, Celeste sees her father pat his
own pass the way he pats his camera or his wallet, to see if
it is there. She hates Jeff. She hates him suddenly for making his own family wait in this awful line. She wants to
leave, but the door in front of them opens abruptly and the
hellish red light from backstage spills out.

"Pink passes only," says a guard who has replaced the
first one. Celeste's mother, Celeste's father, Kenneth, and
Celeste file past him, flashing the pass triumphantly, gratefully, shyly, disgustedly, in turn.

XIII.

It has been fifteen minutes since people have been coming
backstage, and still Ms. Murphy has not come. Annie and
Camilla are chatting and playing with the girls while Tom
signs autographs for the lucky fans who have been let
backstage. Jordan and Kai are still chatting up the three
girls in tight clothes who found them first.

"I like your cross," says Jordan, reaching for a crucifix
that hangs about one girl's neck, finding a resting place
just above the neckline of her shirt.

"Thank you," says the girl, uncertainly.

Jeff can guess her age.

He watches as Kai's eyes shift to the door and move from top to bottom of whoever just walked in; he turns as well to see his sister, Celeste.

She looks miserable. An Asian boy in a suit jacket follows close behind. Jeff's parents walk in last. And still Ms. Murphy is nowhere to be found. Automatically, Jeff goes over to his family and says hello. He hugs his father, kisses his mother on the cheek, puts an arm around Celeste's shoulder.

"You were great," says Celeste. Flatly. She does not mean it.

"Oh, Jeff," says their mother. "You *are* great, honey. Just great."

"I think I'm deaf," says his father, sticking a finger in his ear and wiggling it around. "Was it loud enough for you up there?"

"I'm Kenneth," says Kenneth Wang. He holds out his hand. All he wants is for Celeste to see he is unintimidated by her famous older brother, but his voice cracks when he says, "Nice to meet you."

"Celeste," says Jeff. "Do you have a teacher named Ms. Murphy?"

"No," says Celeste. "Do you, Kenneth?"

"No," says Kenneth Wang, looking lovingly at Celeste as she hands her older brother the bag of burnt, halved cookies.

13.

ELLEN MILLS: TWELVE SIMPLE SONGS AND ARIAS

I.

Ellen Mills begins her first serious relationship relatively late in life, at twenty-four, with a man twenty-one years her senior. His name is Heinrich and he is German. He is a producer who works with Ellen on her second album—tentatively titled *Ellen Mills: Twelve Simple Songs and Arias*—and seduces Ellen one evening at a sidewalk café in the East Village. It is a biergarten of the authentic variety, with waitresses who speak German to Heinrich and call him by name. Ellen smiles at them and blushes a little when she suspects they might be talking about her. Heinrich notices, and politely he switches to English.

"Ellen is just finishing her second album," he says to their waitress. "She is an opera singer. A very talented lady." Heinrich winks at her and reverts to German and Ellen smiles at his formality and at being called a lady. She has had two real German beers in glasses that are as big as her head. She feels drunk and rather lovely; she imagines that her face might be prettily flushed, her hair charmingly tousled. She came here with Heinrich because she had felt thirsty after singing for four hours in a warm Chelsea studio, and because she found him exciting.

After the waitress walks away with their food order— Heinrich has ordered them four different kinds of wursts— Ellen stretches her hands toward the sky in a motion that might be suggestive, and leans casually toward Heinrich. She is thrilling herself with bravery: she feels jokey and unafraid.

"I'm famished," she says, imagining it might be something Katharine Hepburn would say at this moment.

"Fammish?" says Heinrich. He blinks.

"Hungry."

"Ah. Good!" he says enthusiastically, and embraces Ellen abruptly, putting his bear hands on her arms and giving her an affectionate shake. "Good!"

The gesture is so familiar that it startles Ellen, who comes from a family that does not use touch lightly or easily. She gasps a bit, against her will, and withdraws. Heinrich doesn't notice, plunging once more into his third beer, which he drinks with extraordinary vigor. He shows not the slightest sign of drunkenness. Ellen wonders if he drinks this much beer every night—or more. The thought excites her. Heinrich seems vital to her, warm, endlessly human. His odor is pleasantly, mildly rank, and he is hairier than any man she's ever found attractive. Small light curls at his neck escape the collar of his T-shirt, which is old and blue and has holes in both shoulder seams. Sweat darkens the fabric under his arms. He has light and sandy hair, a close-trimmed beard, small laugh lines that frame eyes lined with brilliantly dark lashes. Ellen thinks he's very handsome. He's much larger than she is, for one thing, and his presence is comfortable, almost maternal. He crosses his legs the way ladies do, and bounces his right leg along with the music, his toes wiggling in their sandal as though they are glad to be free.

Ellen sips from her beer while he tells her about Germany. He has a wife there and two teenage sons. He is here in America because the classical division of Titan is paying him to produce a number of albums, Ellen's included. He occupies a small one-bedroom apartment in Murray Hill, also paid for by Titan. He goes home at night after working with Ellen, he says, and puts on the TV and practices his English by having conversations with the characters in the half-hour sitcoms, answering them when they ask each other questions, participating in their lives. His favorite thing is watching reruns of *Cheers*, though he has trouble with the accents. "I'm lonely here," he tells Ellen.

"I miss the little man who sells me bread in my town. I miss my sons."

"And your wife?" asks Ellen.

"Yes," says Heinrich. "I miss her too."

♮ ♮ ♮

The waitress brings their wursts, all four of them huge, white or red and speckled inside with spices and herbs.

"Danke," says Ellen, who would never normally say such a silly thing.

"She speaks German!" says the waitress, kindly.

And Heinrich: "Wonderful! Wonderful!"

"Danke," Ellen says again, laughing, and picks a wurst up with her fingers and bites into it, aware that she is watched by Heinrich.

II.

In the studio, Ellen works quietly. She was not able to befriend the producer who worked on her first album or the musicians who played on it. At the Met, she does not make allies easily. She is younger than most of the other singers, for one thing: she has been studying in conservatories and training with private vocal instructors since she was twelve. Becoming a darling of the press early on in her career has not been easy on her, socially.

Her family—mother, father, younger brother—lives upstate, in a small home in Schenectady. They spend summers at a lake house an hour north. On weekends in the summer, Ellen usually takes an Amtrak train to visit them, buying a trashy novel at Penn Station beforehand and reading it voraciously on the rides up and back. Upstate she sits by the quiet lake and imagines that she is storing up fuel for the city, that she is being blessed, somehow, by the water at her feet. She has romantic ideas about love and sex and uses her time alone to plan relationships with men who do not know her name.

Certainly, her minor fame has brought her admirers, but the men who contact Ellen or her agent are largely older, wishing simply to congratulate her on an opera well performed or to encourage her to listen to so-and-so's version of a particular aria.

Most recently, an elderly pair of Brooklynites recognized her on the street while she was waiting for the bus, and told her that they listened to her rendition of "L'Habañera" almost every night.

"It's so lovely," the woman had said. "Thank you, thank you."

She had been touched by their communal stance, the gentleman with his hand on his wife's back, his hat removed and clutched in a thick-veined hand.

"Our daughter knows you," he had said. But then Ellen's bus had arrived and she had boarded it apologetically, promising them over her shoulder that she would listen to Joan Sutherland's *Turandot*, as they had requested.

She remembers the episode and the couple fondly, as she does all older couples who seem visibly full of love and respect for one another. She has heard from her mother, Maryanne, about the girls in her hometown who are getting married to boys from her hometown, and she can barely believe it. She herself is very far away from marriage. At twenty-four, she has had dates with men who frightened her and she has had a brief fling with a busboy who wanted to be an actor, but she has never been in love.

III.

"Do you like this?" asks Heinrich, gesturing broadly.

"The food?" asks Ellen. "The beer?" She smiles sleepily, and leans her elbows on the table. She's quite drunk now, and she has stopped worrying about hiding it from Heinrich. "I like everything."

"And me?" says Heinrich, and once again puts a bear hand on her arm, and turns her face toward his and wipes something off the corner of her mouth. "Ellen? And me?"

♭ ♮ ♭

Later that night, in Heinrich's bed, Ellen lies on her side and presses her nose into Heinrich's ribs, inhaling deeply. He smells like the earth.

"You have a beautiful voice," he tells her. "May I confess you something?"

"Confess me anything," says Ellen. She is in the midst of noticing things about Heinrich's room: the small framed photo of his sons, both of them adolescent and punkish, which he has placed on the windowsill; the five wooden grocery crates of LPs that line up next to each other on the floor by the windowed wall; the bedside lamp, bizarrely childish, with a boy and a girl that look like Ellen's grandmother's Hummel figurines chasing each other around an apple tree that serves as the lamp's stem. Ellen imagines Heinrich must have brought it with him specially from Germany, and marvels at the difficulty of packing something like that for a plane ride. The lamp must have some kind of significance for him, and Ellen makes plans to ask Heinrich about it later—months later, when they have grown comfortable with each other, the way couples do, when they can walk down the street with their arms slung about each other, hardly noticing the other's presence. This is Ellen's favorite fantasy: When she imagines herself in a relationship, it is never the beginning of things that thrills her. It is the middle—it is closer to the end than anything. That stage of utter thoughtlessness, complete comfort: a stage she has never known.

She is brought back by Heinrich's voice: "I listened to you in Germany," he says. "It was I who asked Titan to let me work on your second album."

Ellen had been under the impression that Titan had asked him—Heinrich is, she has been told, a fairly prominent producer. He has worked with other opera singers on albums that have done well for Titan's German division. She is flattered now, and says so, hoping she doesn't sound stilted or distant (she has been accused of these things before).

"No, no," says Heinrich. "It is I who am flattered, Ellen."

He takes her face in his hands and examines her, as if he might lick his thumb and wipe something from her brow. As if he might pinch her cheeks. Instead, he kisses her on the mouth and Ellen feels the same kind of thrill that she felt as a seventh-grader when some senior boys who lived on her street asked her if she wanted a cigarette one day when she was walking home from school.

"No—I just quit," Ellen had said. Her parents smoked and she had tried a couple of cigarettes once, back to back, the way she had seen her father do it, and she had to sit down abruptly because she felt dizzy, and she told herself she would never do it again. So it was almost true. She kept walking, making sure not to trip or to slow down or speed up, and she complimented herself on a job well done.

Then behind her she heard the worst of the boys say, "Spit or swallow?" which almost ruined it, but not quite. She still remembers it fondly because it was the first time she ever felt like a girl. It was the first time anyone ever talked to her because she was a girl. She felt she had been inducted into a club she had always known existed but could not name—a club with members who roll their eyes at the antics of the opposite sex, and at the unwanted attention they get. Ellen was now part of that club.

She wishes that she could tell Heinrich about those boys, but knows she cannot. Ellen learned a long time ago what makes a story and what does not.

Instead, she places a hand on Heinrich's furry chest and sighs deeply.

"You are all right, my dear?" asks Heinrich.

♮ ♮ ♮

At some point in the night, Ellen wakes up completely sober and realizes in quick succession what she has done and what she is: respectively, she has had sex with a married man and she is a home wrecker. Maybe even a slut. Never before has Ellen thought of herself as anything close to sluttish, but she suspects that overnight she has unceremoniously joined a different club: one with members including everyone from Doreen Geiger—in Ellen's fifth-grade class, the only unfortunate possessor of womanly breasts—to Laney Healey, the high-schooler accused of giving the entire junior varsity football team pregame blow jobs at the back of their yellow bus. Ellen has always felt laughably far away from these girls and their legion. But here she is, and it is four o'clock in the morning, and she is naked, and she is lying in a *married man's* bed. She can picture her mother saying it: a *married man*. Her mother did say it once, in hushed tones to her father, about one of the young women at her office. *She's having an* affair, said Ellen's mother, *with a* married man. It had seemed the worst sin in the world at the time.

But now it doesn't seem so bad. It seems a tiny bit glamorous, even—the kind of thing that one should do once in her life, so she can remember it later when she is old and crippled and very far away from youth. I'm glad that I'm getting this out of the way now, thinks Ellen, aware that she is rationalizing terribly. Glad to be sowing the oats while young.

And then finally, finally, Ellen can no longer stop her mind from turning toward the one thought she has been scrupulously avoiding: Heinrich's unnamed wife, probably waking up now in Germany—or no, she has been awake for a few hours, and she is wondering about Heinrich, and she is missing him and wishing she could call him, but she does not want to wake him because she cares about him very much, and she knows he is a busy producer who stays out late and needs his sleep. And she is cleaning. And her hair is in a kerchief like the hausfrau in one of the books Ellen read as a child. And she is singing a cleaning song, and suddenly, in Ellen's mind, Heinrich's wife becomes Lotte Lenya, cleaning house in a kerchief.

And Ellen is in bed with Lotte's husband—a *married man*. She's having an *affair*.

IV.

In the morning, Ellen wakes before Heinrich and gathers her things together quietly. She is taking a train upstate today to visit her family for the weekend. She observes once more the apple tree lamp, the picture of Heinrich's sons, and then Heinrich himself, sleeping faceup with his mouth open and one arm crooked over his forehead. His right eye flutters delicately, revealing a sliver of bluish white that reminds Ellen of a leechee fruit.

She is uncertain about whether to wake him or simply to leave. First she decides to leave, thinking it would be romantic and unpredictable of her. Then she remembers that she must see Heinrich on Monday in the studio and figures that it might be less awkward if she said her piece now. She closes her eyes and rehearses a speech in her head: *Heinrich, this was lovely,* it begins. *But you're married. You have sons. And I don't want this to get in the way of our professional relationship.* Yes, that would be the thing to emphasize. The studio, the project. Before she can mentally conclude her speech, Heinrich opens his eyes. He sees Ellen standing in front of him and he sits up in bed. The sheet falls down from his torso and in daylight Ellen is shocked at seeing him shirtless: the hair of his chest, his slight paunch, his broad shoulders. She feels he might be a stranger. She barely remembers working with him in the studio. He isn't the same person.

"You are not leaving, Ellen?" he asks.

"I have to go away for the weekend," says Ellen. "To see my parents." She cringes, imagining how young she must sound. "I have to go home to pack my suitcase and then catch a train."

"Ah," says Heinrich, sadly. "Well."

Ellen picks up her bag from the floor and slings it over her shoulder and wonders if she should walk over to him, give him a kiss, embrace him? Just leave?

He doesn't give her the option. He stands, and the sheet falls to the floor, and Ellen stops herself from gasping at seeing him completely undressed. She shuts her eyes inadvertently and forces them open again, keeps them on the floor. Heinrich notices but says nothing. He crosses the small room and takes her hands.

"You are bashful," he says.

"No, I'm not," says Ellen. She remembers her rehearsed speech and opens her mouth to say *Heinrich, this was lovely,* and then realizes the absurdity of a sentence like that.

"May I please call your cellular phone?" asks Heinrich.

"Yes," says Ellen. "I have to go now, really, because my train is leaving soon."

V.

The train is so crowded that two young men stand in the aisle until Poughkeepsie. They are marines and their crisp dark blues remind Ellen of Heinrich's sheets—similarly fresh and pressed when she got into them last night. They were sweaty and wrinkled by morning, and she wonders if Heinrich washes them every day. Or maybe, she thinks, he had just planned to have her come home with him. The thought makes her dizzy.

The marines have their hats tucked underneath their arms. They look no more than eighteen. One of them resembles Ellen's brother. They are touchingly well behaved, scrambling to help an old lady with her luggage when she gets on at Yonkers.

"Oh, nice boys," she says. "God bless you nice boys."

♭ ♮ ♭

Ellen sits at the very front of the car in a backward-facing seat, her knees nearly touching the knees of the man who sits opposite her. Next to him is a woman, perhaps thirty-five, who Ellen thinks must be his wife, and next to Ellen is an older woman. They all know one another, and Ellen hides her face behind her trashy novel so as to give them some privacy, in case they want to talk. But they rarely do, and usually it is to comment on the view. The ride is a particularly scenic one: straight up the Hudson River, which catches the morning light brilliantly and tosses it straight back up in the air.

The three of them fall silent for a long time, and then the younger woman speaks abruptly, startling Ellen.

"Mom, did I tell you?" she asks, sitting forward a bit in her chair. "When Chuck and I—"

"Slow down and speak up," says the old woman, who has been cranky for most of the trip.

"When Chuck and I get married, Mother, we've decided that we're going to have two weddings: one in California, with Chuck's family, and one in Niagara."

"Nonsense," says the old woman. "You're not even engaged to each other."

Ellen, behind her book, feels suddenly conspicuous. She wonders if she should put the book down and feign sleep. But she decides that this might be even more obvious. Instead, she puts her headphones on and listens to Billie Holiday on low volume.

"We are, Mother," says the younger woman. "See?" She extends her left hand, pointing with her right to a modest ring, smiling at Chuck, who looks increasingly nervous and nods awkwardly. "Aren't you going to congratulate us?"

Her mother does not respond, but turns and looks out the window again. The daughter frowns and falls into silence. She bears the aspect of someone who has been slowly collapsing into herself for years: her eyes are deeply set and dark; her lips are barely lips at all, but thin lines of pink flesh that she pulls in with her teeth. She is thin. Her arms are crossed beneath a meager bosom. Her neck is tensed so that the cords in it have become ropelike and conspicuous.

Chuck seems frightened and uncertain of his duty. He makes small birdlike movements with his hands, which he has folded in his lap, but he does not speak.

After perhaps a minute of quiet, the younger woman turns from the window and addresses her mother again.

"What was your wedding with Dad like?" she asks finally.

The old woman lowers her brow. "How you go on," she says. She closes her eyes and leans her head back on the seat abruptly. "I'm sleeping—don't you see?"

♮ ♮ ♮

Ellen wakes just before her stop and sees that her seatmates have gotten off. She wonders how they managed to leave without waking her—she is normally a fitful sleeper—and then remembers that she did not sleep much last night. Then thinks of Heinrich and his wife, Lotte.

She begins to gather her things together. A man in a blue uniform comes by and takes the paper from the place above her seat and tells her her stop will be next.

"Thank you," says Ellen.

The wheels hum against the tracks and the brakes squeal as the train pulls into the station. Through the dim train

window, Ellen sees her mother, Maryanne, on the plat-
form. She is pacing, as she always does: weaving in and out
of people in the crowd, her eyes scanning the train. I'm
here, thinks Ellen. Look here.

♮ ♮ ♮

They greet each other as warmly as they ever have. In the
car, Maryanne asks her about her album, how it's coming.

"I told Margie that you were working with a famous
German producer and she said, 'Well, I never.' You know
Margie was born in Austria."

"Yes, I knew that."

"Your brother is excited to see you."

♮ ♮ ♮

In the middle of the car ride home, Ellen's phone rings,
and she scrambles to answer it. Her phone only ever rings
when someone from Titan is calling her.

"Hello?" she says.

"It is I, Heinrich," says the voice on the telephone. And
Ellen knows, as abruptly as she answered the call, that she
will see this man again outside the studio—she will sleep
in his bed many times over the next months. She will
count the curls of hair on his chest; she will run fingers
over his forehead while he sleeps. In time, she will ask him
for the names of his sons, perhaps even the name of his
wife. Later, leaving his apartment, she will whisper their
names aloud and cry on the way to the subway, imagining

Heinrich and Lotte (whose real name is Ulrike) on their wedding day, at the births of their sons. It will be within her control to end her affair with Heinrich, but she will allow it to continue, knowing herself to be immoral and at fault, and thinking worse of Heinrich each day. The affair will last far longer than it should. It will end when Heinrich leaves.

"Heinrich," she says, "can I call you back?"

"Of course, Ellen," says Heinrich.

Ellen snaps her phone shut and closes her eyes.

"Heinrich," says her mother. "Was that your producer?"

Yes, thinks Ellen, but she feels tired and wants to say more. All of her life she has hidden herself from her mother, and she presumes that her mother has done the same. Maryanne, who is driving with both hands on the wheel at ten and two o'clock, turns now to Ellen, awaiting her response. We keep ourselves from each other, thinks Ellen. We all keep ourselves alone.

What follows is an impulse she is too weary to fight. Unswervingly, Ellen says, "Mom. I'm having an affair. With a married man."

VI.

At the lake house, the breeze lifts the curtains in the hallway so that they touch Ellen's cheek as she walks past them to her bedroom, suitcase in hand. It is a touch that brings her back to youth. She remembers her mother choosing the fabric for those curtains and sewing them herself. They are white and soft, with a tiny trim of cherries that dance around their border.

Her bedroom is just as it always is, drenched in sunlight, carpeted with a deep blue shag that dates the house impossibly. Her bedroom is the smallest, but the only one with a view of the lake. Ellen drops her small suitcase on the bed and shifts her gaze outside. She is greeted with a sense of deep relief. Her mother is somewhere else in the house, presumably crying or smoking or doing whatever a mother does when her daughter tells her she is someone's mistress. Her brother and her father are not home.

Everything is damp here. She knows what the sheets will feel like when she climbs into bed tonight: sticky, as if in need of an extra five minutes in the dryer. The old oak clock in the living room chimes three.

The day is still; the water on the lake looks glassy and golden. Ellen feels that she has lost some innocence since she was there last, and apologizes silently to no one. To herself. I will take a swim later, Ellen says to herself, and then I will go to my mother. But what does one say? The truth: that the affair has not yet started, really, that it was a mistake. A lie: that she will end things with Heinrich. Her mother must have peace of mind. Above all else, her mother's mind must be at peace.

She places a hand on the glass of her window and presses her forehead against it too, wanting its coolness, wanting its smoothness. Ellen will go for a swim and then she will apologize to her mother, who sits upstairs reeling and sweating from the news that her daughter is somebody's mistress, remembering a young girl in her office, long ago, who had an affair that ended badly: she got pregnant, she quit her job. She is making plans to tell her daughter the story of this girl, whom Maryanne claimed to pity when she relayed the story tremblingly to her husband but secretly despised for her tight skirts and for a habit she had of singing under her breath around the office. Maryanne, upstairs, mimics her daughter unknowingly: walks to her window, places a hand on the glass, presses her forehead against it, and the house itself creaks a bit from its basement upward through its roof. Outside, in the distance, a tree releases its topmost branch—an old branch, a large and rotting branch—and down and down it falls, crashing through its lower brush, causing Ellen and Maryanne, on different floors of the same house, to straighten simultaneously. An animal in the woods, thinks Ellen. My husband; my son, thinks Maryanne, mistaking the noise for car wheels on their gravel driveway.

How will I fix this? Ellen wonders. She doesn't know. She turns to unpack her suitcase, there on the bed with the blue and white quilt, but hesitates. She will leave it packed this time, perhaps. She will return to New York sooner than she had planned, perhaps. The lake casts a sudden sharp light against the wall, and she pivots to look at it out the window, wincing midturn at the brightness of the water, telling herself that now she belongs to the city.

14.

LENORE LAMONT IS THE NEXT BIG THING

I.

Lenore Lamont has been crying for days. This is new for her; she rarely cries. She cried once while looking for her prom dress. Once she cried over spilled milk, literally, and then laughed at herself. She cries over the mundane, never over things like this—never over the end of a relationship, never over the death of a loved one. These things do not prompt in Lenore overt displays of emotion, and usually she cannot produce tears even if she tries. Her uncle in

Minnesota, with whom she was particularly close, died last fall, and she fell quiet for a while but did not cry.

But Martin is leaving her, and Martin is kind.

"Martin," she has been telling him as he packs his things, "I'm on a billboard in Times Square. Martin, I'm so messed up."

But Martin seems not to hear her. These negotiations have been going on for days, and today Martin has finally decided to pack his things and leave. He is smiling slightly. It is his Buddhist smile, Lenore can tell. Martin is filled with universal love for mankind, but not for Lenore. Martin was a junkie until he had a semiprivate audience with His Holiness the Dalai Lama in Dharamsala in 1999. He has not looked at a needle since.

Can he not tell she needs him now? Martin: vaguely Teutonic, long-haired, thin-limbed. Martin: spidery. He is leaving and Lenore is crying. She wants to tell him, "Martin, I love you," but the words will not come. Strange that they have never said these words to each other—strange that Martin has never said it to her. He says it to everyone: to dogs, to trees, to Lenore's mother, for Christ's sake. But never to Lenore.

These comings and goings. They always happen in the fall.

"Are you listening to me, Martin?" asks Lenore, and suddenly she is appalled at the way she sounds like everyone she's ever left.

"Baby girl, baby girl," says Martin, turning to her at last, sitting on the bed, placing his gentle Martin-hand on her cheek, "do not be sad. Why are you crying? I have to go because it is time for me to go, but you are going to be just fine, and you are going to keep making your music. You have got to trust me, baby girl."

Martin, since cleaning up, has lost his ability to use contractions. Lenore thinks that at least she won't have to deal with that anymore. Also, she hates being called "baby girl." Still. Martin is gentle and carefree, and if he were an animal he'd be a golden retriever. She loves him; she's sure of it.

She folds her legs under her, there on the bed, and collapses over them, surreptitiously wiping her nose on her pants as she does so. "Martin!" she wails.

Martin has all of his things together.

"My show," she says. "My big TV show next week. I need you."

Martin is backing out the door. He has the nerve to bow a little bit, to press his hands together, the way he imagines Buddhists the world over do.

Lenore realizes this is some kind of last chance and says what she will hate herself later for saying: "Martin, I love you."

He leaves. Lenore has not ever been left before.

♮ ♭ ♮

Two days later, Lenore plays Patti Smith on her iPod and goes for a walk. It is not a whimsical walk so much as a practical one: she has a meeting with Jax Powers-Kline and she has to get to it somehow. She has never been to the Titan building, preferring to meet at cafés or restaurants or, while she was recording, in the studio. But Jax called this morning and asked her specifically to come to the Titan building for a meeting, and the tone in her voice made Lenore think it was important. So she said, "Where is it, again?" and now she's walking outside.

It is crisp outside and autumnal. New York is nice in autumn, and normally Lenore would be excited to wear her new leather jacket, the one she bought with her advance from Titan. It's sharp. But she is distracted by other things. Not Martin, really, just the things she will have to face alone now that Martin is gone. She has already started to get recognized on the streets. She is unnaturally pretty, and also quite tall, so she is used to people staring, but now she must ask herself an added question: are they looking at me because they've seen me someplace?

The billboard in Times Square has been a blessing and a curse. At first, Lenore couldn't get enough of it. She'd walk by it at any time of the day or night, just to see herself thirty feet high. She'd think of herself as a child, dreaming of billboards and magazine spreads of herself. Lenore has always been ambitious. Soon, though, the billboard began to occupy entirely too much space in her brain. She dreamed about it once, about the thirty-foot version of herself climbing down off the billboard and having conversations with people.

Her record comes out next week. In anticipation of this event, she has been booked to play on the *Late Show with Colin McAllister* on Wednesday, six days from today. Before Martin left, she had been looking forward to it in the cool way she looks forward to everything. She had been thinking about the way her face would look on camera. She had been thinking about the backing band Titan has hired for her, whether they would upstage her (she doubted it). Most of all, she'd been imagining Martin in the audience, imagining herself sneaking a glance at him and smiling. She had imagined that Martin would be proud of her, glad to be her boyfriend. Maybe afterward he would say, "Lenore, I have to tell you something; I just can't wait anymore," and the thing he would have to tell her would be that he loved her. All of this had been running through Lenore's mind obsessively prior to Martin's departure. Now that Martin is gone, Lenore doesn't want to do the show. She wants to get Martin back somehow.

She arrives at Titan with five minutes to spare, and goes up to the top floor. She is so consumed by thoughts of Martin that she is blindsided momentarily by the sight of the desk that faces the elevators, and the young secretary who sits behind it. The first thing she notices is that the secretary isn't Cynthia. She has not thought of Cynthia in quite some time, but she used to hear her describe her workplace, and she realizes that Cynthia was very precise. She looks for the ficus tree and sees it in the corner, feels it is a friend. She has heard through the grapevine that Cynthia quit this job a while ago, so on the walk over she wasn't afraid of running into her, but she imagines Cynthia sitting at this desk, briefly gets a visual that shakes her up a little, and then shrugs it off.

II.

Jax calls Theo into her office. Recently Theo has been dreading these meetings with all his might, going out of his way even to avoid running into her in the hall. He has signed only one band in the past year, a surprisingly good girl group called Hype Girlz. They're in the studio now working on their first album. Theo prays that it will do well, but their music is so far outside his realm of expertise that he hardly trusts his own judgment. He signed them impulsively. Thinking about it gives him an ulcer.

His fear of another failure along the lines of the Burn has increased. He still has hopes that the Burn will make a comeback of some sort, but it doesn't look promising. Their first album sold just under twenty thousand copies. Theo has always looked at them as a band in great need of development. Even still, their drop party last spring was at the Bowery, not at Irving Plaza, not at the Roseland Ballroom. And their tour was so sparsely attended that when they came back to New York, they played at Southpaw. Theo heard they packed it, but still—it was Southpaw, and Southpaw is small. Southpaw is in Brooklyn! Not exactly the type of venue that you want your band to play at after a critically acclaimed debut on a major label. He has been working so hard on getting the Burn's second album out this month that he has hardly had time to listen to any of the demos that have landed on his desk recently.

Theo figures that Jax is going to give him another lecture along these lines. Why haven't you signed anyone, why has the Burn been flopping, why aren't you working harder?

Theo does not know this as he walks down the hall toward Jax's office, but something has softened her recently. She is sitting in her office, gazing at her Elvis cutout, fantasizing about taking a vacation someplace by the ocean.

When Theo gets to her office, he mistakes this faraway look for extreme displeasure, and he almost turns around and books it.

"Hey, Theo," says Jax. "Come on in. Sit down."

"Hey, Jax," says Theo, warily. "What's up?"

"I just met with Lenore Lamont."

"Oh, yeah? She's doing well?"

"She's on Colin McAllister next Wednesday."

"That's great." Theo thinks that if Titan would give the Burn one eighth of the attention they've been giving to Lenore Lamont, they'd be on Colin McAllister too.

"Good opportunity for her," says Jax.

"Yeah," says Theo. "Colin's funny."

"But I'm worried about her."

"Why's that?"

"Just met with her. Didn't seem like herself. She seems quieter. I asked her how she was feeling and she said, 'Okay.' I asked her if she was excited for the show, and she said, 'Not really.' 'Not really'! It's Colin McAllister."

"That's weird," said Theo. He's had limited contact with Lenore; she played at the Burn's drop party because she was friends with Siobhan, but that memory was tarnished by the fact that Jax was supposed to come and didn't show.

"I'll say," says Jax. "She's always been a go-getter. I

couldn't get out of her what was bothering her." She swiv-els around in her swivel chair: one full rotation and then she is facing him again. "Theo, I want to ask you a favor."

"What is it?"

"I'm going to be away next week for a long-standing family thing; my parents are doing their anniversary in Paris. I'm going too. Can you keep an eye on Lenore? Baby-sit her a little bit, supervise rehearsal. Be there for her be-fore the show."

"Yeah," says Theo. He gets it. It's a chance for him to redeem himself, to make himself useful in the eyes of the higher-ups at Titan. "Sure. Certainly. I'll do it."

"Great," says Jax. "Thanks." This is Theo's cue to leave.

Then Jax remembers something. "Theo!" she stage-whispers as he's opening the door. He turns around. "What's the new secretary's name?"

"Wanda," says Theo.

"Wanda, Wanda, Wanda," says Jax. There have been so many since Cynthia that it's hard to keep track.

III.

On her way out, after a brief meeting with Jax in which Lenore felt like she was drowning in something sticky, Lenore glances at the new secretary and once again has a vision of Cynthia sitting right there.

Wanda smiles slightly, hoping that maybe Lenore will say something to her. She knows who Lenore is. Everyone at Titan does. Lenore Lamont is the next big thing.

"Hi," Lenore mumbles, before pushing the down button.
"Hi," says Wanda. "Have a good day."

IV.

The next day, Friday, Lenore digs out her photo album,
readying herself for another Martin-related crying session.
Since Martin opened the floodgates, Lenore has hardly
been able to contain herself. Commercials set her off, specific songs, specific memories. Of course she thinks about
Martin-in-bed, because who wouldn't. But it is Martin-in-
the-kitchen that she thinks she'll miss the most, because
in Lenore's mind, Martin's cooking for her meant that
Martin was caring for her. She loved it most when Martin
told her she was too thin. "I'm not," she used to protest,
holding out a limp arm as if to prove his point.

Lenore only started taking and keeping pictures once
she fell in love with Martin. Before, she was careless about
her album, thoughtlessly accepting doubles from lovers
and friends, putting them in when she remembered to or
when they commanded her to. She was with Cynthia for
almost four years, and she doesn't have a single one of her.
But Martin was always a bit out of reach, so pictures of him
became precious.

Here is one of Martin on a mountain in India. Lenore
asked him for it specially because she loved the way he
looked in it, strong and content. Here is one of Martin
and Lenore together at a wedding, Martin in a dress shirt

and tie—the only time Lenore ever saw him dressed up. And one of Martin as a child with his mutt Geronimo. Lenore liked thinking about Martin as a child. She wished sometimes that they had grown up together, that she had been his first and only love.

She flips back quickly through the pages, a fast rewind of her life. In doing so she dislodges a photo that falls to the floor. She reaches for it and sees that it's a picture of her and Cynthia performing onstage. It looks like they're on the main stage at the Knitting Factory. Cynthia is looking at Lenore, and her right hand is raised in anticipation of the downbeat. Lenore is looking at the camera.

She imagines Cynthia must have put the picture in the album, but briefly she wonders if anybody else would have. Or if she herself had and just forgot. She looks closely at the picture again and likes it. She tucks it into a corner of the mirror in her bedroom.

V.

That afternoon, Theo calls an emergency meeting with the Burn. They file into his office one by one over the course of a half hour until finally they are all there before him: Siobhan, Mike R., Mike G., Pete, and Katia. To Theo's chagrin, Katia and Pete have started going out. He has heard this from Siobhan, who told him off-handedly because Siobhan doesn't care about such things. But in Theo's mind, this is a recipe for disaster. They are trying to hide it from him, he can tell. They are sitting on the same couch, but they have left a proper six inches between them. He glares at Pete and Pete smiles back at him.

"What's up?" asks Mike R. when they have finished with small talk.

"Bad news," says Theo, who has in fact just received this news himself. "Your album comes out next week." He pauses. He can't think of how to say what he has to say next.

"Yeah?" asks Siobhan finally. "That's the bad news?"

Theo looks at the Burn and remembers them a year ago. Two years ago. He has never invested so much in any other band. He knows their music is good. He knows they're better than anything new he's heard on the radio in the last five years. But maybe he has been naive; maybe he has fallen victim to his own conceit, thinking he could make something work when it wasn't supposed to, thinking anyone would buy an album just because Theo Brigham thought it was good. The Burn's marketability isn't immediately apparent. They are a scraggly bunch. They just don't look like stars.

"Corporate's really been on my back," says Theo, looking at the floor. "I don't know how to say this. If it's—if this album doesn't sell well, they're dropping us. You, I mean. Unfortunately."

Five band members look at Theo silently. They do not look at one another.

Finally, Mike R. asks, "What's 'well'?"

Theo pauses. "No one specified. But I bet they're thinking gold, at least. They're really trying to revamp the label.

'Cut the fat,' someone said. Focus on bands with more of a shot, bands that haven't already gotten a go." He snorts. How the hell did he get into this business? He can barely remember. He feels like an old man.

Siobhan has suspected this was coming. She feels strangely unresponsive. This is it, she thinks. Probably the end of the road for the Burn. The five of them will split up if they don't make it. It would be too much to bear to go back to drifting along in the abyss of unsigned bands. Maybe they'll get day jobs. Maybe they'll form other bands, try something new.

"But hey," says Theo, and his voice breaks a little, and then he wants to tear at his own skin for this little display of emotion. "Let's not jump the gun. We've got an album to promote!" A pose. A sham.

VI.

Over the weekend, Lenore starts a strike of sorts. It isn't a hunger strike: it's a strike from *not* eating. She has always thought of eating as mildly disgusting, something one must do to stay alive, an activity to be done privately and infrequently. Suddenly, though, she has discovered the joys and comforts of food, and has found herself obeying her appetite's every whim. Spying a plump apple muffin in a store window, she allows herself to go in and buy it and eat it dreamily while walking through the city. A piece of cheesecake? Half of a meat-heavy pizza? Certainly. A friend of hers calls to ask if she wants to go to dinner and she sur-

prises herself and her friend by suggesting, of all the restaurants in New York City, the Olive Garden in Times Square,
because she craves a heaping plate of sauce- and grease-
drenched pasta. She and her friend sit next to a family of
humongous midwestern tourists and she tries unsuccessfully to make conversation in between generous bites. On
Sunday, she simultaneously craves and cannot remember
how to make a dish that Martin used to make for her. She
believes it had something to do with rice and coconut
milk, so she goes to the store, buys both ingredients, and
then cannot stop herself from having first one, then many
sips of straight coconut milk while the rice is cooking. She
drinks the whole can, then loads the rice with butter and
salt and eats that too.

She lies on her bed afterward and unbuttons her jeans
with effort, rubs her distended belly. She has been very
lonely without Martin. She has never been without a lover
for so long—and it's only been days since he left. She turns
her head to one side, wanting to feel the cool pillow on
her cheek, and sees for the hundredth time the picture
of her and Cynthia that she has placed in the mirror.

She wants love so badly that she considers for a moment calling Cynthia, who was wrapped about her finger
for all of the four years they were together. Lenore imagines that she would come running, would drop whatever
she was doing and come as fast as she could. Lenore has
always had this power over people because of her careless-
ness. Not even Martin's leaving her can weaken her conviction that Cynthia is still under her control. But she lost

her number months ago, and Cynthia doesn't even work at Titan anymore. It would be a bad idea anyway, she tells herself.

VII.

Colin McAllister has been on TV for most of his life. He was in commercials as a baby, on talent searches and variety hours as a kid (his talent was having a voice that sounded like an adult female gospel singer's and belting out showstoppers while clutching the mic as if it were a trophy), on soap operas as a teenager, on a few short-lived sitcoms in his twenties, on a wildly popular late-night comedy show in his thirties. *The Late Show with Colin McAllister* has been on for ten years now, and Colin is bored. He has just gotten married to a woman twenty years his junior and he wants children, wants to feel their little feet and hands and heads, wants to take a portrait that looks like a painting of the Holy Family and send it out at Christmastime.

He is due to renew his contract on Monday—tomorrow. No one has had any thought that he might not, and so there has been no negotiation prior to this. But the idea of another five years on TV is too much for Colin. He has been pondering his next step for a while, and over the weekend he and his wife have come to a definite conclusion: Colin is done with the show. The abruptness of this decision startles even Colin, but he is quite sure of what he's doing, and he was to take a break for a few weeks anyway, and it all makes sense to him. He phones his producer with the news on Sunday afternoon.

"Colin," says his producer. "You can't quit. This show's just getting started, baby."

But his contract is up, and he wants out. He has more money than God. He wants to retire with his wife and his babies. He wants to live in Napa Valley, goddamnit, and drink California wine.

"Send out the press release, alert the sponsors," says Colin. "Wednesday's my last show."

VIII.

Lenore's strike against hunger continues unabated until, after a few days, she feels quite ill. At this point she heads to a diner to reassess. She dons an old dress that has no waist to speak of, for her own has expanded considerably.

At the diner, she pulls her long bangs over her face and really lets her anguish sink in. My God, what have I done, what have I done? she asks herself. The way she has felt since Martin left has been almost unbearable, and yet she herself has done the same so many times over that she can hardly count. In high school there was Brian, there was Will. Julia came next, in college, her first girlfriend. A string of nameless girls until Christy the Brit came along and convinced her that she liked boys again for a brief sixth months, and then she dumped him too. All of them had overlapped: she would find someone new and cease all contact with the old. She didn't believe in staying friends with her exes. She wouldn't even allow her boyfriend or girlfriend to meet anyone she was interested in. Christy the Brit, for example, had not been allowed to see her perform because Cynthia had been in her band and Lenore had had designs on Cynthia.

Cynthia. Her longest relationship had been with Cynthia. Four years, and then Martin had come into her life and she left. She had met Martin in a café in Park Slope, the same one she always went to when she was trying to work out the lyrics to a song. She had liked him right away, so—as was her custom—she didn't tell Cynthia of his existence. They had gotten together with increasing frequency. They had started sleeping together a week before she and Cynthia got into a fight. It was a minor fight, the kind of fight they should have been able to fix, but Lenore had stormed off. She wonders now if she had even orchestrated it, to give herself an excuse to leave. She went to Martin's house and spent the night. She told him she was in a fight with Cynthia (whom Martin knew about but had somehow managed to meditate or rationalize out of existence) and wondered what she was going to do.

"Stay with me, baby girl," Martin said. "Just for a while, just until you find a place." Lenore leapt at the chance. She stayed with him until she got signed and got her advance and the two of them found a bigger, nicer place together.

And now it is hers alone. She hates it.

How must Cynthia have felt? Like this? Worse than this? Lenore works hard to push these thoughts out of her mind, but they return and batter her with an odd sensation that she assumes must be guilt.

At last, the waitress comes. "What can I getcha?" she asks, and Lenore must think a bit before she realizes that for the first time in days she is not hungry at all. "Coffee, black," she says. The waitress nods and retreats.

Lenore looks out the window of the little diner and sees a familiar figure walking down the street: a woman in her thirties, short-haired, a slight slouch. Cynthia, thinks Lenore. Oh my God. Cynthia.

She stands and sits and stands again, then runs to the door of the diner and flings it open. Cynthia has passed, and Lenore watches her for a moment, giving her a lead, thinking hard about whether she wants to do this. She realizes that she must, and even feels glad to see her: the familiar walk, the back of the neck—here Lenore has a sudden memory of Cynthia's back, which was smooth and freckled in a pattern like a constellation—the small brown head. It is Cynthia just as she remembers her, and Lenore's feet feel momentarily stuck.

Go, she tells herself, run, and at last she does, waiting until she is only five feet behind Cynthia to say her name aloud.

"Cynthia," she says, but Cynthia must not hear, for she keeps walking. "Cynthia!" she shouts again, and Cynthia glances back at last and Lenore sees all at once that this woman is not Cynthia. The woman smiles, and Lenore looks across the street abruptly, pretending she was calling out to someone else.

She stands breathless on the sidewalk for a while longer, looks back to the diner, and realizes she doesn't even want the coffee. She wants to talk to Cynthia, to apologize, to make everything right. She is convinced suddenly that she must find Cynthia or her life will be ruined forever. She does not believe in karma, but Martin believed in karma, and maybe this is it. She walks home, leaving the waitress with a steaming cup of black coffee in her hands.

IX.

Jax's phone rings Monday morning, but she's not answering her phone, so the call goes to Wanda.

"Jax Powers-Kline's phone. Wanda speaking," says Wanda.

"Hi, yes, I'm looking for Jax," says Lenore. Wanda rolls her eyes. Everyone is looking for Jax.

"She's not available right now. May I take a message?"

"Tell her Lenore called. Tell her it's important."

"Lenore Lamont?" asks Wanda. Her heartbeat quickens. She's still new enough to be fascinated by celebrity.

"Yeah."

"Hang on one second, Lamont," says Wanda, and congratulates herself on being casual, then puts her on hold and realizes that she has called Lenore by her last name. She shudders and transfers her to Jax.

"Lenore!" says Jax. She has been doing not much of anything, for once. She has been speaking with her parents about their trip to France. She and they leave this afternoon. A long black car is due to pick her up in an hour. "What's going on?"

"You had a secretary," says Lenore. "Cynthia?"

"I did, yes," says Jax. "How do you know her?"

"She's a friend," says Lenore. "I was wondering if you knew her number."

"God, no," says Jax. She might, actually, but she is too preoccupied to find it. "Sorry."

"Cynthia Kelley."

"I know her name," says Jax. "I'm sorry; she hasn't been in touch. Did you try calling information?"

Lenore did call information. To her dismay, there were no listings for Kelley, Cynthia, and more than a hundred listings for Kelley, C. Finally, she mustered her courage and took the subway to the little apartment she had shared with Cynthia, breathing in sharply before ringing the buzzer and hearing a man's voice.

"Does Cynthia Kelley live here?" she had asked.

"Nope," said the man.

"Do you know where she is?"

"Nope," said the man.

"Do you know her number?"

No answer.

Lenore buzzed again.

"Go away," said the man's voice.

She did.

Now Lenore simply says to Jax, "Yeah, I tried. No luck."

Jax tries to change the subject. "I talked to Theo and

he'll be with you for Colin's show Wednesday. You're gonna be great. I'm so sorry I can't make it."

"Don't worry about it. Jax, I really need Cynthia's number."

"Look, I'll see what I can do," says Jax, and hangs up, and goes back to daydreaming about France.

X.

The news breaks in the early hours of Tuesday morning: tomorrow is Colin McAllister's last show. The *Post* has a headline: "Colin' It Quits!" The *Daily News* gets the release too late, causing a minor uproar on the newsroom floor and an angry phone call from the owner to the editor in chief. Jon Stewart invites Colin to be on *The Daily Show* and makes a joke about taking over his show for him. "It's all yours," says Colin McAllister, thinking how glad he is to be leaving the business.

In the Titan building, Theo receives an ecstatic phone call from Jax.

"This could not, could not, could not have come at a better time," she says. "Do you know what this means for Lenore?"

Theo says he does and promises to make sure she has everything she needs for the show on Wednesday.

Jax hangs up, satisfied. In the other room, her parents are getting ready for a dinner at the same restaurant they frequented before she was born. Her mother's perfume finds its way under the door and brings Jax back to her youth, reminding her that once she was small enough to think of perfume as something very grown-up and foreign.

XI.

On Wednesday, Lenore wakes with an ache in her stomach that threatens to become unbearable. She clutches it and doubles up. Because of the way her head falls on the pillow, the first thing that comes to her mind is not the massive quantity of food she has been consuming over the past four days, but Cynthia. The picture of them stares her in the face. Cynthia in the picture, looking at Lenore onstage with an expression of pure adoration; Lenore on the bed, looking at herself in the picture with terrible contempt. You had what you needed and you left it, she thinks. Coward. Fool.

She cries again, thinking of Martin's face on the pillow beside her, thinking of Cynthia beside her, Christy, all those men and women, all the boys and girls she has ever tricked into loving her. Her stomach churns and she thinks she will vomit, but she can't bring herself to leave her bed for the bathroom.

She thinks of what she had to eat last night and gags. A sandwich—no, four sandwiches—made with cheese and deli meat that she can't remember when she bought. She would perhaps not have eaten it had she not had five improvised mojitos before that, and two bags of microwave popcorn. And a frozen wiener schnitzel from Trader Joe's.

Frozen, not microwaved; the popcorn was occupying the microwave and she couldn't wait. She gnawed that schnitzel like a Popsicle. It was obscene.

Lenore is sweating. She thinks of the Colin McAllister show tonight and it seems entirely unimportant. Even if she knew that it was his last (she doesn't; she has been cloistered in her apartment and she doesn't read the paper anyway), the news would pale in comparison to her own ailment. When Lenore is nauseated she can think of nothing else. It's been this way since she was small. She closes her eyes and tries to sleep it off.

XII.

Theo wakes up alone in his apartment on Wednesday morning with the feeling that something big is happening, then remembers the Colin McAllister show tonight. Everything will be fine, he tells himself. This will be good for him; Jax has given him an easy babysitting assignment and he will complete it, and at their next staff meeting, Jax will congratulate Theo on successfully shepherding Lenore Lamont, the next big thing, through some very important publicity. Lenore completely lucked out, he thinks. He likes Lenore's music; it's slightly different, hard-edged, but poppy and hooky enough so that the radio will love it. Still, this kind of exposure can't be bought, can't be deserved. He knows that wherever Jax is, she has arranged for some kind of ridiculously extravagant fruit basket or bouquet to be sent to Colin McAllister. He also knows that the heads of every other label are all cursing that it wasn't their artist on tonight's show. Everyone's predicting astronomical ratings for tonight.

Theo looks at his clock: nine A.M. Not too early to call Lenore. She'll want to be up and prepared for tonight. She has hair and makeup at two P.M. and a sound check at three-thirty. The show's filmed at five.

He gets her home number from his Trio and dials. No answer. He's not concerned; she's probably out for breakfast or something. He'll try her again in a bit.

XIII.

Colin McAllister wakes up next to his wife and sighs. She is his third wife and the difference between their ages rarely bothers him, but today it's annoying him. He doesn't like to feel old, and although he had thought that having a young wife would keep him young, mainly it just reminds him of his own age. He regrets leaving his show abruptly for only one reason: he has not had time to really plan his farewell, to think of a really original way to end it. They've got a great actor on tonight, an old-timer who's just coming off a string of good movies, a comeback of sorts that will surely result in an Oscar this year. But Colin's unsure about the music act. It's no one he's ever heard of. Still, he prides himself on being a music aficionado, and he has always made it a point to break new bands. He supposes it's fitting that his final show should be helpful to someone's career.

XIV.

Siobhan wakes up in her father's house in Yonkers and thinks, Tomorrow my career ends. Tomorrow the record comes out. She has known this was coming for a while. When the first record didn't sell well, she tried to comfort herself and the band, saying sales would pick up eventually, saying it was a slow record to start but that their touring would turn it around. When their touring didn't turn it around, she said their next record would do better. She loves their new record; she thinks it's the best thing she's ever done. But she is smart enough to realize when a band is quietly being taken off life support. Titan has done little or nothing to promote this album.

She came to her father's house yesterday to escape her life, the phone calls from friends wishing her luck, the phone calls from bandmates wanting her to reassure them. She has no idea when she became the voice of reason in the band, the leader. She has always avoided leadership positions; in fact, prior to their signing, she hardly ever spoke onstage, leaving the banter to the others. She feels she's bad at it, but Theo makes her do it. She will stay here until the first numbers for sales come in, and then she'll return to her place in Williamsburg to start her life over. It's true that she'll still have connections in the music industry, but she figures she'll have to lie low for a while before trying anything. Maybe get a day job. She and the Burn are in deep with Titan—they've recouped next to nothing of their album advances. She'll have nothing really to take away.

Her father knocks once lightly on the door.

"What is it?" asks Siobhan.

"Breakfast or tea?"

"Not now, Dad, thanks," she says, and rolls over, and waits to go back to sleep.

XV.

It is noon and Theo still cannot get in touch with Lenore. His day has gone from easy to terrifying. He does not believe in God but he thinks, Please, if you're there, please help me today.

He picks up his phone and dials Lenore's once more, unsuccessfully, then calls Wanda at the office.

"Titan Records," says Wanda.

"Wanda, this is Theo. Has Lenore Lamont called you today?"

"Nope," says Wanda.

"I need Lenore Lamont's home address."

Wanda tells him to hang on and looks on her Trio, in her Rolodex, on her computer. "Sorry, Theo. I don't have it." There is dead air on the other end. "Hello?" says Wanda.

"Hi."

"Want me to phone Jax in Paris?"

"No," Theo says quickly. "Definitely, definitely do not do that."

" 'Kay," says Wanda. "So."

Theo is thinking creatively. "I want you to look in your Rolodex for Cynthia Kelley's phone number," he says.

"K-E-L-L-Y?"

"E," says Theo. "E-Y."

Wanda gives him the number and then he takes a breath and thinks about this before he dials. Because of his connection with Siobhan and Siobhan's connection with Lenore, he had heard that Cynthia and Lenore were a thing a while ago, and vaguely the office knew this too, but it was never mentioned. Jax, he knew, was trying to spin Lenore as some kind of rock 'n' roll goddess, a girl that boys would like. Still, Theo was friends with Cynthia, and he had felt mildly guilty about sweeping the whole thing under the rug. He wonders if it hurt her, if she's mad at him. Still, he's desperate, so he dials.

She answers. Thank God.

"Cynthia?"

"Yes."

"This is Theo Brigham. I'm trying to get in touch with Lenore."

On the other end of the phone, Cynthia tries desperately not to react. She wants so badly to be over Lenore, but, as always, a mention of her name produces a physical reaction in Cynthia. Cynthia is trying to move on. She has started seeing someone: a TV producer named Germaine. But she still can't get Lenore out of her head, and when she lets her mind wander it is almost always to Lenore, as if she were the default setting in Cynthia's brain.

"I don't have her new address," Cynthia says stiffly.

"Do you have any other way of getting in touch with her? Do you know anyone who would? It's important," says Theo.

"Is she okay?"

"She's supposed to be on Colin McAllister tonight and no one can find her," says Theo.

Cynthia pauses. She knows she shouldn't care about Lenore's well-being anymore, but it's hard not to.

"Hang on," she says, and goes to her desk and retrieves an address book she hardly ever looks at. Buried in it someplace, she knows, is the telephone number for Lenore's parents in Minnesota. She had insisted on having it if they were to live together. "What if something happened to you?" she had asked a disgruntled Lenore, who was always so private. Cynthia is still not certain if her name would mean anything to Lenore's parents. Once or twice, toward the end of their relationship, she tried to tell herself that surely Lenore had told her parents about them—they'd been together for close to four years! But she had never met them, and she could never be sure, and she could never ask Lenore because Lenore hated questions in general and especially questions that came from insecurity.

There it is, in green pen: Joanie and Lou Lamont of Minnesota. She pauses, looking at the book, and reflects on her time with Lenore. She should slam the book shut, slam the phone down, never look back. She knows how much Titan needs this publicity for Lenore. If she wants to fuck it up, Cynthia thinks, I should let her. Then she conjures an image of the childlike Lenore sitting cross-legged on her old red bed, an image that often presents itself to her in moments of weakness, and lifts the receiver to her ear, and gives the number to Theo Brigham. One digit at a time.

XVI.

Two hours later, Theo is lying flat on his back on the floor of his apartment and trying not to hyperventilate. This is it. His job is over. Lenore Lamont is in the hospital, and she has some kind of third world–sounding intestinal malady that could not possibly have come at a worse time. This is really it.

He considers his options. He can call Jax right now and tell her the news. He can resign preemptively, maybe salvaging his reputation in the business, maybe spend this afternoon trying to get hired by a rival company before word gets out that he's been fired from Titan.

Instead he picks up the phone and dials Colin McAllister's people. He is still in his position on the floor. Colin's assistant answers and Theo chickens out and clicks his phone shut. Distantly, he has an idea that seems too crazy to actually follow through on, but he is a desperate man and for once he feels he must save someone else at his own expense.

XVII.

At four-thirty, Colin McAllister is sitting in his office, wondering what he is going to do with his life after today. He guesses his wife will get pregnant in the next year. Kids are a full-time job. This he tells himself while sipping from the lowball glass of Jack Daniel's he has before every show and staring at the wall opposite his desk at the portrait of

his predecessor on the show. He wonders if his own portrait will be made and placed next to it. He kind of doubts
it. He's sure that everyone's pissed at him; this was an unexpected move on his part, a move that has pretty much
eliminated his chances of ever working in TV again, a
move that has left the network scrambling to replace him.
But he's okay with never working in TV again. He thinks.
Either way, he's made his bed and he'll lie in it. He hopes
tonight's show will be his best. Everything seems to be in
place. He considers smoking a cigar in celebration, but he
thinks that would be a lonely thing to do, and it might
make him cough.

A knock comes at the door. This is unusual, because he
has a strict policy: after rehearsal, after makeup, no one is
to talk to him between four-thirty and five. He takes this
time to sit at his desk and prepare.

"Yes? Come in," he says, and his door opens to reveal
his director and his personal assistant, both looking white-
faced. Behind them is a man he does not recognize.

"What's going on?" he asks them.

"Colin," says the director. He rubs a hand over his face.
"It seems that Lenore Lamont will be unable to perform on
this evening's show."

"Who's Le—the singer girl?" says Colin.

"Yes."

"Where the hell is she?"

"She's in hospital," says his personal assistant, a little
British woman named Malory. "She's very sick."

"Fuck!" says Colin. He looks at his watch. "Do you people realize it's four-thirty? This is the most warning a per-

son can get around here? Was she *just* taken to the hospital? Did the frigging ambulance pick her up from the set?"

"Colin," says the director. "This is Theo. He works for Titan."

Theo steps forward, realizing as he does so that tomorrow he may be in the same boat as Colin McAllister: jobless. But with not nearly as much money.

"Let's hear it," says Colin.

"I have a replacement for Lenore."

"Who?"

"The Burn."

"The who?"

"No, sorry, the Who wasn't available," says Theo, in a misguided attempt at a joke. Colin McAllister looks as if he might throw something. "Seriously, Colin, the Burn is a really hot new band. It'll be perfect: everyone will remember that your last show was their first big one," he says. Is this the right thing to say? He can't be sure.

Colin thinks about the rest of his life. One more show, and then he's done. He didn't leave himself enough time to make it a perfect farewell. He doesn't care.

"I don't care," he says. The director and the PA look absolutely shocked.

"What?" says Theo.

"Fine! I don't care. Where are they? What's their name? The Heat?"

"The Burn," says Theo. "They're in the dressing room. They're ready. They're gonna be great."

XVIII.

Five bandmates sit silently in a small greenroom. Their makeup was done halfheartedly by a disgruntled young Czech girl, employed by the network, who kept telling them, "Normally I just do this for Mr. McAllister." Siobhan tried to do something nice with her hair, but she fears she has wound up looking something like a messy debutante.

Fortunately for them, they've been practicing steadily for the tour that is to follow the release of their album. If their album does well, that is. Also fortunately—miraculously, even—all five of them answered their phones when Theo called with his idea. Siobhan had to take a car to get to the studio from Yonkers in time, which she really couldn't afford. She borrowed money from her father, apologizing, feeling unworthy and excited simultaneously. She wasn't sure if her father understood the magnitude of the event; even if he did, he wouldn't show her. Mike R., who never answers his phone, had been opening the door to his apartment just as the phone began to ring, and answered it quickly and absentmindedly, mostly just to see if he could get to it in time. This was a little over an hour ago. In a half hour, they will face a studio audience—a small one—but six hours later, their electronic images will face the biggest audience they could possibly conceive of. The thought of this is making a few members of the Burn shake. Katia, the drummer, looks at her hands, trembling as they are, and wonders how she is to hold and control drumsticks.

Each looks at his or her friends and bandmates and wants to say something but can't. So it is that not a word is spoken among them before the most important show of their collective career. Each wishes to provide some comfort to the others but cannot; for this reason, sadly, no one enjoys the silence, which later will be remembered as the last truly private moment they had together.

In a minute they will be called to the set to do a brief sound check. In a half hour, they will play—well, very well, better than they've ever played before. Maybe it will be the knowledge that this is their last shot. Maybe it will be Katia's nervous rhythmic energy, which causes her to actually play better and push the rest of the band toward brilliance and excitement. Maybe it will be a glimpse of their own faces on the monitors in front of them, the realization that this is what it feels like to make it. Any of these reasons could explain the way they will play, which shocks even Theo, and makes Colin McAllister happy that this is the band that people will remember as having gotten their big break on his last show.

No one knows this now, though, and the five of them stare at their toes and think of all that has changed and all that might.

XIX.

There are things in the ocean that are so big that on land they would be the size of houses, of whole buildings. A blue whale, upright, would be as tall as an average structure in New York City. Thinking of massive things beneath the sea frightens Cynthia. She has heard of some tribe someplace—Africa, was it? New Zealand?—that builds huge ritualistic elephants and pushes them on wheels into the ocean until their great heads are below the surface of the water, farther and farther until they are obscured by the weight of the sea. Coming upon one of these huge statues unexpectedly is one of Cynthia's greatest fears, though she knows it is irrational. As if they would be off Coney Island, off Jones Beach. Cynthia has no real ambitions to travel to more exotic places, though recently she's been considering France. Now she is watching something on the Discovery Channel about a group of scientists who are trying to take a picture of a giant squid—something that has never been done before. Everyone knows of these squids' existence, but no one has visual proof yet. The clever scientists bait and hook a huge one, sending a camera deep below the surface and taking a series of five pictures that show the creature's struggle: she is spread out like a many-limbed starfish, then the legs are in, then pulsing out again, and finally in anguish the monster tears her own leg from her body and swims away lighter and frightened. The scientists reel in her severed limb, not bleeding but pink enough to make you cry.

Cynthia looks around the hospital waiting room. She thinks she is the youngest one there, but she can't be sure. After hanging up with Theo she had waited a few minutes and then called Lenore's parents herself, holding her breath while introducing herself as "Lenore's friend Cynthia" and hearing no hint of recognition in Mrs. Lamont's "Hello."

The last of Lenore's cruel slights. Four years they were together, and not a mention of Cynthia to her parents. She's
pathological, Cynthia told herself, a mystery of a person.
Still, she told Mrs. Lamont that she wanted to check on
Lenore in the hospital, and Mrs. Lamont gave her the hospital's name, and now here she is. She wants to tell Lenore
that she does not love her anymore. She isn't sure if this is
a lie, but she feels it's the only way she can ever forgive
Lenore, and recently Cynthia has been trying hard to forgive, to get rid of some of the bitterness she carries with
her from day to day. She will enter Lenore's room and say,
"Hello, Lenore, I've come to tell you that I have no feelings for you anymore," and then she can forgive Lenore,
and then she can leave with a spring in her step.

♮ ♮ ♮

Lenore turns over and over in her hospital bed, struggling
with nausea still, though it has dissipated since this morning. She needs saving; she wants to be saved. She wonders
what she can do with the rest of her life—if she has messed
it all up for herself. Now that she is feeling better, she reflects on the opportunity she has missed in not doing the
Colin McAllister show. Jax will be furious. Titan will be
furious. Who will fill in for her? She will be banned from
that network.

Three times she has broken down and called Martin,
and he has not called back. She is filled with self-righteous
indignation. This is a time of great need. She hates Martin. No one is there for her. She can tell that even the

nurses feel bad for her—she is young and single and alone in New York. If only Martin would come and save her. If he saw her like this, wan and beautiful and desperately ill, he would feel sorry for her and realize his mistake. She has not talked to him in a week, and her want for him and for all the other lovers she has ever known builds in her to a great peak.

♮ ♮ ♮

A nurse has led Cynthia down the corridor to Lenore's room and left her outside it. Cynthia's breath comes in quick escapes as she looks through the small glass window on Lenore's door at Lenore herself, turned away toward a different window, the outline of her cheek hollow and graceful, just as Cynthia remembers it. Oh, but she is still so young. Cynthia knows she herself has lost her shot at whatever fame she might once have attained, but Lenore will make it, and for the first time Cynthia feels glad of this.

She places a hand on the door, readying herself for what comes next. Lenore, I do not love you, she repeats in her head. Lenore, I don't care about you. But Lenore turns away from the window and looks to the ceiling and she looks so frail that Cynthia is overwhelmed with compassion; her heart skips beats the way it used to when Lenore was playing onstage, before they were anything, when they were just friends and bandmates. She wishes desperately that she could get those days back. To be four years younger, to be filled with the possibility of musical success, the possibility of the love of Lenore. To be full of anticipation and emptied of regret. Is Lenore crying? No, but her face is crumpled in a way that Cynthia has never seen, and she realizes that Lenore is very alone. If she were to sit on her bed. If she were to place a hand on her cheek, which is feverish maybe, and stroke it just a little bit. If she were to hold a glass of water to those parched lips. All of these actions would be satisfying in the basest way. None would be good for Lenore.

In a moment, Cynthia will open the door. "Hi," she will say. "It's me," as if that needs to be said. But Cynthia will not tell Lenore she doesn't love her, because for the first time it is true and doesn't need saying. Lenore will cry again, for the hundredth time this week, and think of how much she needs to be loved, and all that she is missing, and all that she has given up.

XX.

The Burn walks down the long corridor toward the set for the second time. No one was in the audience for their sound check, but now a small crowd is sitting in red velvet seats, and prompt and enthusiastic applause greets them when they take the tiny stage. Siobhan marvels at how much larger it appears on her TV each night, and then marvels that she herself will appear on TV tonight. She wants to go home after the show and watch it with her fa-

ther and her brother and eat popcorn with them and listen to them tell her they are proud. They may or may not
do this. The odds are about fifty-fifty.

"Ladies and gentlemen," says Colin McAllister. "The
Burn!" and then Katia says, "Two, three, four," and then
they are playing, the five of them together, just as they
have so many times before.

♮ ♮ ♮

Theo Brigham is backstage. He cannot bring himself to
watch from the audience, so he is stuck in the little greenroom, picking at his fingernails, watching the band on the
shitty monitors, praying they don't screw up. He relaxes a
little after the introduction, and congratulates himself on
doing what he thinks was the right thing. Soon the phone
calls from Jax will begin. Soon the phone calls from Corporate. But now Theo sits and thinks that maybe he has
made the kind of difference that he always wondered if he
could make in someone else's life. I have directly helped
someone today, thinks Theo, and puzzles over what he
feels, and recalls a young band he passed over a couple of
years ago—all the young bands he's passed over in pursuit
of better-looking ones, more marketable ones. The Burn
has been his project for nearly as long as he's been in the
business. And here they are on Colin McAllister's last
show.

He doesn't know what will happen to them. He doesn't
know what will happen to him. For the first time in a while,
he feels happy.

♮ ♮ ♮

"Do you know what this means for us, do you know what this means for us, do you know what this means for us?" This is the refrain in Mike R.'s head as he hears the count-in behind him and feels his friends around him and sees the audience in front of him. He tries not to think about how many people will watch this program later tonight. He wonders how many people in his hometown are watching. He wonders if the Cross family is watching, and whether they will bless him or curse him. He wonders if Nora herself is watching; recalls a week that he thinks of daily, hourly; a letter that he keeps in a drawer. Decides that if he were the Crosses he would wish good things for himself, for, after all, he is human—after all, he is young. He makes himself smile for the cameras, then decides that maybe smiling isn't appropriate. He has trouble knowing what is.

♮ ♮ ♮

Siobhan remembers a time long ago, before her mother died, perhaps before Hugh was born, even, when listening to music was the only way she could fall asleep. Up, up, up in her little room in Yonkers, the curtains billowing in and out of her window in time with the breath of the world: here was the three- and four- and five-year-old Siobhan, prone on her bed and drifting in and out of sleep to the sound of her parents' voices wandering up the stairs. Their words, mingled with friendly, familiar strains of music, seemed to Siobhan the most comforting sound in the world.

Strangely, it is this memory that comes to her as she sings in front of Colin McAllister's audience; this memory, and another of her mother brushing Siobhan's hair after a bath, and another of Kurt Cobain's final appearance on television. Siobhan looks out into the audience and feels an emotion she has never been able to name, one that hits her at times like these. Something to do with the word *chaos*. Something to do with sex, or lust. Something to do with religion. She feels she is ready for something bigger. She feels that she has lost herself to something bigger, and her eyes lose their focus momentarily, and before her in the audience she can see a riot of moving colors, each a figure without a name. They will all know hers after tonight, and this frightens her. Feeling her knees go a bit weak, Siobhan is grateful for an instrumental break that allows her to turn from the audience and face the band, and for a moment all five of them are looking at one another; all five of them share something that each will recall later as a sign of something great.

She thinks, This is what it must feel like to be truly happy. She thinks, Maybe this is what it feels like to be in love.